Christmas Cures Everything

✳ **Marie Ralbusky & Diane Belz** ✳

The Quest-CIP, LLC

Cover Design by Jodi Wright

Visit our website: http://christmascureseverything.com/

Facebook page: https://www.facebook.com/christmascureseverything

Scripture quotations marked as follows:
NAB is from New American Bible,
CPDV is from The Catholic Public Domain Version
KJV is from the King James Version.

ISBN 978-0-9912236-0-2 paperback

Acknowledgments

To Our Father, Son and Holy Spirit for His inspiration,
gifts, guidance, and total forgiveness.

To our husbands, Emil & Joe, who were there every step of
the way, providing an endless source of encouragement and
belief in what we were hoping to achieve. To Joe, who was
the first one to read our entire book and deemed it good
enough.

To our children, Heather, Amy, Tyson and Geoffrey, who
listened to us talk about the book forever and were our
inspirations. It took us longer to birth this book then our
five children!

For Diane's daughter, Jessica, who watched over us from
heaven and let us know the meaning of loss and instilled in
her mother a desire to write.

To our granddaughters, Katherine, Jacqueline, Abigail,
Victoria, Claire, Isabella, and Sofia, who are dearly loved,
precious gifts from God and our second chances.

To our parents who taught us we could do anything if we
just put our mind to it. Mom is smiling at us from heaven
and Dad was a gentle reminder each visit, "Is the book done
yet?"

To our friends who believed and encouraged us, they were
our first readers and our first editors.

4

To Marie, my co-author who agreed to go on this ride with me, she just didn't know how long the ride would be! For her putting up with my perfectionism, my endless desire to rewrite and make it just right. For her ability to see a scene and let me run with it bringing our unique gifts and strengths into this collaborative process. Mostly, I want to thank my big sister; I had to say that for her love, belief in me, and for sharing in the laughter.

✳

To my little sister Diane whose vision and gift of encouragement has always been a source of inspiration to me. Without her vision we would not have experienced the joy of working together. Thank you for putting up with my laughter, tears and frustrations as we got closer and closer to the end of writing and editing this book. It was been such a blessing to work so closely with her. I think I understand her gifts and strengths better than before. I've been truly blessed during this journey.

Jo - Chapter 1
Finding the Key

"Take every thought captive to the obedience of Christ"
2 Corinthians 10:5 (NAB)

Sitting on my bed, I hug my knees to my chest, drawing closer and closer into myself. I'm afraid to let go. If I do, my world will explode and I'll lose what little control I have left. Maybe if I keep hanging on for just a little longer, a mystical force will come and rescue me. From what? I don't know, but I know that I need to be saved.

Thoughts are racing through my mind—fast, furious, and uncontrollable. Gently, I rock back and forth to some faint unknown rhythm as I desperately try to quiet my mind. What I can control is how much time and attention I allow each thought to stay. "Josie Beth, treat your thoughts like guests at a party who have entered your front door. Those guests who are unwelcome, causing you distress, and harmful to your peace, laughingly and lovingly show them the back door." That was my Grandma Esther's sage advice, one of so many "Estherisms," as I like to call them. They have ruled my life for far too long. Whenever I'm attacked by my thoughts or unable to quiet my mind...*Estherisms*.

But the unwelcome guests keep knocking. Fragments from conversations that will never happen, memories from long ago, and harsh words recently spoken—they all keep knocking. As I continue to rock back and forth, I imagine myself on Grandma's front porch chair. I review each of my thoughts against my guest list to see if any are worthy of entrance. Then I show each and every one of them to the door and slam it tightly shut.

Desperate to stop the onslaught of unwelcomed guests, I try to find something mindless to focus on.

Something, anything is better than the barrage of *could'ves*, *would'ves*, and *should'ves* that are trying to snap my last thread of control. Glancing over at the digital clock on my nightstand, I find a mindless solution. Analyzing the segments that make up the digits of time becomes a strange source of mental comfort. Not willing to let my focus wander, my eyes burn as I stare intently at time ticking away. How many of those little line segments does it take to make the digits of time? Let's see. It's now 2:14. The two takes five line segments, the one just two, and four, oddly, takes four segments. That's a total of eleven line segments, one and one equals two. As the clock switches to 2:15, I begin the mindless counting ritual.

It's working! My mind is now eerily quiet. The knocking is now replaced by a persistent throbbing in my head. The aching could be from multiple sources—the staring, adding the line segments, or, most likely, the lack of sleep. The pain forces me to lie down. Now instead of incessant thoughts, I can't stop playing the line segment game. There is no peace. As a last resort, I pray out loud. "Dear Lord, I need to sleep. Please, please help me."

Be still and know that . . . pops into my head.

"And know what? Be still? How can I be still with so much on my mind? Please, please! I need real help, not old Bible verses. The tossing and turning tonight is evidence that I can't stay still, especially if I keep having these sleepless nights!"

The unfortunate truth is that over the last few weeks I learned why sleep deprivation is a form of torture; its sheer agony not to sleep. My body and mind can't function. All I can think about is sleep! Every part of my body aches, even my eyeballs. How can my eyeballs hurt? My rational mind, if I still have one, tells me that this eyeball pain is caused from lack of sleep, but this knowledge doesn't offer any relief.

Nothing I've tried, except for drugs, helps. And I am not going down that path. Watching all the former addicts that grace Grandma's holiday parties is sufficient proof that it only takes one weak moment to ruin your entire life. After working all day, running ten miles, and having a glass of wine I thought, no hoped, that sleep would be inevitable, since it's obviously necessary. I'm so exhausted!

Crazy me; I thought by finalizing my decisions, the war being fought in my head would stop. After making my decisions, I usually feel somewhat peaceful, maybe even a little content, but not this time. The dynamic duo, peace and sleep, continue to elude me. My pro/con chart made it clear which choices I needed to make to achieve my life goal, to be recognized as a serious journalist.

After ten long years of writing articles for a small hometown weekly newspaper I was offered a job at the Philadelphia Daily Bulletin. My editor saw the positive reaction and number of readers I have on my blog, Two Sides to Every Story, and he gave me a weekly column under the same tagline. After only six months I was given the opportunity to write a feature article for the paper, a giant step in moving away from writer to becoming a journalist.

My column is bringing some much needed younger female readers to the paper, even if - it is just the online version - with my contemporary perspective. My editor Pete is giving me a chance to finally write something important: why abortion is still causing such a divide among women forty years after Roe v. Wade. If this is what I wanted for so long, why is it causing me so much anxiety?

Since sleep alludes me and not wanting to make the line segment game into a worthless habit and time waster, I choose another addictive diversion – TV flicking. The green glow from the TV casts a cloak of hopelessness and loneliness in my bedroom matching my sleep mode. Flicking, flicking, flicking. I'm not really watching; I'm just trying to numb my mind or even bore myself to sleep. I know sleep is the only way to escape these persistent thoughts running through my head.

So much has changed over the last six months with the successful transition to a major newspaper and a weekly column. I'm working more, that's for sure, and the great part is that I'm finally seeing some results. The column is definitely resonating with my followers, a fact proven by increased readership and followers every week. Researching and writing has changed my life and what I want from it. Ten, five, three, and even one year ago, the choices I made would've been different. It would have been a definitive "No!" to Pete's article on abortion, and an enthusiastic "Yes!" to Earl's romantic marriage proposal, no second thoughts or ultimatums.

The agreement to write the three-part article on abortion was reached after much debate, discussion, and compromise. Pete and I decided to keep the column under my byline, *Two Sides to Every Story*. The first article will be focused on the pro-choice side, the second on the pro-life side. The third part of the series I will offer my opinion and perspective on why the abortion debate continues over forty years after it was legalized. Voicing my opinion straight out *–The Truth by Jo –* will definitely be a risk, but it is also a necessary next step in my career. There is not a downside to it except facing Grandma and hearing her side, which will definitely not be part of the article.

There was also debate and discussion before reaching my decision to refuse Earl's marriage proposal. My acceptance was conditional; we needed to live together for a year. When I told him I wouldn't even think about marrying him without living with him first, he was shocked, and disappointed. But he agreed, moved in, and then stormed out the door one day. What changed his mind I might never know. His response doesn't make sense to me. Why two months into the arrangement did he start feeling guilty, not comfortable with his decision, and even remorseful? He refuses to move back in unless we're married. It is classic "his way or no way," but I refuse to be bullied into marriage.

Stop thinking, it's getting you nowhere. Keep flicking, keep searching and you might find one of Grandma's old movie favorites. Being frugal has paid off, and has let me afford this house, but there are lots of sacrifices, such as only having basic cable, so my TV selections are limited. What a relief it would be to lay back, relax and enjoy a pleasant movie memory, and ultimately tune out the movie playing in my head.

Tonight, my heart longs to be connected to Grandma. Whether I admit it or not, she is my resting place, a safe place I can go whenever my mind is troubled. Even if I don't give her full disclosure, her comforting presence is an antidote for my racing thoughts. Maybe the cord needs to be cut; it's become too long and the break is inevitable, a logical progression to becoming a mature adult and claiming a life of my own.

Oh, but the little girl inside of me remembers the good times when the biggest decision I needed to make was whether to have butter or cheese on my popcorn. Right now I'd like to be at Grandma's house curled up under a mountain of homemade quilts and breathe in the peace that she's always brought me. What has changed lately? Why is it when I'm with her, I can't wait to get away, and when I'm away from her I long for her loving presence? Why did I ever want to grow up? Oh, that's right, so I could be a big girl, make my own decisions, and live life my way.

The critical voice inside my head asks, "So how is that working for you, Jo? You surely can't seem to make them now." The battle in my mind continues; daily skirmishes show up every night not letting me sleep. But what are they fighting for?

Your soul was an answer I wasn't expecting. The realization of these words sends chills down my spine and restlessness into what I am sure is my soul. Not knowing how to react to this newest revelation, I just flick faster and faster trying to race far away from this awful thought.

Tormenting thoughts, torturous sleeplessness, and to top it off, tempting late night TV - there has to be some evil plot to fill the airways with onslaughts of temptation for us poor insomniacs. The temptations to buy with the never-ending infomercials, temptation for sex with provocative programs, and the greatest temptation for me is to keep the

TV on 24/7 watching the same continuous news loops.

Grandma's theory is that the only news we need to know about is the Lord's Good News. She sticks her head far in the sand to avoid the real world news, trying to stop all the evil destruction from reaching her door. What was her latest rant? *The media has convinced us that the world is coming to a gruesome and predictable end and that they are our saviors. They're wrong. Christ is our only Savior!*

Where does she come up with this stuff? She wants to live in the fake world of *Leave it to Beaver* and *Andy Griffith*, especially since Andy was based in North Carolina. She would only let me watch TV shows where good, wholesome, family values were celebrated. Even these two shows would be a welcomed respite to rescue me from all of this temptation. Otherwise, I'll end up buying a workout CD or another useless hair product. Desperately seeking something of interest or amusement, I continue to flick, flick, flick. The mindless, endless flicking is trying to calm my mind, but it only leads me to feeling more agitated and restless.

Then I stop.

"Post-Abortive Women Speaking Out" flashes across the bottom of the screen. This should be interesting; yep, that's why it is airing at 2:43 a.m. with all the other top-rated shows.

Sitting on the panel are women talking about their abortions. They are discussing the usual conspiracy theory stuff, their regrets, and tiresome regurgitations of the abortion industry not being pro-women, but pro-profits. How timely and convenient, another *Godincidence*. I think not. I'm learning that trying to be unbiased is tough; the two opposing sides are so stereotypical. They are either regretful opponents or rigid opportunist for women's rights. I'm impressed with the panel, not full of all the emotional mumbo-jumbo that turns this debate into emotional denunciations and not fact-based discussions.

The camera zooms in on an attractive middle-aged woman as she states that she is still pro-choice even though she experienced some negative consequences from her abortion. She goes on to say that if she were better informed or had received any type of counseling before or after, she wouldn't have experienced post-abortion trauma. Her platform is simple: she wants to help women make informed decisions. She sounds reasonable. She feels the problem wasn't the abortion, but the fact that women go into an abortion uninformed of all the potential physical and emotional consequences.

"Treat abortion like any other surgery and provide full disclosure. Abortion is a life-altering procedure, not to be taken lightly or made emotionally," she said.

It's interesting that she's the only one on the panel who is seeing both sides to this issue. Believing in the right to choose, but wanting, not demanding, that women be provided with information and truth regarding the procedure. She may be the key I've been looking for in bridging this emotional debate. She's intelligent, well spoken, and calm. As Grandma would say, I just know in my gut that this is a woman I need to interview. But what is her name?

Well, maybe this was worth staying up for, but as the clock reads 2:58, they are winding down to a close. "What's her name?" How can they have lines and lines of information running across the bottom of the screen with everything except what I want to know? The program is ending, and I don't know her name. The moderator thanks each of the guests, and as he does the camera zooms in on her face, Elizabeth Betts, Executive Director of W.A.I.T. scrolls across the bottom of the screen. How can I find out about her at three in the morning? Just Google her. My mind has shut down from all this pressure and lack of sleep that I can't even figure out the obvious.

Knowing that sleep will never come if I don't at least check her out, I reluctantly reach over to the nightstand and grab my iPhone. I type in Elizabeth Betts and find her listed as Executive Director of W.A.I.T., **W**omen **A**dvocating for **I**nformation and **T**ruth, a women's advocacy group with a twist. She has a very interesting bio and story. Ms. Betts could add a layer to my research that I was not anticipating. Why would she be on a panel working with pro-lifers if she is pro-choice? Turning off the TV and the light, I crawl back under the blankets and my mind finally gives into sleep.

Chapter 2
Headed to DC

"So with old age is wisdom, and with length of days understanding."
Job 12:12 (NAB)

What is that awful noise? My head starts screaming in pain. Smacking at the alarm clock, I desperately try to shut it off, but the noise continues. Finally, I realize it's not my alarm; it's my phone. I glance at the clock to see the line segments display the numbers 4:58. Panic sets in as I wonder who could be calling at this hour. I squint to find my phone and quickly check the caller ID. It's Grandma!

"Grandma, what's the matter? Are you all right?" I can hear the panic in my own voice.

"Settle down. I'm fine; everything is fine, Josie Beth," she replies calmly. "Are you sure everything is all right?"

"Of course I'm sure," I say, the irritation obviously coming across the phone line. "If you're fine, then why are you calling me at this hour? It's not even five o'clock. Couldn't it wait? You know I'm leaving for DC today to conduct that interview I told you about last week."

"Well yes, Josie Beth, I've been up for hours. I have this feeling that something isn't right. I've been worried about you and can't get you out of my mind. I thought if I spoke to you it would ease this feeling that you aren't all right. Are you sure you're okay?"

Sitting up, I glance out the window and see that the darkness matches my thoughts. "I'm fine except for the lack of sleep. Oh, and being scared to death by your calling me at this hour surely hasn't helped." I shake my head and think that there is no way I'm going to survive the drive and the interview with Liz on two hours of sleep. Grandma has been on my case the last six months. The more successful my column the unhappier Grandma is. Why can't she be happy for me?

"I'm sorry, Josie Beth. I didn't mean to startle you. It's just that when something plays on my mind I need to figure it out. I just want you to be careful today, that's all. Remember, no matter how famous you become, you're still my little girl."

When she calls me Josie Beth, it feels like nails on a chalkboard. Why does she continue to call me by my childhood name when she knows I go by Jo now? Isn't that my byline, Jo Reynolds? Who would take a journalist serious with the name Josie Beth? I'm not twelve.

"Maybe I needed to hear your voice before you left. Are you sure you're okay? My senses tell me there is something wrong. You just haven't been yourself lately. I don't know what is going on, and it has me worried. Josie Beth, please don't let your desire for success get in the way of living a godly life."

I roll my eyes. It takes every ounce of strength I have not to throw this phone across the room. "Why do you have such a problem with me being successful? I've been working so hard."

"I don't have a problem with you being successful. I want you to live your dream, because I believe God has placed this dream in your heart. It is the topics you're writing about and the words you are using. They are in direct opposition to the Word of God. That's what's concerning me."

Gaining some level of composure because I know she means well, I try to reassure her. "Yes, Grandma. Everything is fine. I'm just having a little difficulty sleeping lately." Her constant judgment on my choices, because they're not in line with hers, is really driving a wedge between us. And now she is adding this guilt trip. I don't need her worrying about me. I'm not a little girl. I'm a grown woman who finally is getting noticed in her career.

Why can't she see that?

"Can't sleep? Josie Beth, are you capturing every thought? Remember this is where Satan likes to work on you, your mind."

Why does Grandma think every problem is an attack by Satan? Even scarier is how she always knows when something is working on my mind. If I didn't know better I would swear that she has my house wired with surveillance cameras, or she actually does have supernatural powers.

"If anything is playing on your mind that is causing you not to sleep, you know that you can talk to me . . ."

Why the twenty questions? No sleep, high anxiety about this interview, and now her relentless religious talk? Falling back on the bed, my pillow drops to the floor, and my head hits the headboard with a loud bang. Remembering that Grandma is still on the phone, I squeeze my lips tight so I don't let the curse word escape from my lips. I drop the phone onto the bed so I can rub my head.

"Are you okay, Josie Beth? It sounded like you hit something!"

I pick up the phone and grit my teeth. "I just hit my head on the headboard. I'll be fine." At least the headache in the front of my head is now balanced by the bump on the back. When is this conversation going to end?

"Did you hear what I said before you banged your head?"

"Yes, Grandma, I know I can talk to you about anything." Sure, I can talk to her about anything, but lately all it ever does is result in an argument. She's gotten so judgmental. Everything that I say, or do, has her overreacting and jumping down my throat.

"Grandma, I'm really fine, really. Please, I have to go. Your call might be a blessing since I need to get ready and on the road. You don't want me to miss this meeting do you? I'll see you in a few weeks. Love you and thanks for caring." I hang up the phone not waiting for her response. I don't want her to stop caring, but can she do so without the constant judgment? Is she capable of doing that? Only time will tell.

I shove my other pillow over my head; I want to go back to sleep. Then I remember the time. I reach over to turn the light on. Suddenly, I see what looks like snowflakes flying around my room. Maybe that's why it feels so cold in here. As the focus fog lifts from my eyes, I realize I knocked over the stack of last night's musings. These little papers are now sprinkled all over the floor. What can go wrong next, and where's the heat? I see my robe hanging off the other side of the bed, evidence of my restless night. Reaching under the bed, I grab the slippers and as many papers as I can before leaving the comfort of my bed.

"Got them," I proclaim in victory. As I pull myself back onto the bed, victory is short lived. I smack the side of my head on the nightstand. This time the curse freely escapes my mouth. Once again I see the papers scatter across the floor.

"Is everything and everyone against me this morning?" I scream. I watch those tiny slips of paper run away from me. If I didn't desperately need them I would have just left them there on the floor to freeze. Unfortunately, they are precious notes for my conversation with Elizabeth Betts.

"What else can go wrong this morning?" I mumble.

Wrapping my robe tighter, I move from the bed, put on my slippers, and bend down to collect the allusive papers once more. This time I secure them with a paper clip I've retrieved from the nightstand drawer. For extra security, I put my phone on top of them.

"Stay put," I order. Walking into the bathroom, my mind wanders to the place that I had fought so hard not to go last night—Earl. Every room in this house reminds me of him. My precious robe and slippers were a few of the Christmas gifts he gave me last year. Part of me never wants to wear them again, but this house has been so cold since the day he moved out. The robe and slippers are a source of comfort and warmth–just like he had been.

I glance out the frosted windows of my bathroom to see skeletons of leafless trees standing at attention almost as if they are sentries guarding my house. "Stop it! I don't need you or anyone else watching over me."

Splashing cold water on my face, it happens again; a primal urge to scream coming from deep down inside of me. A scream that will somehow re-adjust my psyche, to ease this unnamed pain I am feeling; a real scream of desperation and release. I recall the scream I need to scream. I felt like that little boy in the *Home Alone* movie who yelled to high heavens when he put the shaving lotion on his face. Remembering this scene from the movie brings a quick laugh, but I still feel like screaming.

What's new? That's how I start most mornings lately. Why not scream? It would only resonate through the empty house; no one would hear it, and the scream I want to scream is directed at me anyway. What's the use? I am so tired of talking to myself, especially since it gets me nowhere.

After taking a quick shower I take out my best navy blue suit from my closet and lay it across the bed. My challenge is always trying to look the part, even when I don't have the budget. One day I will be able to buy the clothes I want without scavenging through thrift shops and the clearance racks at department stores. Quickly I grab and pack my overnight bag, just in case the interview takes longer than expected, or the weather turns. Sad to say I'd rather be alone in a hotel than alone at home.

Chapter 3
Liz the Almighty

"Entrust your works to the LORD, and your plans will succeed"
Proverbs 16:3 (NAB)

Being late for my appointment with Elizabeth Betts is not a good way to start the relationship, especially since she was willing to meet me on such short notice. After finding her on TV, I called and talked to her about my article. When I asked if I could interview her, Liz initially said no. Then after my silent prayer she then asked if she could think it over and call me back. I really wasn't expecting to hear from her. To my surprise the next day she not only called, she agreed to the interview. Just one caveat, we need to meet in person.

Maybe the "in person" caveat was to try and stop me. I agreed on the spot. DC is a drivable distance from my home in Yardley, PA, or so I thought, until I hit this awful traffic. I've been sitting in a traffic jam for over an hour. But bottlenecks seem to be everywhere I go, especially in my career. After ten long years of writing fluff articles for small town newspapers, I'm finally getting a shot at writing an article that could earn the long sought after title of "journalist". This is an awesome opportunity and I'm not going to blow it.

"Patience is a virtue, Josie Beth" rings in my ear as I honk at the car in front of me. When I least expect it, and maybe sometimes need it most, Grandma's little Bible verses or Estherisms come to mind to either haunt or help me. Timeliness is also a virtue, but right now these two virtues cannot co-exist within the small space of my car. I need to move! The exit for W.A.I.T. is just a quarter mile away, and I am less than a mile from the building. I hate being late! This interview is important to my series and making a good impression is imperative. Should I call the office to let them know I'll be late or wait?

Geez, all this time waiting and rubbernecking was the culprit. With all the car crashes in the news, the movies, and video games, you would think people would have had their fill of wrecks and keep driving by, but we are curious by nature. *Don't look, don't look, keep your eyes focused ahead.* I restrain myself from looking at the pile up and keep driving to ensure I'm on time and the images of the wreck do not get stuck in my mind.

The W.A.I.T. office is located in a nice part of the city. Thankfully they even have their own parking garage because I'd never find street parking at this time of day. I check the building directory and see that W.A.I.T. is located on the third floor. This building also has doctors, lawyers, and accounting firms as tenants. Definitely not the rundown storefront I was expecting. The elevator doors open to an office space with contemporary sleek lines. Abstract prints line the walls to the reception area. A wall fountain displays trickling water behind the receptionist's desk creating a Zen-like atmosphere. The receptionist immediately stands up to greet me, extends her hand, and introduces herself.

"Good afternoon! Welcome to W.A.I.T. I'm Sheila. How can I assist you today?"

"I'm Jo Reynolds. I have an appointment with Elizabeth Betts." Why do I feel so nervous?

"We've been expecting you," Sheila replies perkily. "Can I get you anything while you wait – coffee, tea, or some water? Liz should be with you in about five minutes."

"It's been a long ride. I would love to freshen up, and a bottle of water would be great."

Sheila directs me down the hall to the restrooms. From the looks of the office, Ms. Betts runs a very professional, high-energy, and friendly organization. Before arriving here, I had assumed only women Elizabeth's or my grandmother's age would be working here. Surprisingly, I see a diverse mix of friendly, energetic ladies from the receptionist to the staff members who greeted me in the restroom. What is attracting people from every age and ethnic group to this cause? Their conversations are upbeat as if each one has a personal mission to be nice. Maybe I'll need time to talk to some of the staff to better understand what goes on behind the scenes. I'll clear it with Elizabeth at our meeting.

Everything from the artwork on the wall to the amenities in the bathroom demonstrates a casual elegance and sophistication. Where do they get the money to have a place like this? Is W.A.I.T. one of those fraud non-profits that siphons off its contributions? I hope not, because this place makes a great first impression.

Within five minutes of arriving, and right on time for our appointment, Elizabeth Betts is standing in front of me. She is surprisingly warm and more attractive than I remember from TV. Casual yet professional, warm yet authoritative. Her smile mirrors the friendliness of her office.

"Good afternoon, Jo. I'm Liz Betts," she says, extending her hand toward me.

I stand up, remember to smile, and wipe my hands across my pants to eliminate sweaty palms before accepting her hand. Her handshake is firm, yet welcoming.

"Thank you for coming down to DC to meet with me," she continues. "I find face-to-face conversations much more effective and efficient, don't you?"

"Yes, I love technology to expedite work, but I still prefer face-to-face conversations. Blame it on my Southern upbringing." I let go of her hand and gesture around the room. "Your office is beautiful, and not at all what I was expecting."

"The office does make a statement, and we're all proud of that. I'm a born bargain hunter. Just because it looks expensive, doesn't mean it is. Where in the South are you from? I didn't detect an accent."

Why do I find it so difficult to talk about my upbringing? Maybe it's the years of being made fun of for how I grew up. Kids would call me a Jesus freak, bookworm, poor little orphan girl, and they would constantly taunt me about my out-of-control hair. I've got to learn the art of small talk and become more comfortable with combining personal and business.

"North Carolina, outside of Asheville, in a little town called Saluda. It's quaint and claustrophobic all at the same time, and that's the only good thing I can say about Saluda."

She gives a nod of agreement, though I seriously doubt she has any idea about growing up in small town USA. "Haven't heard of that town, but I'm sure it's lovely. Bob, who's on our team, is from the eastern part of North Carolina."

Liz graciously offers to give me a quick tour of the office, including the hotline call center, which she says is the heart of their operations. Once inside the room, it's immediately evident that this is true as I hear the quiet hum of machines and see the gentle nods of understanding.

"Jo, ninety-five percent of our telephone counselors have had abortions. They have a gentle and non-judgmental way of approaching everyone who calls. They've been trained to walk a fine line between offering counseling and offering their opinion and experience. This is not about them, but about the client on the phone."

We enter the hallway where small offices outline the perimeter. An expansive library for reading and research is at the other end of the hallway – an indication that W.A.I.T. is taking the "information" part of their name very seriously. We pass a room with a sign on the door – Silence Please: Re-energizing in Progress.

"Is that the coffee-break room?" I whisper to Liz.

Liz shakes her head no and puts her finger to her mouth asking for silence. She leads me into the company lunchroom.

"That's our meditation chapel. This work takes a toll on our employees. Some companies offer gyms, but we offer the opportunity for silence, prayer, or meditation. Call it what you want, we just know that sometimes our employees need to get off the phone and come to a safe place to recharge, let the tears flow, or think. If we don't take care of our employees, we cannot expect them to take care of our clients."

"Sounds like you're running a business."

Liz laughs. "We are. It's just our business to serve our clients and not focus on profits. It's still a business."

Fifteen minutes later, we leave the building to walk down to a deli for a late lunch. We're hit with a wind so biting cold that it sends shivers right to my bones. It feels like the temperature has dipped another ten degrees. What did I expect? It is November. Liz walks out in front of me and is moving fast. Is it because she's hungry or wanting to get in from the cold as quickly as possible?

Finally, we enter the warm, coziness of DiNardo's Deli. The hostess greets Liz personally and lets her know her favorite table by the window is available. Liz creates a buzz in the deli, probably due to her beauty and grace. She moves like a celebrity with confidence I would do anything to have, especially today conducting this interview. I'm sure no matter where Liz goes; she gets this same level of attention.

The waitress is immediately at our table.

"Will you be having your usual today, Liz, or can I persuade you to try one of our soups? Our special pumpkin squash bisque is perfect for taking the chill out of this weather."

"Betty, you can try all you want to persuade me, but I have to have the Greek salad. Could you give me a tiny cup of the soup, just so I can taste it?"

"Sugar, you can have whatever you want. You won't be disappointed."

I scan the menu quickly to make sure I'm ready. "Do you have other soups today, or just the pumpkin squash bisque?"

"We have split pea with ham, which is our specialty, and we have some turkey noodle."

"A bowl of the split pea would be great, please."

Betty lets us know that our meals will be right up, and that she will bring some bread and butter as well. I start to tell her I don't want the bread, and Liz shakes her head at me. "It's worth the calories. Trust me."

Before her coffee and my tea arrive, I ask Liz if I could record the interview. She agrees only if I promise to give her a copy.

"Of course. I can download it and have it to you tonight. Will that work for you?"

Liz nods in agreement, so I continue.

"Liz, you probably remember from our phone conversation that I caught you on a segment from a panel interview with pro-life advocates. I'm writing a three-part series on the continual debate on abortion forty years after *Roe v. Wade*. How did you come to the place you are now? How did you go from being pro-choice to pro-life?"

"I've never moved away from my position of being pro-choice; choice just has a much different meaning for me now."

"Okay, I'm confused. When I heard you on the panel you said how much you regretted your abortion. W.A.I.T.'s mission statement is 'Saving lives through informed decisions.' What do you mean you're pro-choice?"

"You have beautiful curly hair. If you were moving to a new city, would you walk into any old hair salon and get your hair cut?"

"Of course not. Do you know how few stylists can cut curly hair? I guess you would, your hair is curly as well. I try to find someone with similar hair and a great cut and find out who her stylist is."

"I did the exact same thing when I moved here. Jo, how do you make other choices in your life, from buying a car, finding a home, or what over-the-counter medication to take when you have a cold?"

"I feel like we are getting off track. I thought we

were talking about abortion rights?"

Betty stops by and delivers a basket of bread. The smell is glorious.

Liz reaches over and opens the breadbasket. "You've got to try these rolls; they're heavenly."

Reluctantly, I reach for a roll. It's a warm, soft and fresh, just like Grandma would make with her soups. Liz is right. Fresh bread is always worth the calories. I follow her lead, pull the warm bread apart, and place a slab of soft butter in the middle. "This is so good," we mumble almost in unison. We look up and laugh at our perfect timing, which instantly puts me at ease. *Relax Jo, she's human.*

After taking another bite of the warm roll, Liz continues her explanation. "I apologize if I am taking the long way around to answer your question. Please let me take you on a little tangent. It's been my go-to way of explaining my position and making it a little clearer. Believe it or not, this method helps get me to the point while framing my position in a way that anyone listening can understand why I'm pro-choice. That was your initial question, correct?"

"Okay, I'll try to follow your line of thinking. How do I make decisions? Well, being a writer, I gather as much information as I can in a reasonable amount of time. I do my research, ask friends, weigh the pros and cons, and exhaust all possibilities before I make a decision."

"I'm glad to hear that. What if you were making a life-altering decision—would you need more or less time to make your decision? Do you need more or less information? Where would you go to do your research? Who would you ask for their opinions?"

"What do you mean life-altering decision? Like getting married?" The minute I say it I wish I could pull it back. How can such a simple question knock me out of this conversation and bring my thoughts back to Earl? Gazing out the window, I try to deflect direct eye contact with Liz. Getting all teary-eyed is not how a professional should be handling herself.

"No, I was thinking more life threatening like treatment for breast cancer or gastric bypass."

"I'd do research. This wouldn't be an easy decision. I'd want to know all my options, medical alternatives, possible outcomes, and side effects. Then find the best doctors or treatment centers."

"Why do all the research? Why not just take the advice of a trusted friend or do whatever your doctor tells you to do?"

"Because it's my body! I'd need to know all the ramifications and side effects. Like you said, these are life-altering decisions. The outcome is critical to my life and how I live it. I'd need to make sure it was the right decision for me, both short and long term. I'd ask advice, but the bottom line is that I need to have as much information as I can to make the right choice. Because . . . it would be a life or death decision that I am making, right?"

"Jo, you sound very passionate and persuasive, and I agree. With these invasive, life-altering procedures, the provider needs to give you full disclosure of the risk, implications, and side effects—correct?"

"Yes, all the laws, guidelines, and information must be provided to save lives and allow individuals to make the best informed decisions."

"So, that's why I'm pro-information, pro-truth, and pro-educated choice."

"But, you're really pro-life."

"Well, yes, I am. It sounds like you're pro-life, too," Liz says with a laugh.

Liz has a pleased expression on her face. I'm almost expecting her to proclaim touché as she lifts her cup of coffee and nods at me. Did we just make some secret pact that I'm not aware of? I think she misread my response.

"How did you draw that conclusion?" I say with obvious irritation in my voice. Is she laughing at me?

Liz looks at me so seriously and lowers her voice.

"When you're about to make critical decisions, your goal is to stay alive. Isn't that pro-life?"

"Yes, I'm talking about my life."

"So am I!" she states empathically.

"Do you know how many women go into an abortion not knowing all the ramifications, both the physical and emotional side effects? I'd say over ninety percent of them."

"But pro-choice is about protecting women's rights to choose and not interfering with her reproductive rights."

"Did you get that statement off an abortion clinic's website? Look, I'm infertile. Do you think anyone was looking out for my reproductive rights when I had an abortion? That's why my pro-choice is about protecting women's lives *and* woman's rights."

"Infertile? How are they connected?"

"Jo, you really need to do the research. Remind me when we get back to the office to provide you with some data. I'm not the only woman who has experienced this. An abortion is a lifetime decision, and too often it has been viewed as a short-term solution. That's why education, information, and truth are essential to choice."

"What about your pro-life stance?"

"I can't separate the two."

Thankfully, our soups are delivered. Taking a deep breath, I take a sip of my soup and enjoy the warm heartiness. *Breathe Jo, breathe,* I keep reminding myself. I have to maintain my composure, and I really need to take control of this interview. Maybe I'm not as prepared as I thought I was. Obviously I'm not prepared to have Liz steer the interview in this direction.

Before I can ask a question, Liz jumps right back in.

"Jo, do you know women who have an abortion are sixty-five percent more likely to be at high risk of clinical depression? The percent jumps to 138% if the woman is married. Post-abortive women are sixty percent more likely to receive mental care within ninety days of an abortion compared to women who carry their baby to term. Why? Is there some common thread?"

Not sure whether this was rhetorical or if she actually wants me to speak, I resign and take another sip of my soup before I answer. Apparently, I made a good choice, because she lobs another question at me.

"Jo, what got you interested in journalism?"

This woman isn't letting up. I need to get to *my* questions so I can write *my* article. Maybe if I placate her while we eat she will allow me some talk time.

"I've always been interested in the truth because of its amazing power even when it hurts, and it often does."

"So, what truth are you seeking to tell with this article?"

"What do you mean by that question?"

"Over the last thirty years, most journalists I've worked with see truth through their own lenses. They gather just enough information, even a sound bite, to prove their truth, and they rarely listen to my truth."

"I came here with a very open mind, willing to listen, even allowing you to take this interview in your own direction. I think I've been fair and reasonable. True?"

"We'll see when your article is written."

Frustration takes a front seat. *Take back control, Jo, now.* "Can you elaborate for me how you feel journalists push their preconceived notions about you in their writings? What has been incorrectly written about you and your work?"

"Journalists from the pro-life camp sometimes make me into a feminist Nazi because I'm not pro-life enough for them. My mission, my personal mission, is to save the lives of mothers, fathers, grandparents, aunts, uncles, and anyone else who has been hurt by an abortion – not just the babies. If through the information that W.A.I.T. provides the mother changes her mind, well that's a bonus. On the other side, journalists who write from the pro-choice camp make me out to be anti-women's rights activist because I'm not one hundred percent for abortion either. The pro-choice camp doesn't want me using words like baby, complications, and full disclosure, which I will not stop using. Both sides try to box me in, and I'm not to be boxed. Life is not either, or. There is a whole lot of gray in all of our decisions."

"Then why did you agree to this interview?"

"After your call I did some research myself. You've written some fluff pieces, and with your *Two Sides to Every Story* column I can see that you're attempting to venture into more controversial issues. You've done a good job in providing alternative points of view and not editorializing. I've not trusted my gut in a long time, but my gut is telling me that you really are seeking the truth."

"I am seeking the truth. I'm always seeking the truth."

"Let's talk about the first article you wrote on this debate, which was a contrast from your weekly column. I noticed that your writing perspective shifted from two sides to the story to defending one side. How I read it, from the tone and words you used, was that you felt that pro-choice had already won the battle and that pro-lifers should get over it. The war has been fought, legislation is in place, and pro-choice has won."

"Maybe you didn't understand the intent of the column. It was to give the pro-choice point of view. My next article will provide the pro-life point of view. That article was picked up by the wire service, and they are committed to publishing the whole series."

"So, you measure the veracity of your articles by how marketable they are?"

"That's an insult to my journalistic integrity."

"No, it is a comment on the naïveté of a young journalist trying to make her mark on the world."

I'm so taken back by her comment that I can't respond. Who does this woman think she is? Sure, I want to make my mark on the world, but I want to seek the truth, first and foremost. I need to get her to see my side.

"Jo, I've seen so many women hurt by the manipulation of the women's movement. If you really want to know the truth, I'll give it to you. You need to set your agenda aside, whatever that is, and you must admit you have one. I want to lay out some facts and research for you to hear, not my version of the truth, but some hard facts. Let's look at what the pro-abortion movement has done to support their industry. In many ways, it has hurt more women than they have helped. Are you willing to hear the facts, just the facts?"

"What about your agenda, Liz? You have an agenda, too. Why is that okay?"

"Absolutely I have an agenda! It's okay because I'm not a journalist. My motives are out there for anyone who wants to know what I stand for, and what I'm trying to achieve. By doing that, I'm being truthful. So I guess were both pro-truth."

Maybe we are. I decide to give up the fight to control the interview and just let her talk. Maybe I'll learn something. Why not let the tape recorder do its work, so l can just listen? She holds my attention with her passion and commitment to women, so I guess she really is pro-women.

For the next hour, Liz talked about the strength of the women's voice in this country from the beginning of our nation to women's suffrage and what has brought us to the present. She explained that whenever women worked together with a focused purpose they have accomplished so much. Women now have the freedom to choose where to put their time, treasures, and talent. She feels the world is a better place because of these choices: the freedom to choose their purposeful path whether running large companies or running the PTA, powerful in national politics or powerful in their community. There are no roles too big or too small if we are making a difference in the lives of others.

My tape recorder runs out before Liz does. When she hears the warning beep, she grows quiet, but not for long.

"That's the first time that's ever happened. How long have I been talking?" She was so involved in her own monologue that she's acting as if she just woke from a nap, not knowing if it's day or night, who she is with or what she has been talking about.

I wait, not sure how to respond or if another question is coming. "There's usually two hours of battery life," I tell her when the silence becomes uncomfortable.

Liz checks her watch and jumps from her seat. "I had no idea of the time. I have a four o'clock meeting. Let me get the check so we can head back to the office. Can you come back with me? I know you haven't gotten to all of your questions. The meeting shouldn't run longer than thirty minutes. I have a rule about that!"

Exhaustion is setting in, but Liz is right. I need to get my questions answered. I agree to stick around until after the meeting. When Betty comes back to take Liz's credit card, I ask if I can have a coffee to go.

Walking back to the office, our conversation takes on a different direction when Liz points out something very interesting.

"Jo, do you need to be told that that cup of coffee you're holding is hot and could burn you?"

"No, I hope it's hot. That's the way I like it." Too late I realize that I've just been lured into another topic trap with the Mighty Liz Betts leading the way.

"Do you need to be told that putting your hand in a running snow blower can cause you to lose your hand? Or that you shouldn't ride a bike at night without reflectors? Or power tools can cause bodily harm?"

"Of course not, that's just common sense."

"Look at your cup. What does it say?"

"'Caution, contents may be hot,'" I read loud. "I've never even noticed that before."

"Not many people do, but there are disclosures on almost every product you buy and almost every service you receive. I'm waiting for my favorite candy bar to have an audible warning, 'Beware this may cause addiction to chocolate, weight gain, and wild mood swings.'"

"What else needs a warning label?" I ask with a laugh.

"Abortion – that's for sure. I want to believe that we save lives by letting people know the different risks to their various options. Some are important. Others may seem a little ridiculous, almost begging you not to use the product. 'This product may cause choking,' or 'This product may cause anal leakage.'"

Liz stops dead in her tracks and looks at me. "Who wants to take a product that causes anal leakage? So I am thankful to know what kind of product or procedure could cause that kind of messy problem."

Liz is way out there, but she has a way of pointing out the absurdity of it all, and it's making me see a different perspective. My mind runs through all the lawsuits I thought were ridiculous in recent years.

She can't seem to stop herself. Before I know it, I can see why her staff and the people at the deli are so enamored with her; she's funny.

"How about a drug for heartburn listing headache, nausea, abdominal pain, diarrhea, gas, and constipation as common side effects? It sure makes me think twice about taking that product. Now I can make an educated choice, do I want heartburn or diarrhea, heartburn or abdominal pain, heartburn or gas? Let me tell you. They're not great choices, but at least I have them. Why do all the drug companies fully disclose possible side effects?"

"They want to cover their butts and avoid being sued. Bottom line is always money."

"You might be right, but lawsuits and wrongful death claims also hurt a company's reputation. Drug companies are required by law to fully disclose side effects. Drugs save lives, but they also can cause some pretty serious problems. Legislation has been put into place to inform us of that truth."

"What are you driving at? How does this have
anything to do with abortion?"

"When I went in for my abortion, no one told me that
I might suffer excessive bleeding, hemorrhage, endotoxin
shock, cervical and uterine injury, infertility, or chronic
abdominal pain. That was over thirty years ago. Guess
what? They still aren't providing that level of information in
most states."

This weird feeling overcomes me. *Am I going the wrong
way?* The next article will be the balance, I remind myself,
and there really are at least two sides to every story. "Liz, I
have to admit I am surprised about all of this. I want to take
you up on your offer to use your library and do more
extensive research."

"Of course, Jo! That's why I wanted to talk to you.
The truth needs to be told, and you might be just the one to
do it. Remember I told you I was infertile? It's a known
possible side effect from the abortion, and that is why I am
pushing for information and truth. Just like with any other
medical procedure, or when you buy a cup of coffee, let the
patient and consumer decide. Give them their right to
choose, but let it be an informed choice."

With the sun making its descent, the temperature
continues to drop. I pull open the office door appreciating
the warmth of the building. Getting into the elevator, I turn
to Liz. "Are you looking to stop abortion or provide
information?"

"Stopping abortion . . . I don't believe will ever
happen. Women have found a way to abort since the
beginning of time. Abortion has a sacred shroud of secrecy,
which leads to shame. I want the shroud of secrecy lifted. If
it was any other issue, trust me, women would unite and
take care of one another.

"We've had some luck in a couple of states, such as
providing an ultrasound and providing information on post-
abortion trauma, etc. Let them know the truth. If there were

a disclaimer covering all the possible ramifications of an abortion were posted in treatment rooms, hanging from the ceiling, or posted on the stirrups, it would reduce the number of abortions and the number of women who suffer post-abortion trauma. Why don't we respect their ability to make educated choices, and let them decide? It would have made me think twice."

"Are you telling me that abortion clinics are not required by law to disclose side effects of this medical procedure?"

The doors to the elevator open, but Liz presses the hold button. "Yes, that's exactly what I am telling you. When my husband was in a motorcycle accident, he was taken to the hospital. Before he was treated in the emergency room, he had to sign a waiver giving the doctors permission to amputate if the surgery did not go well. They told him all the ramifications of the surgery and gave him the opportunity to make an educated choice. The hospital would not operate until he signed the waiver acknowledging they provided him with this information. For heaven's sake! I received more informed-consent counseling when my cat was neutered than when I had my abortion."

I nod solemnly. Why did I not know all this information *before* I spoke to her? One thing I do know now, Liz is an impassioned expert and a mighty force for her cause. Her passion alone is probably why W.A.I.T. has lasted this long. She could argue the devil right back to hell, so why hasn't she been more successful?

At times today I wasn't sure if she was trying to teach me, convert me, or if she was incapable of talking about anything else. However, she's making more sense than I would like to admit. Maybe this topic is out of my league and I should just stick to writing the fluff pieces for my column.

Chapter 4
Lonely Hotel

"Those who spare their words are truly knowledgeable, and those who are discreet are intelligent."
Proverbs 17:27 (NAB)

As I take the short drive to the hotel, my mind keeps reviewing all the information that Liz provided. My head feels like it's going to explode from the details. While in the library at her office, Liz provided me with articles and studies from a multitude of medical journals like *Journal of Psychiatric Research*, *Journal of Child Psychology and Psychiatry*, *Medical Science Monitor*, and *Journal of Medical Ethics*. What surprised me was how much has been written on both the emotional and physical adverse effects of abortion. *Maybe I did come with some preconceived ideas.*

Work awaits me, lots of work, but the desire to relax, even if for a few moments, is necessary to recharge what little battery life I have left. With little to no sleep, the commute into DC, Liz's incessant tangents, and the piles of research she suggested I review, I'm exhausted and overwhelmed. Slipping into my warm flannel pajamas is the first step to winding down. My fear is if I stop now, even for a few minutes, I might not be able to start up again.

"Where do I start?" I say out loud.

Oddly, when the overwhelming feeling of details and deadlines sets in, rather than focusing, I become highly distracted. Is this some sort of protection mechanism, or is it something else like laziness? I've been programmed to believe if I'm not working every possible moment, I'm not a hard worker.

Picking up my cell phone, I look to see if I have any calls. One flashes on the screen, Earl. Why is he so persistent even when I haven't returned his calls in weeks? He acts as if nothing has changed and checks in with me almost daily, always leaving a thoughtful message highlighting the details of his day and reassuring me of his love. If he loves me then why did he leave me? Is he the only man in the world who refuses to live with a woman he supposedly loves? Each time I hear his voice, I vacillate between anger and hopeful anticipation that he's changed his mind.

Stop it, Jo, and focus! Taking out a pad of paper, I jot down all that I need to do: questions for Liz, review the research from W.A.I.T, and develop an initial outline for the article. When the list is finally complete, I look at it and wonder how I'm going to get everything done. The thought overwhelms me, and anxiety settles into my chest. I pick up my cell phone again, staring at it, ordering it to ring, hoping for a distraction from everything that I know needs to get done.

What is wrong with me? My weekly column is so easy to write. Why am I struggling so much with this feature article on abortion? Have I developed attention-deficit disorder over the last month, or does sugar really impact your ability to think clearly? That will have to be my next story, the two sides to sugar addiction. I put down the phone and try, once again, to focus on the article.

Why today, why now do I need to talk to Earl? What's shifted? But the urge is so strong as I again reach for my phone. I know I won't be able to focus until I talk to him. I dial his all-too-familiar number and wait. It rings once before going straight to voicemail. Who is he talking to? Why does the sound of his voice have such power over me? Even his recorded voice saying, "This is Earl. Please leave me a message" is emotionally dangerous and why I've been avoiding him. I need to hold my ground. I hate leaving voicemails, but I want to make sure he gets the message. He either needs to stop calling me or be willing to make some compromises with our relationship.

"Hi Earl. It's Jo. I don't know if I'm ready to talk yet. That's why I haven't returned any of your calls. I've got too much to do, and right now I'm overwhelmed with work. I feel pressured by deadlines and by you. Give me a few more weeks, let me get these articles completed, and then we can talk."

Would this push him away forever? Thankfully the voicemail lady asks me if I am satisfied with my message. I'm not! It's not like I want him out of my life. I just want the guilt from rejecting his marriage proposal to stop. I delete the message and hang up before I change my mind.

Too much pressure from too many sides is squeezing me to the point of exploding. Maybe a break is what I need. I order soup and a sandwich from room service. Soup could be a miracle cure; it sure warms up my body and relaxes me.

With the call made and food on the way I am able to refocus on work. I begin to separate the papers in some sort of order: stories, legislation, history, and advocacy groups. The realization that this isn't going to be as easy as I initially thought sets in and an overwhelming feeling rises up again. This is not the black-and-white issue I thought it was, or was led to believe, by my editor, Pete.

The pro-life side has some good arguments against abortion, so why aren't they being heard in the mainstream media? It isn't all about religion, or the sanctity of life, which was always the basis for Grandma's adamant opposition to abortion. It's interesting to me that Liz, with all the passion she has, never once mentioned religion as the basis for her advocacy. For her, it's about why treat abortion differently than any other medical procedure. On that point, I have to agree, and I'm curious to discover more.

The knock on the door is a welcome distraction, even if I know who it is and why they're here. I make some space on the nightstand before answering the door. The room service attendant walks into the room and looks at the piles spewed across two beds and the desk.

"Looks like it's going to be a long night. We offer room service up until 10:00 p.m. if you need more energy to get through all of this."

I look around and agree. "I might need more than food to help me get through these piles. But I'll keep that in mind." I sign the room service receipt and give the pleasant waiter an additional tip.

After finishing up my soup I decide to save my sandwich for later. The waiter was probably right; I might need a midnight snack to get through all this research. Speed-reading would be a wonderful skill to have tonight.

The soup gives me some fuel to get started. After several minutes of reading the medical journals, I now have a dramatic twist for the second article. How could this be true, and why did I not find this level of detail before? I write down the citations and additional questions I now have for Liz. The excitement of uncovering this information is propelling me to keep going. Satisfaction sets in as I realize this article could stoke the fire of debate. Isn't that what I want for my career? The ability to open minds, change perceptions, and get to the truth? My vibrating cell phone pulls me away just as I'm making real progress. My mind says, don't stop now, but my heart wins.

"Hi, Earl!" I answer the phone almost giddy. Is this what you call holding your ground?

"Jo, I saw from my caller ID that you called. How have you been, and how is Grandma?"

Like a lovesick teenager, I get up from the desk and sit back on the bed, relax into the pillows, and enjoy the warmth of his voice. For a brief moment I let myself believe that everything is okay between us. Attempting to stay in control of my emotions and the conversation, I answer. "Grandma is still a fireball. She called me this morning to check on me at 5:00 a.m. She said she's worried about me. I just feel she doesn't want me to be successful, unless it's on her terms."

"She just loves you, Jo. That's why we're worried, especially since you seem out of sorts lately. All work and no play."

"Earl, did you call to give me a lecture? Don't bother. I already got one from Grandma this morning about my work. Can't we have a conversation about my work without your judgment? I'm being doubled teamed, and I don't like it."

"That's fair, can I start over again? Jo, how are things going with your articles?"

I relax a bit. Talking about my research is safer ground than talking about Grandma. "I'm down in DC. I've been really busy researching and did an interview today for my second article on abortion. The pressure of this deadline is not fun, and this issue is not as cut and dry as I thought it was going to be. Did you catch the first article I wrote?"

"Yes, I did read your first article. You've picked a tough topic, and I'm sure the second one will raise some controversy as well. I agree deadlines are never fun. I remember the anxiety I had when I was trying to meet someone else's unrealistic deadlines. So who are you meeting with in DC?"

Giving Earl some insight into W.A.I.T., my conversation with Liz, and how she communicates in tangents, especially the anal leakage comments, gives us both something to laugh about. Earl has a great laugh. It has a way of resonating through him and right into me. It was even greater to feel the intimacy of talking, laughing, and sharing the day. I do love and miss him. This separation is harder on me than I want to admit.

Feeling I'm on safe ground with Earl, I continue to share how confused I am by what Liz stands for, pro-choice, even after claiming her abortion was devastating. Hopefully Earl, with his logical lawyer mind, can help me sort out aspects of Liz's abortion story. How can she still be pro-choice after pouring her heart and soul into W.A.I.T. and from the information she has shared? Maybe Earl can help me understand.

"Jo, this sounds exactly like what you have been hungering for – a meaty topic that you can pour yourself into. Liz sounds like a handful, but I'm confident you can steer the interview tomorrow and get your questions answered. Lead with curiosity. It always helps me answer your questions. It's a great surprise tactic to get to the heart of the discussion and debate."

There he goes again, being Earl: sweet, understanding and selfless. He gave up his law career to help his sister when her husband was redeployed to Afghanistan. His sister Deb has four boys and one has special needs. According to Earl he thought they needed a male presence. I'm not sure if there is more to that story he's not telling me. If what he said is trued, am I giving up him for my career? Will it be worth it? What will I regret more in my life, not being recognized as a journalist, or not being Earl Broden's wife? So much is going on in my head that I can't seem to quiet my mind even to have this conversation.

"Jo, are you still there?"

"Yes, my mind keeps wandering. It's gotten so bad lately that I can't even sleep. That's how I found Liz one sleepless night flicking through TV channels."

"You're watching late night TV? I know you don't want to hear this, but maybe you *are* working too hard. I'd hate for you to be going down this path for another ten years and realize that you're going the wrong way. I learned that lesson the hard way. Sometimes we chase our dreams and then find out they were just that, dreams. Mine became a nightmare, and I don't want you to repeat my mistake."

Why did I think my research and conversation with Liz would be a safe topic? I get off the bed, stand up, and yell back at him. "At least you had a chance to get there, and then turn back. You don't know how it feels, Earl. You grew up with two parents, a whole family, money, and a sense of stability; that's not my life. It was only Grandma and me! Since I was young I wanted to do something significant. I have to believe that there's a reason I survived the car accident when my parents didn't."

Earl keeps his cool, which at times is more frustrating to me than if he blasted me back. "Jo, you are already significant to me, to Grandma, and to God. I hope you know how much you're loved, whether the rest of the world loves you or not. I love you, and I always will."

Why do I fight against the love I receive from both him and Grandma? He's right. I am loved, but why is his love not enough? Why do I need to prove myself when it's so exhausting?

"Jo, are you still there?"

I flop back onto the bed. "Yes." I wipe a tear from my eye and take a deep breath reminding myself not to give in to my emotions. "How can you say you love me and then leave me? It still doesn't make sense to me. I'm so confused and talking to you makes me more confused. Nothing makes sense anymore."

"What doesn't make sense, Jo? "

"That you love me but won't live with me. You love me but won't stay in the relationship unless we get married. That being successful is causing such strain on my relationship with you and Grandma. None of it makes any sense. I feel you give me freedom to pursue my dreams and then put constraints on the relationship. Don't you see how that's confusing to me?"

Earl's voice is so soothing. He lowers it to his reassuring tone. "Yes, I can see how it's confusing. I want you to be free to pursue your dreams. I respect what you are trying to achieve. I also want the best for you. And to me, that's not living together, unless we're married. Jo, you were the one who said it would be over between us if I ever left your house. I didn't issue the ultimatum; you gave it to me. I want to be in your life, but you set the final parameters."

How does he do that? How does he tell me the truth in such a gentle, loving, and calm manner? It makes me want to scream!

"What do you really want, Jo?"

"That's the million-dollar question." And I wish I knew my answer. Too often I want to run away, give up on my dream, and say yes to his marriage proposal. Other times I'm so focused on this goal that I feel I will die if I don't achieve it.

"Jo, did I lose you again?"

"No, I'm just thinking. I'm not sure what I want, maybe that's the problem. If I don't do it your way, I feel like a petulant child and that unsettles me. If I do it my way, I might lose the two people I love most in this world, and that scares me. I just don't know. Sometimes both yours and Grandma's love makes me feel smothered. That's crazy, I know. I just need more time to sort this out. Doesn't time heal all wounds?"

"Jo, if I've wounded you in some way, let me know. I can't fix it if I don't know what I'm doing to hurt you."

I've confused him; I've hurt him. I can hear it in his restrained tone.

"That's probably not what I meant. I don't know how else to describe how I'm feeling."

"Can we take one step at a time? Jo, I've lived under anger and oppression from my father. The last thing I want is to put you through that. What demands have I put on you? How am I smothering you or making you feel like a child? I want to be your husband, not your father."

I start to cry. I didn't want to, didn't plan to, and now I'm sobbing like a big baby. I can't even respond to him because I don't know the answer. He's right. Grandma's right. I am out of sorts, but I don't know why?

Oh, God please help me!

"Jo, please don't cry. Please. This conversation is not the one I wanted to have with you, especially after weeks of not talking. Maybe we need to take a break and let you get back to work. I know you've got a lot to do, and I don't want to be a negative distraction. I also don't want this divide between us to get any wider."

This is not the conversation I wanted either. My stomach is in such a knot. My head is pounding, but I don't want him to hang up. "It's not just you, Earl. I feel like something inside of me is splitting, or pulling me apart. It's exhausting. I'm so out of sorts. I don't know who I am anymore or what I want. What I do know is that I don't like feeling this way; not sleeping, watching TV late into the night, and being apart from you. What's happening to me? I just need to finish these articles. Maybe it is the stress of the deadlines, doing research, finding information I knew nothing about. I feel over my head right now. That's it! I'm just overwhelmed with work. Can you give me the time?"

"Yes, I said that I would. I'm here for you. Whatever you need Jo, let me know. Remember I use to work in the corporate world. I could be a good sounding board for your ideas and even help you review some of the research you've been doing. You don't need to do it all alone."

"Thanks, Earl, but I *need* to do this on my own. If I succeed or fail I want it to be mine, to own it. Give me a couple of weeks . . . please? Thanks for your calls. I appreciate them more than you'll ever know, even if I don't return them."

"Good night, Jo. Get some rest."

How does he do that? Love me and respect me even though I totally frustrate him? Fighting is better than not talking to him. I didn't even realize how much I needed him tonight.

My heart screams, *Jo, run to him!*

But if I don't finish this project, try to make it as a journalist, I'll always wonder what my life could've been if I reached my dream. He said he'd wait. But opportunity is not that kind, and I'm not sure I'll get another chance with the paper if I don't nail this series. Timing is everything.

When did my life get so difficult?

Reluctantly I go back over to the desk, pick up the last article I was reading, and get back to work. With what I've been finding in the research from Liz, the truth I've been seeking might be closer than I realized.

Earl - Chapter 5
Salve for an Aching Heart

"Better to be poor and walk in integrity than rich and crooked in one's ways."
Proverbs 19:1 (NAB)

Hearing Jo's voice on the phone after weeks of no contact was salve to my aching heart. I don't know how much longer I could have held out not hearing from her. Right before Halloween I was ready to drive over to her house, just to hear here scream at me. She's struggling, and I, more than anyone, can identify with that struggle. I've been there. I've lived her pain of trying to prove myself worthy, good enough, or whatever term you want to use, for pleasing the world.

Putting on my jacket, I decide to go sit out on my back porch to enjoy the brisk air and beauty of the moon lit sky. Mulling over tonight's conversation with Jo I wonder if I made progress with her. Are we still stuck? Restraint, she calls it. Jo has no idea how much energy it takes to sound nonchalant, not demanding, or broken-hearted. Keeping our conversation about her work was safe ground, or is it? Remembering the heated argument that put me here, alone on my back porch, tells me that maybe discussions about Jo's work are not safe territory.

It started so innocently. We were snuggling by the fire, sipping wine, and discussing some ideas for her column. Someone had recommended she write about couples living together versus marriage. Stepping back from the situation and reviewing that night from Jo's point of view, I realize I had more to do with the outcome of the argument then I wanted to believe. Jo's rejection of my proposal two months before was still stinging, that much I do know.

The wine and the warmth of the fire had lowered Jo's guard. This, I believed, had created an atmosphere to win her over to marriage. What I don't know was what tempted or prompted me to ruin this perfect evening. "Jo," I whispered in her ear, "just because something's socially acceptable doesn't mean it's right. What about denying women the right to vote or slavery? They were all once legal, and accepted. Does that make them right in God's eyes?"

She pushed herself away from me. Anger welled up in her, and hurt covered her face. My words had as much sting to them, as if I had slapped her. It felt like the right thing to say at the moment, almost perfect timing to get my point across. Now I can see how much I hurt her that night. My attempt to show Jo that socially acceptable and right in God's eyes are not always the same had pushed too hard. My desire to be right, or righteous, about marriage did not allow me to loving and graceful with my argument.

Before that night I never knew we were on opposing sides to the marriage discussion. How did I miss her intentions? Jo said her decline of my proposal was for us to wait and spend more time together. She was curious why I wanted to rush into marriage; we'd only been dating for a year. I guess loving her and wanting to spend the rest of my life with her wasn't the answer she wanted. When she suggested that I move into her place, it made sense. I was already staying there three or four nights a week, so I agreed. I also believed that this would speed up the marriage process. Now I'm not so sure if that was Jo's intention, or just my wishful thinking.

My attempt to calm the situation failed miserably. "Jo, maybe you're working too hard. You're trying to do too much in such a short period of time. I'm afraid that you are going to burn yourself out, and I won't be able to pick up the ashes."

"In case you haven't noticed, I'm not getting any younger. The window of opportunity is getting smaller and smaller each passing day. I want to reach my goal before I'm too old to appreciate it. Why aren't you supportive of my work?"

"Where did you come up with that conclusion?

Seeing you so stressed and on edge these last six months makes me want to protect you, even if it's from yourself. I think you need a voice of reason from someone who really loves and cares for you. I know what you're feeling."

"How could you? Being a journalist is different than being a lawyer. There's always someone to sue, but there are only so many newspapers to write for, and the number is rapidly decreasing. My goal has been, and it will remain, to have a weekly syndicated column by the time I'm thirty-five, and time is running out."

"What's the magic in that number?"

"That's my goal. That's what I've been striving for since I was in college. So you want me to throw it all away, is that what you're suggesting? Just dump my dream so I can be a merry little housewife. It's not going to happen!"

The accusations kept flying, and our voices kept getting louder. "Are you implying that I'm trying to stop you from reaching your dream? I want to be part of your life, and that includes your dreams. Is that what you think? Have I showed you in any way that I was giving you an ultimatum, your career or me? I would never do that. I know how important this is to you. All I'm saying is that when I watch you, I see myself three years ago trying to prove how great a lawyer I was. In the end, it was a soul-selling decision for me. I'm not a lawyer anymore and for good reason. It wasn't worth it, trust me."

"That was you, not me. This is for me, not to make my daddy happy. Remember, I don't have one. I know what I want, what will make me happy, and I will fight to get there. I will not turn back now. So either support me, or leave me because marriage is no longer up for discussion."

What pushed me off the couch and up the stairs to pack my bags I'm not sure. Even now I know I made the right decision. The biggest mistake I made in our relationship was saying *yes* to an intimate relationship outside of marriage, and *yes* to moving in with her. My sister Deb had warned me of this, but I didn't listen. What did

Deb call it, the slippery slope? That first step, that one
decision to live outside of God's plan is the first step into
saying *yes* to the world's values and *no* to God's plans for us.
How easy it was to slip back into the old worldly routine
after spending two years building and strengthening my
relationship with God. God help me, God please forgive me.

Now I wonder did she really not ever want to get
married, or just not to me? That thought never entered my
mind until tonight. I still honestly believe if I give her the
space she requested, allow her time to focus on her career,
we will be together. Hopefully Jo will learn the truth that
doing it God's way is the only way.

Jo - Chapter 6
What is W.A.I.T. All About?

*"Seeking the good of his people, and speaking out on behalf which
pertained to peace for their descendants."*
Esther 10:3 (NAB)

Liz called at 7:30 this morning to ask if she could move our appointment back to 1:00 p.m. I agreed, and I'm relieved. This will give me a little more time to finish up the last research article I was reading. Meeting her at our previously scheduled time would have meant a cold shower and a carafe of coffee in order to wake myself up after yet another sleepless night.

At 12:55, I arrive at the W.A.I.T. office armed with questions, my questions that need to be answered if I'm ever going to meet this looming deadline. Sheila, the receptionist, lets me know Liz is expecting me and directs me down the hall to her office. When I reach Liz's office, I see that she's talking to this tall, very attractive, black gentleman standing next to her desk. He caught my eye yesterday in the library. He's handsome and distinguished with a touch of gray at his temples. Boy, if he was dressed in a tux, he could pass for the next 007. Unfortunately, he didn't have an English accent, but his slight Southern drawl added to his attractiveness. Maybe he's Bob from North Carolina that Liz spoke about yesterday.

They are deep in conversation, so I step back to give them some privacy even though I am curious to hear what they are saying. I debate whether to go back to the reception area or wait until they're finished. From the few seconds I had to assess him, this man has an air of compassionate confidence. There was something gentle and strong about him that I could sense without even talking to him. I know he needed the confidence to deal with Liz, that's for sure. The compassion was probably a necessary balance to redirect and guide his co-workers after they got caught in one of Liz's whirlwind conversations. I'm thankful that I don't work for her! I silently cheered him on, sensing that he wasn't letting Liz get the best of him; he was actually doing most of the talking. Practice does develop expertise, and he's obviously had some practice dealing with her style. Maybe he can give me some tips for how to keep Liz on track.

Liz finally looks up and sees me standing at the door. She holds up her hands signaling that she needs ten more minutes. Stepping back out to the reception area I take a seat, pull out my notes, and go over my questions one more time. Not sleeping, the anxiety of the deadline, and trying to sort out all the information that Liz provided has left me feeling exhausted. If I had known she was running late I would have had another cup of coffee, or a triple shot of espresso. Caffeine could be a major reason for my sleeplessness or the cure for the exhaustion. Some days I wish there were one cure for everything. Just take the miracle cure daily, and I would be able to face whatever is thrown my way. Boy, I could use one of those miracle cures now, because Liz is a power to be reckoned with, and I don't have any power left today.

After waiting for about five minutes I hear someone approach me and I look up. It's the handsome man I saw standing in Liz's office.

"Excuse me. Hi, I'm Bob. Liz asked me to spend a few minutes with you while she wraps up some business. Would you like a cup of coffee?"

I stand up and extend my hand. "Hi, I'm Jo, but you probably already know that. I'd love a cup of coffee; you must be a mind reader. I'll need all the energy I can get to keep up with Liz this afternoon."

He gives me a fabulous smile and shakes his head. "I'm not a mind reader. Liz told me that you had a cup of coffee yesterday afternoon. I was just assuming that you like a midday energy boost, and it does help to be on your toes when meeting with Liz. So, did you get a chance to ask her any questions?"

I guess Liz told him about the entire conversation we had yesterday. "Not all of them. That's why I'm back today."

He nods his head in understanding. "She's focused and wants to make sure no one gets her off track, which generally means she is taking the other person in directions they had no idea they were going to be going in."

"She did let me get in a few questions, but I've got a lot more to ask, especially after all the research she provided me. That's why I'm here for round two. Surprisingly, I have different types of questions to ask than I did yesterday, so maybe her taking control of the meeting was actually a blessing in disguise."

"I'm glad that the research was of help. All the evidence citing complications with abortions is out there, you just need to know where to look to find the facts that you need. How do you like your coffee, or would you prefer coming with me to the kitchen and selecting it yourself? We have so many different varieties; I think we're trying to compete with most coffee shops."

"I'll go with you. Liz gave me a tour yesterday, and this is a great workplace. I might have to try one of the flavored coffees. I've already had a pot of coffee this morning and a little variety might be a bonus to the caffeine."

Bob and I chat as we make our way down to the kitchen. It's so much easier talking to Bob than Liz. I even start asking some personal questions, like where Bob's from in North Carolina. Find common ground, and like Earl said last night, curiosity.

We select our coffee, and Bob recommends that we take them into the library so that we can sit comfortably until Liz finishes with her call.

"The library is my retreat," he tells me. "When things get too hectic, I can step into this room and feel a sense of peace. It's almost like I can feel the pages of history turning, reminding me that even when bad decisions are made, righteous men and women can stand up and justice prevails."

I sit down at the conference table and start by asking him, "Can I ask you a few questions while we wait? And do you know if it's possible to speak to some of the other W.A.I.T. staff?" I feel the red rise in my face. "I'm sorry that came out wrong. I mean I wanted to talk to some of the other employees or volunteers."

Bob chuckles. "Jo, we are servers in this organization, so maybe W.A.I.T. staff is an appropriate way to describe the work we do." He obviously is trying to make me more comfortable, which I appreciate. "Would you mind if we use that when answering the phone? 'W.A.I.T. staff speaking, how may we serve you?'"

He is charming that's for sure. "I don't know if I'd use that one. Someone might think they've called a fast food restaurant and hang up the phone." I take a sip of my coffee and catch myself in the childish act of twisting my hair in spirals. Stopping in mid-twist, I pick up my notebook to refocus my attention on the interview.

Bob laughs again. "You've got a point there. We don't want to confuse anyone; we're here to help. You said you had some questions for me."

"Yes, thank you. I'm just curious. I haven't seen any other men around here but you. How are you affiliated with W.A.I.T?"

No sooner did I get that question out before I fire off four more questions. "How long have you been involved with W.A.I.T.? Why did you get involved in the first place? How do you know Liz? And why are you working for a woman's advocacy group?"

"Hold on, Jo. One question at a time," he says calmly. "I'll give you all the time you need. I'm at your disposal, well at least until Liz finds and redirects us."

"Thank you. I'm more excited about this article after reading all the information, and I don't want to miss anything."

"Liz said that this series is for your first featured article. I'm sure you feel that the weight of your entire career is on your shoulders right now. Liz and I have both been there. W.A.I.T was a career detour that we didn't plan on taking, but we are very glad we did. Treat the anxiety as a reminder that the work you are doing matters."

I nod my head in agreement. "Yes this is an important interview to me, but I didn't realize it was that obvious."

"Jo, I'm in the business of reading between the lines and finding the real intent in people's messages. You're right; there are not any men in the call center. We do employ men. We are an equal opportunity employer. They are in our IT and finance areas. We've been searching for some men to man the phones, but so far no luck."

He is easy to talk to, and I do appreciate his calmness and politeness. Hopefully I will be able to get some answers from him. "So when did you start working here?"

"I've been with W.A.I.T. since its inception. Liz and I started the group together back in the 80's. I'm a lawyer, so I took on the role of legal counsel, and that suits me. Liz is the public name and face of the organization, and rightly so. This is after all a women's advocacy group.

"As for why I got involved, I believe this is my calling – advocating for truth. When that truth can help women, men, and families to prevent the pain of abortion from occurring, it's even better. And if that's not always possible, then we're here to help our clients heal, and hopefully, to become whole again.

"How do I know Liz? It sounds like she did not give you this part of the story. We met in college, and married the summer we graduated."

"I'm sorry. Did you say that you're married to Liz? I thought the two of you just worked together."

"That doesn't surprise me. Liz doesn't reveal the personal side of our relationship. She assumes people already know. I guess if I introduced myself as Bob Betts that would have made it clear from the start. I apologize, seems like I was assuming myself."

"Okay, that puts an interesting twist to the interview. I was hoping, like I said before, to talk to W.A.I.T. staff. So let me see what else I can ask you. Did you know Liz when she had her abortion?"

Bob seems uncomfortable and pauses before he answers the question. "I was married to Liz when she had the abortion."

"I'm really confused. I just assumed, again, that Liz was not married and that's why she had the abortion. And you supported her decision?"

"To add another layer of confusion into this discussion, I didn't know about the abortion until after Liz had it."

How can two people be married and not know what is going on in one another's lives? "Let me get this correct. You were married, you knew about the pregnancy, and Liz had an abortion without telling you. I'm sorry but this story doesn't make any sense."

"That's what's so hard to explain with our story. Liz and I were having some relationship problems. For some couples absence makes the heart grow fonder, not with us. Living apart was causing a great strain on the relationship and on us individually. At times I didn't think we were going to make it. The pregnancy was adding another layer of complexity. Liz had gotten to a crushing point from all the pressure with school, with our distance and with our career aspirations. She felt an abortion was the solution to our survival."

"So were you pro-choice at the time?"

"Yes, both Liz and I were pro-choice."

"Are you still pro-choice, like Liz, or have you changed your mind?"

"I'm now pro-life after seeing the woman that I love suffer from her abortion and through a rebirth in my faith."

Isn't that always the way? They come to Jesus after they make major mistakes and want to stop everyone else from living their own lives. Thankfully, Liz did not mention faith at all. "Interesting that you're pro-life and Liz is pro-choice. Doesn't that cause a whole lot of conflict in what you do at W.A.I.T.?"

"You're right about that," he says with another chuckle. "What we do agree on is the mission of W.A.I.T and that's why we decided to form this women's advocacy group. The battle that's been waged on both sides of this discussion has hurt women. W.A.I.T's mission is to empower women through truthful information. We believe that will lead to an educated and informed choice, and hopefully less abortions."

"Is that why W.A.I.T. is an advocacy group and not a women's rights group?" I ask.

"Yes, an advocate is one that defends, supports, or pleads the case of another—someone who is trying to help people better themselves or deal with the circumstances that they were dealt. My role model for advocacy is Jesus Christ. Did you realize Jesus was a great advocate for women?"

"Jesus? An advocate for women? Now that's a stretch. My grandma made sure that I knew the Bible inside and out, but I don't remember Jesus as a women's advocate."

"Good, so you have a background that will help with my explanation. Would you mind if I share the story about the woman being stoned for adultery?"

"I do remember something about that story. A typical story of a woman getting stoned and the man is nowhere to be found."

Bob nods in agreement. "Yes, and sadly that still holds true. Jesus, however, was there with her and advocated for her. He didn't condemn her or even the people ready to stone her. By His actions He made them look inward, and He changed their hearts. He pointed out that we all have sins and that only those who have none could cast a stone. All the accusers left, and Jesus stayed with her, comforting her and releasing her from her sins. Doesn't that sound like an advocate to you?"

Great, I feel like I have a male version of Grandma sitting in front of me. There is not a problem, in her mind, that doesn't have a Jesus cure. "That's just one story, and I will trust your version for the sake of this discussion. I can see your point of view as to why W.A.I.T. is an advocacy group. But you seem to be positioning this from a religious standpoint. That doesn't sound like Liz's approach to W.A.I.T. She's advocating for women's right to full disclosure based on what?"

"That question is best for Liz to answer. What I do know is that she is advocating based on her own experience and the limited information, guidance, and counseling she received prior to her abortion. We come from different religious backgrounds, but we are both advocating for truth."

"So you do not support women's right to choose?"

Bob takes a deep breath. He seems either uncomfortable with the question or he's being tentative in how best to respond. "Jo, I'm for human rights. I'm for life, liberty, and the pursuit of happiness. What I've learned is that sometimes giving rights to one group you invariably take away rights from another. That's why we need to be careful when we fight for group or individual rights, it's never easy. Slavery is an excellent example. Slave owners by law had the right to own slaves, which then took away the slaves rights to live freely. The law deemed slaves as property without human rights. The law then took away the slave owner's right to have slaves. By the stroke of a pen, we can claim the rights of some and take away the rights of others. So which right was right?"

"Well, I can see that you and Liz share a common interviewing style, you do not directly answer the questions. So I'm not sure what you're driving at, taking away someone else's rights. Whose rights are we taking away through abortion?"

"Jo we both want you to think and see issues from all sides. Just like with slavery, one person's rights should not supersede another person's rights. The child is a human being. You're taking away his or her right to live, and you may also be taking away the father's rights. True equal rights will be when we are certain that everyone's rights are protected and accounted for, not just those with voting power."

"Why should the father have rights? It's the woman's body. She's carrying the baby for nine months, getting sick and fat. A woman is not a man's property."

I think I just crossed some invisible line with that question. The expression on Bob's face is one of pain, sadness, and grief mixed in with a little anger. Maybe I was a little insensitive by asking that question, but I'm curious.

Bob's voice moves up a notch as he tries to remain composed. "The law gives women the right to make her abortion decision immediately and without regard to the baby or father's rights. My wife made a decision that she felt was her right, and the law supported her decision to abort **our** baby. She took away my right to be a father, or for me to have any say in the decision to end the life of my child. Liz at least got to hear the sound of our little girl's cry. I was denied that right."

"What do you mean she heard your little girl cry? Is that what they called a failed abortion? I read a little about that last night, but does it really happen that often?"

Again, Bob appears tentative. Is he guarding his words or his emotions? This is after how many years, over thirty? It's very apparent the pain of losing his daughter has not gone away.

"Liz had her abortion in the third trimester. It was illegal then and should stay illegal. Because of Liz's distressed situation and my perceived absence, a doctor agreed to perform the abortion. Labor was induced, so Liz gave birth to our child."

With that declaration, Bob pushes himself away from

the table and walks over to the window. Boy, did I ask the wrong question! His temperament changes from sad to mad. You can definitely see why Bob is so passionate about W.A.I.T. He lost, from what Liz said, his only child. How could they have reconciled such a deep hurt? Maybe his rebirth in faith was necessary.

He is still over by the window but continues to talk. "I really don't want to go into the details, so please excuse me. It's still too painful. Together I know we could have gone for help, to seek advice or look into other alternatives. We could have had a better ending to this story. Unfortunately we don't have the luxury of time machines to go back to change our choices. Abortion is permanent!"

His passion for advocacy is making sense. Once the abortion happens, there is no chance to rethink your decision. Thankfully he comes back to the table and seems to have regained his composure.

Sitting back down, Bob apologizes. "Jo, I'm sorry. My hurt over this part of my life can still stir up old anger and resentment. This is just too painful and personal a topic."

"Why wouldn't you be angry? I don't know how I'd feel if the roles were reversed." Be careful here. I'm not supposed to be interjecting my opinion into the conversation. Your job is to ask questions only. How do I get out of this uncomfortable discussion? I look at the questions in my notebook, but I need to know what really happened while being careful not to get tangled up in Bob's emotions. That's what will make being a journalist so hard— staying neutral. And right now I'm on Bob's side.

"Bob, so you are saying that the abortion was due to your separation, not being planned, and Liz feeling so distressed? Liz didn't want to talk about her abortion. She said it was old news. So how did you two work through this crisis? Can you fill in the rest about when you found out?"

"That's painful history for both of us. Every day for over thirty years I've watched my wife and seen the sorrow and regret in her eyes. I'm the only one who would ever notice. You think Liz is strong now; you should have seen her before the abortion. She was even more of a whirlwind. The physical and emotional repercussions from the abortion took years of healing for us both. Starting W.A.I.T. was part of that healing. Taking our struggles and working to make a difference from what we experienced saved our marriage. We became a united force again for a cause that we believed in, truth."

"That seems a little too simplistic. If abortion is the trauma you say it is, how could advocating for truth heal your marriage?"

"I don't mean it to sound simplistic. It was very difficult, and there were times I thought we wouldn't make it. When Liz called to tell me what she had done, I was so angry I told her I never wanted to talk to her or see her again. I thought we shared everything, that we were partners and equals. I never felt so diminished in my life, and with my background, that says a whole lot. A week later she was admitted into a psychiatric hospital. I really thought about leaving her. What else could I do? I didn't even think I could look at her again, let alone love her."

"This is obviously painful, and I'm so appreciative to hear your perspective as a father. I still can't understand how a divide so deep can be healed."

"I'm now a firm believer that any divide can be bridged if you have Christ walking alongside you through the pain. The other part that got me through was my family. I had a strong family growing up. We stick together. We share our fears and struggles, and we get through it. My dreams were destroyed by that one decision, or at least that was how I felt at the time. I loved my wife, but I was lost, covered in grief, and wasn't sure where to turn. Fortunately I turned to my family, who directed me back to the Lord. Without the support of my mother, brother, and sisters, I don't know where we would be today."

"Faith and family? That's what helped you get through. You sound like my Grandma. It's just the two of us, and she believes the same thing." So why do I fight against her faith and my family?

Bob seems to be now on safe ground. How quickly his mood changes; he's even laughing as he tells me the rest of the story. "I laugh every time I think about it. I know the hand of God was with us. Can you imagine my black Southern Baptist family telling me to stay with my white agnostic wife after having an abortion? We didn't even get married in a church. They counseled me to stay with Liz and trust God to heal our wounds. They were Christ's hands and feet for me during that time."

"I've become a little skeptical about my own faith. Is faith the cure to everything? What about Liz? She seems to be doing okay without it."

"Faith is not fact, and it is hard for those of us who need to see it or prove it to believe it. For me, yes, it was critical to my healing. My faith has allowed me to forgive her, erase most of the pain, and see the good that God can create when we say yes to Him. It helps me to know that the Lord has forgiven her as well. Without faith, Liz has not yet totally forgiven herself."

I ponder Bob's word for a few seconds.

"Aren't you being a little over the top with faith? It's like you've got it all together and Liz doesn't. I've only just met you, but it seems you're both pretty strong. Why are you any different than Liz?"

Bob checks his coffee cup. "Would you mind if I got something else to drink? Between the emotions, yes I admit that I have them, and all this talking my mouth is dry. Can I get you something while I'm up?"

Smart man, trying to diffuse the situation, but also being confident enough to admit he is vulnerable. That's a quality I admire in anyone, and one that Earl has. "Sure, something cold and without caffeine would be great."

We get up from the table, and Bob walks beside me and answers the question. "I think it's because that's the only child we were able to conceive. The burden was even

heavier for her. That's why she works so hard, advocates
for waiting periods, pre-abortion counseling, and
ultrasounds before every abortion."

"So all of this is very personal. You've both felt pain,
though different, from the abortion and your only goal is to
inform, not to stop abortions."

"Yes and no. We want to expose the truth in the
light. I'm not naïve enough to believe we have the power to
stop abortions. We're both terrified that abortion laws will
be even more liberal with absolutely no restrictions, then
what will happen? More lives lost, and I'm not only
speaking of the baby's lives. I'm also talking about the
mothers' and fathers' lives that are affected. So, yes, it is
personal."

"Is that how your counselors feel? Are they trying to
stop the clients from having an abortion or providing
information and truth?"

"Good question. Our counselors are here to support
and encourage our clients to understand the full implications
of their decision. They've been there, so they know the pain
and that allows them to counsel without judgment. If there
were an easy answer to this, W.A.I.T. wouldn't exist. Our
counselors go through intense healing support. The training,
our support systems, and their counsel to women in need are
very cathartic for them."

"I'm not sure I got that question answered.
Are they supportive counselors no matter what the decision,
or are they trying to talk them out of an abortion?"

Bob opens up a well-stocked refrigerator, picks up
two bottles of water, and loosens the cap of one before
handing it to me. He is a Southern gentleman.

As we walk back to the library, he takes a detour into
the call center. "If you want, you can listen to what the
counselors are saying and hear it for yourself. It is mostly
support. If the client asks a direct question, such as, did you
ever have an abortion? The counselors can share their
experience. I was really lucky to have had the support of my

family to help me through the grieving process. How many men and women are not given that support? We will never truly enlighten women and men to the full extent that abortion hurts if we don't have more people telling their stories. But as you can see from my own emotions, these stories are told with a price."

"Maybe if I have time before I leave I can sit in. It doesn't seem right to listen in on a conversation."

Bob heads us back to the library. "I guess I should have clarified what I was recommending. You would only being hearing what the counselor says, not the client. Would that make you more comfortable?"

"Thanks for the offer. But I am working on a tight deadline for the article and need to focus." Bob is a good man, that's for sure. His kindness, love for Liz, and even his grief about his daughter make him an even stronger man than I first believed. Is it his faith, his personality, or his intelligence that makes him so attractive, or is it his passion for the cause? Maybe all three, he is a lot like Earl.

We sit back down in the library. The little walk was helpful in calming my nerves. Interviewing is tougher than I thought, especially on such an emotional topic.

"Jo, legalized abortion has been around for over forty years, and still this is not cocktail or family dinner discussion. The victims are shrouded in hurt, pain, and shame because no matter what the law says, a human life was taken."

I see Liz standing in the doorway listening to our conversation. She motions to me that she'll be right back.

I want to get the rest of my questions answered. Maybe I need to speed things up. "I'm beginning to see what W.A.I.T. really means to you both. You both want women to wait and think through their options. I can see where waiting is a giant obstacle since we are such an instant-gratification society. I hate waiting for anything – traffic, downloads on my computer, or standing in line for my coffee. Once I make my decision, I want it now. An instant fix. Too often I've not understood the ramifications of my decisions. I remember reading somewhere when you need to make an important decision that you should ask yourself: how will this impact me ten days, ten months, and ten years from now? I don't always ask myself those questions, and I have to admit I've made some poor decisions. Buying my big old, fixer upper house is one example. That was definitely an emotional decision. I'm sorry a costly purchase is not at all in line with the gravity of an abortion."

"Jo, our challenges are our challenges. Whatever they are there is a lesson to be learned. What we try so hard at W.A.I.T. to do is to share both the facts and the feelings. Too often the facts aren't presented and are difficult to find. But that is where the truth is; it's in the data. A survey of post-abortive woman found that sixty-three percent say they regret their abortions. When we make decisions in haste, there may be repercussions that we never really expect. And they can last a lifetime. So, Jo, can you see why we're advocating for information and a waiting period?"

"You're saying that in the long run, you are trying to protect the well being of the mother. That you want to help women make the best decision, not just now, but forever."

"Yes, waiting allows time to think and consult with others as with any other invasive medical procedure or major decision. Laws protect people from making bad decisions. Do you know that you have a three-day rescission period on home equity loans? This allows people to sit back and not have buyer's remorse. Why not have the same for abortions? If it isn't an emergency, and you have time to research the procedure and doctors, why wouldn't you? This ensures your protection and that a well informed decision can be made."

"Bob, if you are only proposing laws that will protect women, why are you getting so much opposition?"

"I'll answer that one," Liz chimes in as she comes into the room with three bottles of water. She hands me a refill and gives the other to Bob.

Bob stands up as Liz comes over to join us. She looks like she just came from the spa, not a conference call. I guess her call must have turned out in her favor. Bob excuses himself, wishes me good luck with my article, and leaves me alone with Liz. I think I could have sat all day and listened to him. He is gentle, but strong with a faith that seems to be working for him. Maybe there are lessons to be learned not just about abortion, but faith. He seems peaceful, and that is something that has not come easy to me over the last several months.

Liz sits down. "Was Bob helpful to you? Did he give his perspective on why he cares so much about advocating for women?"

Was this planned? It is interesting that I get to hear both sides to the story. Maybe they are polar opposites that attract and join forces. "Yes, he did, and I have to admit it was very compelling. He is a very interesting man."

"You've got that right! He is my strength, my safe harbor, and my sanity. He's a good man, Jo. He has done so much good with W.A.I.T., even if at times it feels more like we're the cleanup crew rather than the lead of the parade to change. I'm baffled how we could be doing such good work, have all the research to support our cause, and still not have gotten more traction and attention. But, we believe if we can't change laws maybe, just maybe, we can change some people's minds and hearts on this topic."

"That was exactly what I've been thinking. With the two of you, all of your counselors, and I'm sure the other support you've gotten from your clients – why are we not hearing more about this? Something just doesn't seem right. Can you clear that up for me, or do I need to do more research?"

Liz laughs. "Did I overwhelm you? I have a nasty habit of giving so much information that I might overload, rather than inform. I might need to change my tactics. I think it would be a good idea for you to talk to some of our clients. We've gotten permission from several, which is interesting considering we have talked to millions over the last thirty years, who are willing to share their stories. Just let me know, and I can put you in touch."

I thank her for her offer, but I would rather not. I'm sure she can find a handful, like she said of people who can support their position. What I need is someone I can trust, and who will tell it to me straight. "Thanks Liz, but I'm on a tight deadline with the next article due in a couple of weeks. Bob and you have given me a good perspective and with all the research, I guess I have enough to go on."

Liz is much more gracious this afternoon and lets me lead and ask my questions. She doesn't reveal anymore about her abortion, again saying that this is not about her, it's about her work. An hour later, Bob comes back into the library to inform Liz that they have an unexpected visitor, a congressional aide who wants to talk to them. They both apologize for cutting my time with Liz short. Bob promises that he will be available to answer any further questions as he hands me his business card. Liz does not.

I'm disappointed, that's for sure. I wanted more time with Liz. Having a male perspective is helpful, but it's Liz that I want to know more about, especially why she really aborted the baby. Maybe she was sparing Bob's feelings and not telling him the whole truth. What makes me think she would tell me?

Bob escorts me out to the reception area. He shakes my hand with a two-handed shake and looks me in the eyes. "Jo, this is a tough topic, and I'm not sure why you are taking up this challenge. We need to have our message get out; we need to let people know that there are two sides to this debate. I hope that we've given you enough information to know the impact that Liz's abortion has had on both of us."

He lets go of my hand and walks away. Maybe I'm reading him wrong, but I think he wanted to share something with me. What I'm not sure. Maybe it was another lesson, another Bible story, or something else that would've changed my mind. I'm not so sure he could have said anything that would have, but I still wish he'd told me.

No, maybe there is something he could have said, how much he misses not having his child.

Chapter 7
Fork in the Road

"Wherever arrogance may be, there too is insult, but wherever humility is, there too is wisdom."
Proverbs 11:2 (CPDV)

Who are all these people on the road? Where are they all going at 8:05 on a Tuesday night? By delaying my drive home until after dinner I assumed, which is always a bad thing to do, that I would miss the crazy traffic on Interstate 95 trying to get out of DC. After the intense meetings with Liz and Bob, and then being cut short after she promised me all the time that I needed, I decided to collect my thoughts and transcribe my notes at a Starbucks before getting on the road. I'm still reeling from Bob just sashaying into the library and calling an end to our meeting. Being dumped for a Senate aide makes sense, even to me; but I still have questions to ask Liz, and I'm running out of time.

Even an additional hour with Liz did not provide me with the chance to ask the questions that were really pressing, like what happened to the baby after she heard it cry? After hearing Bob's story, I am amazed that they are still together. How could he ever forgive Liz? Maybe it was his faith. I see Grandma's faith has taken her places I would never go. No matter what happened, she was always harping to turn the other cheek and asking, "What would Jesus do?" They are both better people than me because I still think that sometimes forgiveness should not be an option.

In some ways it feels like I opened up Pandora's box and can't contain all these new ideas, insights, and information about abortion. This article is not going in the direction it was supposed to go, and if what Liz and Bob say is true, maybe there is another story that needs to be told.

Just when I thought it couldn't get any worse, traffic screeches to a halt. All I see is a line of brake lights in front of me. Searching the radio for a traffic report is no help. I just missed the traffic report and they only report traffic every ten minutes, on the twos. Frustration wells up as I look down at my gas gauge and see there is only a quarter tank left. My plan is to stop after Baltimore, grab some gas and a coke for the final trek home. Plans are great, but not accomplishing them is painful.

Banging my head on the steering wheel, a lame attempt to release the pressure building in my head, causes a powerful chain reaction. The bang not only hurts my head, but my car horn is squealing as well. Raising my head, I hear a symphony of liked-minded, angry horns blasting their wrath back at me. Everything I touch, even my steering wheel, is turning into a disaster.

"Josie Beth, what's the lesson in all of this?" Another Estherism pops up in my head. Out of habit, I search to find the lesson. None, nada, nothing. I suppose the lesson could be don't slam your head into the steering wheel. Another good lesson is don't drive on I- 95.

Grandma would have a list of at least ten lessons or blessings for this situation. How does Grandma always do it? Maybe it's another of her supernatural gifts to find a lesson or blessing in every bad thing that comes her way, and she sure has had a whole lot of practice. Her response to the parking lot situation on Interstate 95 would be to thank God we are here and not in the accident, to be grateful that I don't have to go to the bathroom yet, and to be happy that my car is running and the heater works. She thanks God for everything, and I am thankful for nothing. Well, I will be really, really thankful when I get home safely.

"How much longer are we going to sit?" I shout to no one and everyone at the same time.

Turning back on the radio, I glance up to see it is 8:13. I missed the traffic on the twos again. Grabbing my iPhone, I turn on the GPS and see if there are any traffic alerts. There are none. Well, since I'm stuck with nowhere to go, maybe I will glance at my messages. I can't be breaking the cell phone usage law if I'm not actually driving. Just to make sure, I do a quick check to see if there are any cops in the area. With my luck, this is a cell phone checkpoint, and I'll be caught red-handed. It appears to be all clear. There are no flashing lights, so it's safe to scan my phone for messages. Spam, ad, spam, and then "Josie, can we meet? Nicole" in the subject line. I open the email and see a short message from my college roommate.

Nicole contacts me after ten years. My emotions are running the gamut from sadness to anger, excitement to disappointment, and then the one that really gets to me, curiosity. Why now and what does she want? Wow, how long has it been since I last spoke to her? A feeling of regret comes over me as my thoughts drift back to the closeness of our relationship. Now I can't even remember when I last spoke to her, or more accurately when was the last time I reached out to her and got no reply.

She wrote that she will be in the area next week and would like to see me. My heart actually jumps as I realize she used my work email to contact me. Maybe she obtained it from my column. The roller coaster of feelings quickly returns. Why does she want to talk to me? Maybe I should just ignore her, as she ignored me so many times. Why is she interested in me now? Because I have a column, I wasn't good enough for her before?

The honking noises start up again, but this time they aren't coming from me. They're directed at me. Looking up, I see that traffic in front is finally moving. How long have I been distracted reading this message? Checking my rearview mirror, I see my lane of cars is at a standstill. Shifting my car into drive, I move into the flow of traffic, but my mind is still parked, back at Nicole's email.

Part of me wants to feel flattered that someone from my past saw and read my column. Another part of me just feels the anger from her abandonment. Nicole was the only friend, true friend, I ever allowed myself to have. After all the friend troubles I had throughout junior and senior high school, I believed college would be a fresh start with my history quietly tucked away in North Carolina. How we were selected as roommates I will never know. For me it felt like a stroke of luck, much needed luck. Grandma didn't buy that. She called luck a "Godincidence" believing that all things happen for a reason and for God's purpose in our life.

Well, at least I knew what Nicole's purpose was in my life. She taught me how to loosen up and have some fun. Interesting how our differences never divided us; it always brought us together. We were two different ends of a magnet, and I was most definitely the negative pole. With absolutely nothing in common, except the fact that we both were only children and grew up in Christian households, we still became fast friends. Coming up north to college was a little bit scary for me. Make that very scary. If it weren't for Nicole, I would have left after the first semester. She took me under her wing and helped me integrate into college life. She made friends so easily. People were drawn to her because she had exuberance for life, and every encounter with her was fun. Whether we were going to the cafeteria for lunch, the library to study, or one of her many impromptu excursions into Philly, everything became an adventure.

So if we were such good friends, why am I so angry with her? Maybe because I opened up to her, shared my life with her, and she slammed the door shut with no reason or explanation. It looks like I have a track record of becoming vulnerable, letting people in, and then being tossed aside when I am no longer wanted.

Curiosity wins, it always does. Maybe there is a silver lining in all of this. Maybe it's more than just a coincidence. I can ask for her perspective on my article. She has direct insight and experience; getting her side would be a much-needed boost to this project. To hear about how she feels ten years post-abortion might provide the balance that I want and need for this article. Who knows? Maybe it's another Nicole and Josie "Godincidence"?

Finally and gratefully, I pull into my driveway. That drive was a killer. The traffic added another hour to an already merciless commute. The darkness that surrounds my house is eerie. I love the solitude of my home's location, but when it's dark, it's really dark.

I feel warmth as I open my front door, and for that, I have to admit, I do feel thankful. The old beast is still running. Putting my keys on the foyer table, I look around. I'm still in love with this house. It's mine and whenever I'm in it, I can be me.

I put some water on for chamomile tea to quiet my restless stomach. Walking to my office, I turn on the light and see my safe writing haven, an old antique desk that Earl refinished for me. It looks rich and expensive, but it really is merely a garage sale find from one of our many antiquing trips. Taking my laptop from its case, I place it gently at its rightful place on my desk. I turn it on and listen to the soft sound of the laptop coming back to life. Opening the file I completed at Starbucks hours ago, I double check to make sure that my work is still there. To be safe that it doesn't disappear I sent it to the cloud and emailed it to myself. A little excessive, but I want to make sure it does not go MIA. I've worked too hard to lose this work.

The kettle whistles beckoning me back to the kitchen. After pouring the tea, I glance in the refrigerator to see if there is anything to eat. Nothing of interest, but I open the freezer and see a container of Earl's split pea soup. Just what I need, something warm and hearty! Reheating the soup in the microwave gives me a few minutes to run upstairs, change, and get into my sweats. A very late night snack is ready and the scent of homemade, love-kissed soup fills the air. That's what Earl would say each time he put a meal in front of me, "It's love-kissed." He was always trying to impress upon me how wonderfully he took care of me, and he did. Earl's a much better cook than me, so I enjoyed every meal he made and every kiss he gave me.

Stop this trip down memory lane before it brings you to a dead end, Jo. Ruminating always does.

"Capture your thoughts, Josie Beth, or they will take you hostage." Another Estherism. Grandma had all these little sayings that she used to help me with my ever running mind, and all the other problems that plagued me as a kid. Capture my thoughts I will, and then tie them up and kick them out the door.

Heading back to my office with my midnight snack, I get ready to work. I open Nicole's brief message again. How could one email, from a long-ago friend put me on this emotional roller coaster? Curiosity again gets the best of me, and I take some college photo albums off of the shelf. I take some time to remember Nicole and our adventures in college. These pictures capture the truth about our times together. Nicole was the most beautiful and self-assured person I've ever met, and in college she was very much the exception. The rest of us were so uncomfortable in our own skin. Not Nicole. She wore both her skin and her clothes very well. She looked great in t-shirts and old jeans, her staple, even though she had an entire wardrobe of designer clothes.

Funny, I looked better than I remember. That had a lot to do with Nicole. One of the best parts about being her roommate was that we were the same size. Her closet was my closet. Was her generosity because she cared so much for me, or so little for her clothes? Whatever the reason, it doesn't matter now. Her wardrobe sure came in handy. Work was an essential part of my college life. Nicole's clothes gave me the illusion of confidence whenever I interviewed for a job. Her wardrobe might not have done much for her, but it helped me land much more professional internships than I could have gotten with Grandma's homemade creations. For that reason alone, I should be thankful and give her a bit of a break on the betrayal.

I send her a quick email message. "Sounds great. I'll meet you at Turning Point on Wednesday at noon." I include the address and provide her my cell phone number just in case she needs to change her plans.

With the interviews done, the outline to the article written, and a chance to speak with another person who had an abortion, I feel like I have things under control. I can do this and write a solid article that will make an impact. I shut off the lights as I head upstairs. Feeling satisfied, maybe I can even get some sleep tonight.

Chapter 8
Turning Point

"A joyful heart is the health of the body. But a depressed spirit dries up the bones."
Proverbs 17:22 (NAB)

Wednesday came around so quickly. I'm vacillating on how I feel about my lunch meeting with Nicole. Both excitement and trepidation lobby for my attention as I rush around preparing to see her for the first time in ten years. It's so hard to believe it has been ten years, ten long years missing and resenting her. What has kept her away, and now, what is bringing her back?

"God's timing is perfect." Another Estherism tries to take over my mind and send me to a place that I no longer fit in or believe in. Did I ever believe in God's perfect timing, or have I heard Grandma say it so many times that it feels true?

If I documented what I do all day, ruminating and worrying would be top on the list. If only I could find a cure for a wandering mind. That would be my ticket to fame and fortune. The only remedy I know of is fresh air and exercise, like long walks or runs along the river. Both have always helped me clear my head and prepare myself mentally and physically for what lies ahead. Putting my car keys back in my purse, I decide to take the two-mile walk into town and enjoy this cold, but sunny November day.

Even if the reunion does not go as well as I hope, at least I will have had a meal at one of my favorite restaurants, Turning Point. The name alone gives me fuel to keep moving forward. Soon, very soon, my turning point is coming. Walking is the best idea I've had in a long time. The crispness of the air, the crunch of brittle leaves, and the bright sunshine-filled day ensures nothing can go wrong. Or at least I hope so.

I see the typical lunchtime crowd filling the seats as I open the door to the restaurant: ladies lunching, businessmen bragging, a few retirees looking for some company and comfort food. Wanting to collect my thoughts and keep away from the frenetic pace in the front of the restaurant, I ask the hostess for a table in the back corner. The table provides a clear view of the front door and some privacy. Glancing up at the clock on the stone fireplace I can't stop feeling a little nervous. What am I so apprehensive about? Since the last time I saw Nicole, I'm doing pretty good for myself.

Due to my fretfulness minutes pass slowly as I wait for Nicole. I begin to worry if she's going to show when I see that it's now ten after the hour. *Did she change her mind?* But then I remember that Nicole was always late, and I suspect that part of her hasn't changed. Why am I feeling so anxious today? Is it excitement to see Nicole again, or knowing I will probably be stood up? Hard to tell anymore what I'm feeling and why.

For four years Nicole was like that sister I never had. I always thought she felt the same about me. What happened, what did I do that she chose never to return my calls, or answer my letters? Was it something I did or said? Was she tired of the country bumpkin friend constantly tagging along? Had she wanted to return to her more sophisticated, country club, New England buddies?

For the first time in a long time, I begin to worry about how I look. No designer suits yet, but this is a good knock off. My curly hair is hopeless, but I remember how Nicole loved my curls as much as I loved her straight blonde hair. As for my weight, I have slimmed down since college. I can thank Earl for that since he encouraged me to run with him. Running and some weekly trips to the gym have me more toned and fit than when I was in college. Odd, I never cared about appearances when I thought of Nicole, why now? That was not what our relationship was about. It was about two girls who bonded like glue until she pulled us apart.

My focus time is about ten seconds. I keep checking my phone for emails, missed calls, or text messages.

Nothing. As the waitress comes around for the third time, I ask for a cup of chamomile tea and let her know I am still waiting on my friend. What's ten minutes when I've been waiting ten years?

I scan the restaurant looking for signs of her. Maybe she's already seated and looking for me. *It's only ten minutes. Take it easy.* Distractions, even friendly or family, are getting in my way of finishing this article. Hopefully our lunch will help me discern the truth about abortion from someone I know. Then even if the relationship is not rekindled, I will at least get some information for my article.

My eyes are now focused on two tables in the front of the restaurant with loud businessmen. The noise up front suddenly quiets down, and I stand up to see if Nicole arrived. Nicole had a shut-up factor to her. When she opened the door and glided into the room, it quieted to a hush as everyone watched her walk, if you could call it that, across the room. Grandma would always say, "Nicole is a head turner." No Nicole, it's just the arrival of food. I watch with a growl in my belly as the wait staff places hot bowls of soup, colorful salads, and warm toasted sandwiches in front of the hungry customers.

My tea arrives and I glance up again as the clock strikes 12:15. I hear the jingling of the Christmas bells on the front door welcoming someone new into the restaurant. In walks a girl with short blonde hair, a huge mauve-colored puffy coat, and large sunglasses. The blonde girl takes off her sunglasses and scans the tables looking for someone. She glances over at me, stops, raises her hand, and waves. Could this be Nicole? It can't be. If I hadn't been looking for her, she could have walked by without me giving me a second glance. Well, that isn't true; I would have noticed a giant coat on such a thin girl. As she hands her coat to the hostess, I notice something else. She's not just thin - she's emaciated. Where did my Nicole go?

Shaking the anxious thoughts out of my head, I walk over to make sure it's her. The hollowness of her face makes her huge blue eyes look even bigger. She brightens up as I come forward. This really is Nicole. We embrace, longer than I expect, she holds so tight I fear she will never let go of me. I relax my hold for fear I could break every bone in her back. Even at emaciated, I underestimate her weight, she's sickly thin. A million questions cross my mind at that moment. What's wrong with her? Great, I don't see my friend for ten years, and she looks months, maybe even weeks away from death.

How do you restart a relationship, especially when it is on such obviously unsteady grounds? Should I comment on her weight, ask what the hell is wrong with her, or take the avoidance approach, which is totally unnatural for me? Under these circumstances, it's the only approach I am comfortable using. Her appearance has rendered me speechless.

Just like old times she grabs my hand to make sure I don't run away from her when her tales become too long, detailed, and exasperating for me. Together we walk over to my table.

"Josie, you look fabulous! You're going to be one of the lucky ones who get better with age. Unfortunately, I hit my peak in college and the road ahead doesn't look so promising," she says with more joviality than her appearance would expect.

How do you respond to that comment with the truth written all over it? "Nicole, you will always be beautiful," I say with more conviction than I feel. How did she become this skeleton of who she once was? No wonder she's been in hiding.

"You're probably wondering why I decided to get in touch with you after so many years," she continues. "Most people think I fell off the face of the earth, and I kind of did."

"Yes, you did pique my curiosity but how could I say no to my very best friend?" My comment, which was not planned, seemed to put her at ease. Kindness balanced with curiosity is a much better approach to gaining trust. I'll have to use that tactic more often.

"In my email I told you that I read your article at my doctor's office. To be more specific, it was my therapist's office. Let me reassure you, since I saw the look on your face when I walked in, I'm not terminal or contagious. I have an eating disorder. Don't go pitying me, girl. Believe me when I say I look great compared to six months ago."

Again I am rendered speechless now by her comment. Aren't eating disorders for the weak, not someone as strong, popular, and exciting as Nicole? The waitress walks over to take our order, and I welcome the interruption. How do I respond to that bit of news? Do I appear grateful that her condition is not terminal, or respond truthfully–perplexed that Nicole could allow this to happen to her?

The waitress taps her pencil on her notepad, which snaps me back to attention. I guess I went on another one of my rumination tours to gather my composure. "I'll have whatever she is having," I blurt out without thinking. Oh, great, what if Nicole didn't order any food? She'll think I lost my mind, or that I'm making fun of her.

"Great choice," the waitress responds. "We have been getting a lot of thumbs up with our new salad menu. Would you like dressing mixed in or on the side?"

Looking at Nicole I decide to take a risk. "Mix it in for me. Thanks."

The second the waitress leaves, Nicole starts up exactly where she left off. "I'm on the road to recovery, and this time it will stick. That's why I needed to talk to you. I misled you into thinking that I was traveling in the area. This was a very intentional trip. After I read your article on abortion, this nagging feeling that I needed to talk to you wouldn't go away. So I gave in to it. You know my past, and I think you need to know the rest of my story, including my post-abortion experience. "

I was wondering how I could get her to talk to me about her abortion, and she opens up immediately. I'm starting to believe in these little "Godincidences." What a gift! Now I don't have to look like I have an ulterior motive in saying yes to the meeting. No matter what her reason was for reaching out to me, my heart aches for her. Not knowing what else to do, I gently squeeze her hand. It's my lame attempt to show my acceptance while encouraging her to go on with her story.

"This is so hard for me to talk about. My therapist is encouraging me to express my feelings verbally and as often as I can. Internalizing this anger has been destructive. I mean, look where that has gotten me? You were there, Josie, so you know the ultimatum my parents gave me. I was coerced into having that abortion."

She stops almost as if she is backtracking. My mind begs her, *Don't stop now, Nicole. Tell me the truth.*

"The truth, and I have to admit it, is that I said yes. I didn't have the courage or strength to say no, to stand up for myself and the baby."

She never told me that. I knew her parents. They were perfect in my eyes. This seems too hard to believe that they would coerce her into an abortion, but she said she was going to tell me the truth.

"At the time, my parents appeared more concerned with their reputation than me. They were so freaked out by my pregnancy, which confused me since women were having babies out of wedlock every day, even within their circle of friends. I thought the baby would help me grow up and find a focus and purpose for my life. My parents just saw me as an airhead, who made too many mistakes. This mistake, they believed, would ruin my life. An abortion would ensure that I would get a fresh start and leave this problem behind me."

"If you were your parents, what would you have done?" I ask.

"That's what my therapist is helping me come to terms with. I'm starting to see myself through my parents' eyes, and I'm disgusted with who I allowed myself to become. I didn't even know for sure who the father was and did not want to go through the painful process of figuring it out. How do you tell a child that you don't know who their father is? Somewhere along the discussion, I lost my will to fight for my child. So an abortion, at that time, did appear to be the best option."

That comment was a real shocker. Did I have my head buried in the sand during the last year in college? I thought the father of her baby was Sean Fitzpatrick.

"I had no allies in my corner. I know you were there for me, Josie, I do, but my parents and the abortion clinic counselor were powerful forces. They had all the right words, the answers. They won the argument. Who could argue with the sentiment that the abortion was going to be easy, painless, and over in a matter of hours? The best part was that I could then have my life back and do whatever I wanted. The problem would be behind me forever."

"Nicole, it sounds like you made the right decision. Maybe your parents saw all of these problems coming for you and wanted to avoid the added problem of you having a child in the mix."

The look on her face is so distorted. It looks like she's ready to kill someone, and that distorted look is directed right at me.

Nicole's face turns red and veins are throbbing in her neck. I've never seen Nicole respond this way. "That's why I need to talk to you," she spat out. "That type of attitude and the article you wrote presents abortion as important of a decision for a woman to make as a new hairstyle. Let me tell you, it's a decision that you cannot turn back. No one, not then, and certainly not now, gives you the truth about the personal ramifications that are caused by this 'choice.' I am so tired of the bullshit rhetoric on abortion and giving women freedom to choose."

I try to calm her down by asking her to lower her voice. The exact opposite happens. Nicole's words get louder and louder. They hit me like poisonous darts. The venom lethal and painful, hitting me in places I did not know existed.

"Well, you should be in the room when they suck out your baby. When you feel your child unwillingly being pulled from your body, you know right then and there what you're doing is wrong. You and those like you, who pretend to be pro-women, should know the truth. It's all a lie. My life has been destroyed because of the abortion! Do you remember me looking or acting like this in college? Well, I don't. The spiral downward started after the abortion." She punctuates the last sentence by banging her fist onto the table and spilling water all over our placemats.

My mouth drops open, and I look around the restaurant trying to divert her intense glare. What I saw were all eyes staring at me, like I had done something wrong to cause her outburst. Nicole was out of control. I hope she had her therapist's number on speed dial. She might need to check in with him right about now.

"Nicole, please." I plead, "Quiet down. This is a small town, and I don't think this conversation is G rated. Why don't we ask the waitress to pack up our salads, and we can go over to my house? It's just two miles away. It would be more comfortable there, and you can talk freely without getting anyone upset." I hope I'm convincing her because there is no way I'm going to sit here in public and listen to her rants. Thankfully, she reluctantly agrees.

"I'm sorry, Josie. I have had this anger bottled up for so long and directed it at myself. Just look at me. I have been punishing myself for ten long years. I had no right talking to you that way, directing my anger at you. You don't deserve that."

Maybe, just maybe she hasn't lost her mind. One more tirade and we're done. Who does she think she's talking to? Little, helpless Josie is gone, I think as I wipe an unexpected tear from my cheek.

The waitress boxes our salads, some rolls, and our drinks in a flash. She's in just as much a hurry, to get us out of the restaurant, as I am to leave. I don't blame her. It's hard enough for me to be in the conversation, let alone witness it, especially when I had hoped for a nice, relaxed, lunch with my old best friend. We walk over to where Nicole parked. I tentatively get in the car, somewhat afraid to be in this small space with her alone. Walking would have been my preferred mode of transportation.

Nicole is in no state of mind to take directions. The thought of having her follow me in the car makes me shudder. With her emotional state, a car would be her next weapon, and today I seem to be her target of choice.

We pull into my driveway, and she turns to me. "Josie, your home is beautiful. It has all the charm that your Grandma's house had and not like the cookie cutter McMansion that my parents prefer. How long have you been living here?"

"I've had the house for about two years."

"This house looks like it's taken care of and tended to by very loving hands," she says.

A tear streams down my cheek as I realize that those loving hands no longer live here. *Stop it, Josie. Don't get all emotional; this is not the time or place to enter into a conversation about Earl.* Someone has to have her wits about her in this conversation, and that someone is me.

Nicole admires the staircase and beautiful woodwork as we enter the foyer.

"That's why I had to buy this house. I got the same warm feeling when I walked through the front door. The wraparound porch was the selling point. And yes, it does remind me of home."

Hoping a more relaxed feeling would help turn this conversation around, I set our lunch in the living room. Nicole seems to agree with that decision and sinks, or should I say disappears, into the overstuffed sofa. Strategically positioning myself, I sit in the side chair across from her. This allows me the opportunity to keep an eye on her while providing a quick escape through the front door if she starts acting crazy again.

After a few minutes, Nicole apologizes again for the outburst. "Josie, I've missed you so much, I really have. You were a true friend, and if you remember, the one, maybe the only one, who supported my decision to keep the baby. I'll never forget that for as long as I live."

Her comment startles and confuses me. "I've missed you too, Nicole. Why did you stay away? What did I do?"

Tears stream down her face. "Josie, you did nothing wrong. I just couldn't face you; I didn't want to let you know you were right. I shouldn't have had the abortion. I thought you would hate me."

"Nicole, I knew you had the abortion. Did I ever say anything or do anything that made you think I stopped loving you or supporting you?" I ask with more anger and hurt in my voice than I should have considering her weakened state.

She shakes her head. "No, not at all. I've been projecting my thoughts and feelings onto others. I've needed you, your friendship, and level-headed thinking for so long. Thank you for forgiving me, I hope, and meeting with me. I just hope you will be able to hear what I need to tell you, I won't rest until you know."

I nod, prompting her to continue. "When I saw the article I knew it was you, even though the byline said Jo Reynolds. I could not believe the position that you were taking. I know you, or thought I did, and this is not how you were brought up. You were the one encouraging me to have the baby. If you've changed your position on abortion in ten years and moved away from your Christian pro-life stance, anyone could. I want to know what changed your mind. And I desperately need to know what I can do to change it back."

I am now getting angry with her indignation and insinuations. "What do you mean the position I was taking? I was reporting the pro-choice side to the story. That is what my byline is *Two Sides to Every Story*. The second article is due next month from a pro-life standpoint."

Nicole looks me straight in the eyes. "Josie, you and I were in the same classes. We both know the power of the press. People are writing their opinions as facts and only including the facts that support their opinions. This is editorializing, but without the guts to say, 'This is my opinion and I want you to share it and believe it as fact.'"

Who is this woman? Really, who is she? Nicole never cared about anything the least bit political. She cared more about personal feelings and parties than opinions. Yes, at times, I felt she was shallow, but she was always lovable. Now she is a woman on a mission. She doesn't take a breath but continues on her soapbox. I'm too amazed at the physical, mental, and emotional change in her that it is hard to hear anything she's telling me. I need to somehow capture her story on tape.

"I am so sick and tired, literally and physically, of how this country has twisted the truth to support an agenda called freedom of choice. People like you are leading lambs, innocent precious lambs, to the slaughter all under the guise that this will be good for them, it will give them the life that they deserve. Why let this one mistake ruin your life? Well, that decision, that precious choice you want me to be able to exercise, has ruined my life in ways that you can never imagine."

Nicole's anger dissipates as tears being to run down her face. "I'm so sorry, Josie. This is not how I wanted our reunion to be. You were the one constant bright light during my college years. You were so grounded and self assured."

I look at her and just start laughing. "Nicole, you can accuse me of a whole lot of things, but being self assured in college? You've got to be kidding me! Now I know you've lost it."

For the first time, I see a glimmer of the old Nicole, and she starts to laugh as well.

"Josie Beth Reynolds self assured? You seem to have a whole different memory of me in college than I do. What I remember is being a Christian geek Southern girl in hand-me-down clothes that had to study every waking minute to make sure I didn't lose my scholarship. That is who I was. Why did you think I was self assured?"

"Josie, you made good decisions: decisions that were based on long-range plans, not impulsive ones like the rest of us. You weren't sleeping around, partying, dabbling in drugs; you were studying."

"Yes, I was studying because I was hanging on a financial thread. One bad grade could be the difference between graduating from an elite college that had a strong reputation, or going back home in defeat. I had no choice."

"You know what, Josie? Not having a choice would have been the best thing for me. My problem was that I had too many choices. If one did not work out, well, I knew that my mom and dad would pick me up, dust me off, and take care of it. That's what my parents were good at, taking care of things and whitewashing my mistakes. I was never allowed to own or learn from my mistakes, because they always had the broom and dustpan to clean up right behind me. How else can you explain why two good, God-loving parents would ever recommend an abortion to their daughter? They actually believed that they were doing what was best for me."

"Your parents adored you. I was so jealous of you for so many reasons, but mostly because your parents were so cool."

"They are great people. I actually think they've suffered more than me for their part in the abortion decision. Watching their precious daughter self-destruct right before their eyes was exactly what they were trying to avoid. Unfortunately, the pregnancy problem could not be solved so easily. Maybe I just need to tell you about what's been happening over the last couple of years. Then I promise I want to hear all about your fabulous life. I didn't even tell you how great you look or how much I have missed you. Josie, I wish that I had called you back."

"You did tell me I looked great," I remind her.

"Thank you. Jeez, Nicole, I wish that I had been more persistent. I regret giving up on you. It sounds like you needed a friend." The last thing I wanted to do was tell her about my life. I was not close to where I wanted to be but the less she knew, the better. It's too complicated to even try to explain.

"It wouldn't have mattered, Josie. I needed more than a friend. I needed real help and finally, thank God, I'm getting it."

Nicole asks if she could tell me her story from the beginning. My heart stops. Should I ask her if I could tape our conversation? With the emotional intensity, I want to be able to hear her perspective. Listening is tough enough. Listening with a highly emotional component makes me want to put on my running shoes. Sheer boldness comes over me. "Nicole, this sounds like a really important story to you, would you mind if I recorded it? I am writing a follow-up on the first article, and your insights are exactly what I need to hear."

Surprisingly, she agrees and tells me that is why she contacted me. She wants me to know the truth. Well, isn't that a "Godincidence." Before she can change her mind, I jump up, go to my office, and grab my recorder and a pad of paper. I quickly run into the kitchen and bring us both back some iced tea. As I sit down ready to listen, really listen, Nicole starts to fill me in on the last ten years of her life.

Chapter 9
Get Me to the Airport on Time

"Who among you is wise and understanding? Let him show, by means of good conversation, his work by a good life in the humility that comes from wisdom."
James 3:13 (NAB)

Who in his right mind travels on the Wednesday before Thanksgiving? The traffic to the Philadelphia airport will be bumper to bumper. *Get moving, get out of bed, or you'll be late.* The airport shuttle is due in an hour.

Mustering what little energy I have left, I roll out of bed. I flinch at the coldness of the hardwood floor.

Turning on the shower, I run my hand under the water waiting to feel the warmth. After about two minutes, I realize it's not coming. Great, what if the heater is broken? Who's going to fix it? I will not give Earl the satisfaction and call him for help. I'll figure it out myself.

I trek down to the place I hate the most in this house, the dreaded basement. The silence of the mighty beast confirms my suspicions; the oil burner is not working. Its silence is deafening. Why didn't I listen to Earl? I had more faith in the old beast than in Earl's expertise. Well, at least the beast didn't leave me. It just isn't working.

Now what? No heat, no hot water, no Earl. Who can I call at this hour? Running upstairs I grab the phone book and call the first 24-hour plumbing and heating service I can find. *Great, the 24-hour plumber isn't even answering.* How do they get away with the false advertising? Does anyone tell the truth anymore? I'm forced to leave a message.

Why didn't I listen to Earl last spring when he strongly advised me to have it serviced to see if it needed to be replaced? Too stubborn, too little time, too sure it would hold out for another year. Now I have to deal with a crisis, and it will probably cost me double. Maybe I need to start listening to all the free advice I usually refuse to take. Then I wouldn't be regretting so many of my decisions.

I jump when the phone rings. Please God, let it be the plumber and not Grandma. Did she sense that my heater wasn't working? It wouldn't surprise me.

"Are you the plumber?" I answer curtly.

"Yes, ma'am. I'm John Cross. What seems to be the problem this morning?"

"Well, it's twenty degrees outside, and I have no heat. It must have stopped in the middle of the night, because I had heat when I went to bed."

"Before I can help ma'am I need to ask a few questions. What kind of heating system do you have?"

"An old one that doesn't work very well. I call it the beast."

"Okay let me try another question? Where does the heat come from, is it a vent in the floor or ceiling, through a baseboard heater or do you have radiators?"

"Radiators – those big clunky things that look like an accordion. That's what I have!"

"Okay good. Do you know what powers the beast - oil or gas?"

"That's easy! Oil!" I say it like I just won the heating bee contest. I got all the answers right.

"You probably have an oil fired-boiler."

"Can you fix it?"

"I'm not sure. Those old beasts, as you call them, need a specialist. Do you know when was the last time you got your tank filled?"

"The last delivery was at the end of September."

As he asks more diagnostic questions, I go back into my bedroom and start throwing things into my carry-on bag. Time is running out, and I'm not anywhere near ready to go. With only my laptop and carry-on, I won't need to check my bag so that will save some time. There is no one at Grandma's I need to impress anyway, so why is it taking me so long to pack? Even if I go wearing my pajamas and robe, I'll still be the best dressed at Thanksgiving dinner.

"You could have an oil leak," I hear him say.

"Can you come right over and plug it up?"

"I wish I could. If that's the problem, then this isn't a patch job. Oil leaks involve the EPA."

"EPA, are you nuts? I don't have time or money for that."

I hear Grandma's voice remind me "You'll catch more flies with honey than vinegar." So I change the tone of my voice, turn on all the sweetness I can muster, and ask, "John, can't you just come over and take a look for me?"

"Sorry, that's too big of a job for me. I'll give you the number of someone who can help or you can call your oil company."

I quickly abandon the sweetness tactic. "What do you mean you can't help me? It's freezing in here, and I'm flying out for the holiday in less than an hour."

"Calm down, ma'am. Maybe you're just out of oil. We had a pretty cold October, and it's the end of November. Why don't you call your oil company and have them check it out?"

"Didn't you hear me? I'm leaving in an hour." This conversation is going nowhere fast.

"Okay, let me offer you a suggestion. Since those old oil boilers supply both heat and hot water I would recommend that you shut off your water main so the pipes don't freeze while you're gone. To be on the safe side, open up all the spigots to let the water drain out of the pipes so nothing freezes while you're gone. You'd be hard pressed to get anyone to come out in the next couple of days anyway."

"You must be crazy. I don't have time for that." Then from out of nowhere the tears start coming. Mr. Cross apologizes, wishes me a Happy Thanksgiving, and quickly hangs up.

If I didn't have bad luck, I wouldn't have any luck at

all. Having no choice, I trudge down the steps to shut off the water. Thankfully, I did pay attention to Earl when he showed me the breaker box and water main. At first, I protested when he made me go into the basement. Basements scare me. Why do you need them anyway? They smell and they're filled with spiders and other creepy things. Every time I go down there I get this strange feeling that something or someone is going to jump out at me. I don't want to find it, and I don't want it to find me. *Get a grip on yourself, Jo.* "It's just a basement," I proclaim aloud with more courage than I feel.

Thinking of what a flooded basement will cost me is enough to propel me forward. As I creep down the steps for the second time, I pick up a shovel that is leaning against the stair post. Feeling a little more fortified with shovel in my hand, I cautiously walk over to the back corner and shut off the water main.

Walking back toward the steps I glare at the old beastly boiler that has ruined my morning. Running right at it, I lift the shovel and beat it as hard as I can. It feels so good to be taking out my vengeance. My thought was to give it a mercy killing. All of a sudden, a loud belch and a big puff of smoke blast out of the vent. Smoke fills the room. Grabbing my chest to hold back the heart attack I'm sure will follow, the boiler groans and comes back to life. It's working!

"There! That will show you who's boss," I shout over my shoulder. I run up the stairs dropping the shovel behind me. Breathing a sigh of relief, I let out a quick, quiet, "Thank God."

After running up two flights of stairs, I look at the clock hoping that time has stood still. Nope, I have no time left. I rush to the bathroom. Glancing at the mirror, I groan realizing how crappy I look. Great. I can't get a shower, and my hair is out of control. One side is smashed flat, and the other side is a ball of frizz. Taking a quick sniff under my armpits, I realize I'm especially stinky this morning – a pleasant combo of BO, soot, and smoke. Slaying beasts does work up a sweat.

I open the spigot and showerhead to let the cold water flow out just to make sure nothing freezes. Moving closer to the mirror, I notice that the sleepless nights are making their mark. Wrinkles are drawing their fine lines around my eyes and frosting is starting to coat my hair. Some days I want to put a paper bag over my head. No, invisibility would be even better. I could see them, but they couldn't see me.

With the last bit of water left in the pipes I finish brushing my teeth while reviewing the events of this very crazy morning. I have a sad realization that I hate everything and everyone in my life. The beast has moved to the number one spot on my list, but to be honest what I hate the most is my attitude for feeling this way. No matter what I do, I have not been able to get rid of the loneliness I feel since Earl left me, and the hurt from Grandma's constant judgment.

Picking up my cell phone, I check the time. It can't be 6:15 already. How long have I been staring in the mirror? "Go, Jo, go," I coax myself to keep moving and stop thinking. My limited time left is confirmed by the knock at the front door.

Looking out the front window, I see the Rapid Transit van outside. Running to the top of the steps, I yell, "I'll be right there!"

At break-neck speed, I throw the essentials into my bag before running out the door. Thankfully the van is still there in my driveway waiting. Handing over my carry-on bag, I greet the driver with a smile and an apology for my delay. I breathe a sigh of relief as I slide into the backseat. I feel somewhat in control for the first time this morning. "Louie," I say after reading his nametag, "how many other passengers are you picking up this morning?"

"Only one other passenger," he informs me. "I had a van full on the 4:30 run. You're lucky traffic is light, and we should be at the airport by 7:15. What time is your flight?"

"9:30," I say with a smile. I close my eyes and put my head back knowing that I am somewhat safe for the next half hour.

Chapter 10
Holiday Memories

"There is an appointed time for everything, and a time for every affair under the heavens."
Ecclesiastes 3:1 (NAB)

As the van pulls over, I open my eyes to see that we are at the next passenger's house. Good, the other passenger is outside waiting. Not so good, he's stamping his feet and pointing at his watch. The safety sign just went off in my head as Mr. Business Man, carrying only his briefcase, gets into the van.

No good morning from him, he just barks out. "My flight is at 8:30. I better make it on time, or your manager is going to hear about this."

Mr. Business Man throws a glance over at me. He probably knows that I am somehow responsible for the lateness. Well, let's see, checking my phone I realize I've had a full fifteen minutes of peace. Slouching down in my seat, I pull my wayward hat over my head. Invisibility would really be great right about now.

"You know how long these security lines are? I specifically asked for a 6:30 pickup. The airport is insane today, and I am not traveling for pleasure," he starts in on Louie again. He glares at me. "I can't miss this flight, or my meeting."

Louie glances back at me in the rearview mirror. We both know it's partially my fault. But like a true gentleman, Louie takes the brunt from this brut.

Give it a break. I keep my eyes focused out the window, but he won't let up. He's going to blow a blood vessel. Where is my handy shovel when I need it? I've hated bullies my entire life. Mr. Business Man is a classic bully using power and threats to cower his target. Thankfully it looks like Louie has better skills at dealing with this behavior than I've developed, even after years of practice.

That could be one of the reasons going home is so hard; bad memories of the bullies I dealt with everyday throughout middle and high school. Success will be sweet revenge.

"I better make it through the security line on time or this will be my last trip with Rapid Transit. I've got your name, Louie, so I will let your supervisors know exactly who was responsible for me missing my flight."

His anger is making my tension rise. Really, no, *really*, could this day get any worse? Reviewing a few scenarios in my head, I relax realizing Mr. Business Man is the least of my problems. How is it on the holidays that we either see the best or worst side of human nature? Sounds like a great topic for my column. I could've had a good night's sleep if I'd known that the topic for my next column would be sitting right next to me driving to the airport. A chuckle escapes from my mouth as I think that maybe there are three sides to every story, not just two. I hear a grunt coming from Mr. Business Man and remain still as a mouse for the rest of the trip.

Louie makes it in record time as we reach the airport by 7:10. Mr. Business Man exits the van and runs toward the terminal not offering a thank you or a tip. Knowing that tips are a big part of Louie's income, I feel obligated to make up the difference and hand him a 20-dollar bill.

"Thank you, Louie. I'm sorry I was late this morning. You're a real gentleman and did not deserve what he was giving you. Happy Thanksgiving," I say much more jovially than I actually feel.

See, Jo, you can be nice when you want to. If I ever find that voice in my head that's always giving me etiquette lessons, I will permanently shut off the switch. It's bad enough I have Grandma telling me I'm not good enough; I don't need to be telling myself.

Checking the flight board I see that my plane is on time. Things are looking up as I breeze through security. What was Mr. Business Man thinking? Of course they'd have extra staff for the holiday. My plan is to stay close to my gate. With my last-minute booking, I'm afraid I could be bumped from the flight. My nose lifts to the smell of coffee, and my tiredness draws me into the caffeine line. It was worth the wait. Taking a sip of the warm coffee, my body temperature finally stabilizes from the very cold start.

After the wild morning rush, I finally relax. I settle down into the first open seat I see. The plop causes my hat to start sliding off my head again. Oh, no you don't. One look at this mangy mop of unruly, unwashed hair and the fashion police will be all over me. Trying to gain control of something in my day, I firmly grab both sides of the hat and yank it down over my uncontrollable hair.

The person next to me suddenly gets up, and I immediately place my laptop bag on the vacant seat. Thanks to Mr. Business Man's un-holiday spirit I can start outlining my column. It has taken me ten years to get this column, and I'm not about to let anything, even Earl, get in my way. My byline has enough edge and controversy to get me the recognition I have been working toward. It's fun to take the arguments that are always happening in my head and put them onto paper. People are following me, and the debates are lively on my social media accounts.

I wish I could somehow obstruct all the hustle and bustle of those around me. Focusing is tough and would be much easier with one more cup of coffee. I stop that thought right in its tracks. Don't want to lose my seat, here or on the plane. Focus, there is my ever-present column deadline and Pete, my editor, will not be as kind to my lateness as Louie was this morning.

Why did I agree to even think about taking on this feature article when my column is just starting to take off? Keeping up with social media for ideas and insights, researching, and following up with comments on my blog I have enough balls in the air. Why do I even want to throw another ball into the mix?

Pride! My mind says.

Shut up! I silently scream back to the incessant voice in my head.

Pete made it very clear that holiday, or no holiday, the *Two Sides to Every Story* column needed to be in his inbox every Tuesday. It's amazing how you dream, hope, wish, and work so hard for something and when you finally get it; well, it's not exactly like your dream. The dream has now become a deadline prison. If I write it too early, it may not be relevant the day it goes to press. If I wait, I may not have enough time to get it done. Pressure is fuel to me, but I don't like Pete, or anyone else, setting the deadline. Trying to stay compliant to the established rules, I emailed my column to Pete at 11:55 last night. Maybe that had something to do with my inability to sleep.

Closing my laptop, I decide to give in to all the distractions. I'll have an hour and a half on the plane to do some actual work. With the holiday and travel time, I do lose three workdays this week. Every minute counts.

Maybe I'll observe all the holiday travelers to get additional ideas for columns and discover what causes all the festive craziness. The house I'll be staying at this weekend alone would provide enough material for ten columns.

In my desire to accomplish something, anything, today, I take out my iPhone to send my first tweet of the day.

"Unthankful list cold house, no shower, bad hair, mean traveler; thankful list cool hat, warm coffee, corn bread, Grandma. Happy Thanksgiving." Thankfully I was born in the age of social media, which makes it easier to build an audience, but never allows me time to rest.

Looking around I see I am not the only one texting away. I guess writing is a welcomed distraction to the mayhem of the airport. Couple that with the fake cheer being forced upon us with the never-ending loop of Christmas music. Why are they jamming Christmas down our throats when we're not even through with Thanksgiving? One holiday at a time is all I can handle.

Maybe that can be the following week's column why we have to mush together Halloween, Thanksgiving, and Christmas into one gigantic holiday that we could call "Hallgivingmas." I'm starting to sound like Grandma. Who knew I would get two or three week's worth of inspiration just from a drive to the airport?

My mind drifts back to Grandma's phone call. Her heaping guilt on me, by insisting we spend Thanksgiving together, will make this trip home an irritating inconvenience. She really doesn't ask for much, and I know it's my responsibility to be there for her; she has definitely been there for me. But I have better things to do with my time than to visit Grandma and her "friends" every break I get. Come to think of it, I can't remember the last time I had a real vacation.

It's not like she is supportive of what I am doing with my career anyway. She's always knocking my articles. I keep telling her, "It's two sides to every story, not my side of the story." The knock-down, drag-out fight from last week over the pro-choice article vibrated through the airways. Her judgment and strong Christian values would never allow her to see another side to this debate.

"His way is the highway to happiness," she would always say. How can His way and free will co-exist? The thought of the argument that will ensue confirms why I am doing it my way, and not His or hers.

The song "Grandma Got Run Over By a Reindeer" blasts through the airways and penetrates long forgotten memories of happier times. I feel the pangs of remorse for the distance I have placed between Grandma and myself these last few months. The constant judgment of my life has become harder to deal with each time we talk. Face-to-face contact gives Grandma more opportunity and more ammunition. *Just shut your mouth, Jo,* I keep telling myself. Don't give her any more fuel to stoke the fire. Keep the peace at any price is not my mantra, but if I don't, this could be my last visit home, or at least until Grandma calms down. I'll bite my tongue and do it her way while I'm home, but it doesn't mean I'll like it.

"Excuse me. Do you mind if I sit here?" Looking up, I see a young mother with a toddler in her arms begging for a place to sit. I smile, place my laptop bag on the floor between my feet, and relinquish the coveted seat.

The young mom tries to engage me in conversation. "Are you flying to Raleigh? I don't like flying and I'm a little nervous. My husband been deployed to the Middle East and Little Jimmy and I are staying with his relatives for a few weeks waiting for his return. I hate being alone on the holidays. How about you?"

I try to keep the smile firmly planted on my face. "I'm going to visit my grandmother. I'm sorry to hear about your husband. Thank him for his service to our country. I hope he'll be home soon?"

"We are all hoping he will be home for Jimmy's first Christmas. He's been gone for over six months, sand we really miss him. You're so lucky to have a grandmother. Both my husband's parents and mine have passed. So Little Jimmy doesn't have a Mom-Mom or Pop-Pop. Mine were such a big part of my life."

All of a sudden a stench permeates the air and the young mother excuses herself to change Little Jimmy's very dirty diaper. I'll never understand why strangers feel the need to engage you in conversation. It's not like I'll ever see her again. I know I need to get better at small talk since probably more than half the population engage in it and like it. Isn't that what building a platform and audience is all about? It's inviting others into the conversation?

Another classic holiday song "Jingle Bell Rock" booms across the concourse immediately sparking another holiday memory. Closing my eyes, I slip back in time to Grandma's fragrant kitchen. I remember the joy of our cookie-baking days. It's amazing how a song or smell can trigger such vivid memories. I feel my shoulders relax as the familiar, pleasant smells drift through my memory. There I am dancing on the well-floured kitchen floor with Grandma.

One particular holiday jumps out at me.

We were baking cookies, and I was barely able to reach the cupboards to retrieve the ingredients. I must have been around twelve. Until I reached puberty, I was vertically challenged. Grandma said I was small for my age since I was a preemie. Thankfully, when my hormones kicked in I grew to 5'4." I was still below average, but tall enough to stop the name-calling...well at least about my height.

Grandma and I were making cookies for everyone; we were baking, singing, and dancing to all the carols on the radio. What a sight we were, twirling and swaying to the Christmas tunes. Flour was flying everywhere and our kitchen looked like the North Pole, quite appropriate for the winter festivities.

"Grandma, teach me to do the Jinglebug."

"The Jinglebug?" she chuckled with that wonderful laugh of hers. "Do you mean the Jitterbug?"

I remember feeling the color rise to my cheeks; I hate making mistakes, then as much as now.

"Josie Beth, I love when you get the words mixed up like that. The Jinglebug will be our special dance. I'll show you as soon as the right song comes on so we can cut a rug."

She said *I* used words incorrectly, but what in the world is "cutting a rug"? We continued baking, slipping, sliding, and laughing until the timer went off for the next batch of cookies to go into the oven. Then back to the dance floor we'd go. Finally the song she was waiting for came on, "Jingle Bell Rock." Grandma grabbed my hands and guided me through all the steps. She started moving faster than my feet could follow. Our legs tangled up and on the floor we went. I tried to get up, but she insisted we stay on the floor never missing an opportunity to have fun.

"Josie Beth, how about I teach you to make snow angels?"

"What? Where are we going to get the snow?"

"Guess we will have to make our own," she said. She

reached up to grab the sack of flour and tossed more onto the floor.

"Watch me." She swished her arms and legs back and forth across the floor.

"Voila," she proclaimed as she stood up and proudly pointed to her work of art on the kitchen floor. "Flour Angels – my newest creation," she said with that big belly laugh of hers.

"Grandma, can I make one?"

"Sure, baby girl. Here let me put some more flour on the floor for you."

As I lay on the floor swishing my arms and legs back and forth, I saw "that" expression cross Grandma's face. It was that look she got when she was going to ask me a question. What had my face said that my brain was not even thinking? I swallowed knowing that a tough question was coming. Grandma was very intuitive; she could always read me like a book. With all the laughing and singing that day I had forgotten the altercation I had yesterday at school. I was foolish to hope she wouldn't notice, because she always does. Her sixth sense was getting stronger and scarier with age.

As almost a reprieve from the tension that was growing from that long ago moment of truth, I am jolted back into the present when I hear a page go over the loud speaker announcing some flight delays. Standing up to check my flight's status, I try to erase the unpleasant parts of this memory, while retaining the moments of joy. Just when I thought I was going to catch a break, I see the time for my flight changing. Wasn't it on time a half hour ago? What now!

Returning to my seat, I close my eyes and again allow the joyful memories, sights, and smells of baking cookies to pleasantly whirl through my mind again. Cookie baking was sure good for the soul. Well, doing almost anything with Grandma was good for the soul; at least it was when I was a kid. I recall a defining moment in my life. I replay that moment of truth and look for the hidden clues to tell me how

I got to be who I am today.

"Josie Beth, do you want to tell me what's been playing on your mind?"

Getting up off the floor, I looked down brushing the flour from my pants as I pretended to admire my "Flour Angel."

I respond with a shrug. "What do you mean? Nothing's bothering me." I sounded less convincing than I hoped.

"I know when something is bothering my little Jinglebug. Now tell Grandma what's going on in that mind of yours." She took my face in her well-worn hands and looked directly in my eyes with so much love and concern. I looked at her and reluctantly molded into her arms.

Grandma is one of those people you can really pour out your soul to, but with each passing year it was getting harder and harder to talk to her about how I felt. When I was twelve, all the secrets began. Things were changing, and I didn't want to hurt her. That particular holiday season was especially difficult. I made a big mistake after Grandma encouraged me to invite some girls over to the house for cookies. She didn't understand that I was a misfit in school. I was different from the other girls in many ways: the way I dressed, the way I looked, my height, my hair, my focus on school rather than gossip, my lack of boy knowledge, and my faith. All attracted unpleasant attention from some of the girls in my class. Many things I wore were handmade, and my wardrobe brought some harsh joking. Being an only child, or rather grandchild, with no cousins or any other relatives I didn't have a clue about boys, or for that matter, girls.

Not wanting to go into detail with her as to why this wasn't a good idea, I agreed and invited those that I thought at least tolerated me. How could the life and home I loved become a source of ammunition to taunt me? They called my Grandma a Jesus Freak and a Holy Roller. I never thought of her in that light. She loved the Lord and was willing to share His joy. They were mean spirited and not only hurt me; they were saying awful things about Grandma. To this day I have never told her; I preferred letting her think I was just a shy bookworm and wanted to be by myself, in my head thinking, or writing. She did not deserve to be talked about that way. That day all of the girls were bragging about their Cabbage Patch™ dolls. They wanted to know if I had gotten one. Grandma overheard the discussion and brought in the antique china doll that was my one and only Christmas present. After that revelation, life at school was never the same.

On that day I vowed never to get close to anyone again. Why have I let the judgment of a few teenagers define my life? Am I trying to prove them wrong? Am I still allowing these young girls, wherever they are, to rule my life? Oh, God, help please me if that's true.

Maybe I wasn't gifted with riches, athletic talent, or a particularly engaging personality like Nicole or Grandma's, but what I lacked in these areas, I made up for with my power source, words. I could always win an argument, which helped in backing down the ridiculers, but didn't do much for winning over friends. Words became my number one survival skill. I tried to stay out of the wrath of the popular girls, but everything I did gave ample ammunition for my classmates to pick on me, even when I won writing contests or became part of the debate team. It seemed everything in my life that I considered succeeding equaled teasing or so some sort of judgment.

"Grandma, some of the girls have been picking on me. That's all," I whispered into her chest. "Even the ones I thought were my friends."

"What do you mean picking on you? What are they doing or saying?"

I remember pulling away and moving to the other end of the kitchen, pretending to straighten up the counter. I didn't want her to feel or see the lie.

"Grandma, it's nothing." I didn't want to hurt her by

telling her how they laughed at my clothes and how we lived. "The teacher asked for the truth, and I gave it to her, that's all. I wasn't trying to get back at them." Was I trying to convince her, or me, with that last sentence?

Grandma knew there was more to the story. She moved closer to me. All the dancing and baking probably left me more open and vulnerable than I wanted to be. The words began to spill out.

"Some of the girls started writing about . . . you know boys, boys and kissing. That's all my classmates ever talk about. They're passing around boy notes and saying some things that I know we shouldn't be talking or writing about, especially during class. I got a few of them in trouble when I found some of the notes and gave them to the teacher."

"Josie Beth, is this all of the story?"

"Well, yeah. When the principal asked who wrote the notes I told him."

To protect myself from her chastisement, I left out the part that I added a few more powerful notes to the bunch.

"They were the ones in the wrong," I defended myself to Grandma.

My heart sank when she looked me straight in the eyes. "Josie Beth, your tongue can be a two-edged sword. Who were you trying to help, and who were you trying to hurt, with the truth?"

Tears welled up in my eyes, and I hugged my grandma until the tears were all gone. I just buried myself in her, accepting her consolation, freeing myself from the pain of my classmates' taunts and from disappointing Grandma once again. I also came to the realization that the truth had the power to hurt or to heal, and I wanted to hurt those girls the way they were hurting me in the only way I knew how, words.

Looking back I realize that Grandma wasn't judging or condemning me; she was trying to set my compass in the right direction. Is that what she's trying to do now?

"Josie Beth, you have the gift of seeking the truth," she told me in the flour-covered kitchen. "You always want to know the truth and, for the most part, tell the truth. You have to know that the truth can hurt and not everyone is ready to hear it when you are ready to tell it. Step back from the situation for a moment and think first, that's all."

It felt even worse, because I know I wasn't telling Grandma the whole truth. It was too painful to let her know that being me had never been easy.

Stop! Don't go there, I command myself. Go back to the cookie baking, the laughing, and the fun times. Remember to think happy thoughts and walk the other thoughts right out the door.

Chapter 11
The Dynamic Duo

*"But woe to you who are filled now, for you will be hungry. Who to
you who laugh now, for you will grieve and weep."*
Luke 6:25 (NAB)

Standing up again to check my flight time, I ask
myself why I'm calling this trip an untimely inconvenience.
The love Grandma gives me is . . . I'm not sure there are
words for the unconditional love she has for me. If I love
Grandma so much, why do I have this attitude about visiting
her now?

"Flight 3239 is now boarding for Raleigh/Durham," a
woman's voice says over the loud speaker.

Thank God.

Slinging my laptop over my shoulder, I drag my
carry-on behind me as I inch my way down the aisle. Lucky
me, I have the most desirable seat on the plane, middle seat,
in the last row–right by the bathroom. One day I'll be
making the big bucks and sitting in business class. Nearing
the back of the plane, I look in horror. I'm in the middle of
two people that should have bought an extra seat each! How
can I relax, let alone work on this flight squished between
the two of them? Quickly looking around the plane, I realize
there is no escape; the plane is completely full.

I hear one of my seatmates talk to me as I open the
overhead compartment. "Sorry, sweetie, there's no space left
up there for you. We are bringing Thanksgiving dinner to
our mom." They have not only taken up most of my seat, but
the entire overhead bin as well? Perfect.

The flight attendant reads my look of unhappiness.
"I'll take that for you, Miss," she says quickly.

Great, now my bag is going down into some
unknown "black hole." So much for the quick exit! With my
luck, they'll lose my luggage and with this holiday frenzy,
and they won't find it until next year. Let's keep this day

rolling along. Do I even have clothes at Grandma's? I don't have any unless I want to wear my high school hand-me-downs, or Grandma's granny panties and a housedress for Thanksgiving. Neither one is a very good option. What else can go wrong today?

The large woman in the aisle seat gets up to let me in. I walk forward, she backs up, and through some weird plane dance I squeeze into my seat.

The three of our bodies are now touching like conjoined triplets. My personal space preference is at least two feet. Now there's not even an inch between our bodies. Their bodies have a vice grip on me. Wiggling around in my seat I hope to find the most tolerable position. I give up, lean back, and close my eyes in defeat. Feigning sleep is my only defense not to engage in their conversation.

My mind races through various scenarios as I try to find a solution on how I can get some work done on this flight. I imagine myself trying to open my laptop, elbows pressed firmly into my belly button, my arms at a precarious angle. To accomplish this feat I would have to turn my laptop upside down and type with my hands facing up. I can't seem to make any progress. With a sigh of resignation, I realize it's hopeless. I'm trapped for the next ninety minutes. What does this sight look like to everyone else, or am I just blowing it way out of proportion? Here is proof again that fact is stranger than fiction, and you never know when or where your next story idea will show up. Maybe I should get these two ladies version of this story!

The food smell permeating from the overhead and the chatter of my seatmates ensure there will be no work, no sleep, or peace on this flight. The headache I have been fighting all morning returns with a vengeance. It has now reached a category 8 on my headache scale. Opening one eye, I realize their chatter is now directed at me.

"Honey, I know we're big. Our hope was that we would take the last seats in the plane, and no one would pick the middle seat," the window lady says.

"Cheaper than buying the full row," the aisle lady laughs.

"We're sorry about hogging up the overhead bin with our feast. You've gotta admit that it does smell like Thanksgiving in here. Maybe the smell will put happy faces on people," the window lady says.

The smell isn't putting a happy face here is what I want to say. But remembering my encounter with Mr. Business Man and Little Jimmy's mom, I put on a fake happy face. "It does smell like Thanksgiving, that's for sure."

"We know this looks a little crazy," window lady continues. "People are jumping to conclusions seeing Mindy and I hauling in these food bags. They probably thought we were packing our lunch."

They both start laughing. The up-and-down movement of their bodies makes me feel like I am in some weird massage chair. My body shivers in revolt.

A loud snort pops out of aisle lady and that brings on a tidal wave of snorts and laughs between the two of them. Passengers turn to look at me and shake their heads. So now laughing has become a crime.

Wiping tears from her eyes, window lady continues. "Our mom just had a real bad stroke. You never know if this holiday will be her last. Don't we always say that, Mindy? So we wanted to make the best of a sad situation. Poor woman can't walk, talk, or even eat. But the doc says she can smell, and isn't that the first part to eating anyway? Smelling? So our two brothers and their wives are meeting us for Thanksgiving dinner at the nursing home."

"Won't believe this, but we made the whole Thanksgiving dinner last night and brought it with us," the aisle lady pipes in.

"So we bought these hot/cold bags. They are the greatest invention since the microwave. You should have seen us try and get all of this through security," window lady laughs. "The look on the TSA agents' faces was something to see. Cindy pleaded our case, and they let the bags through.

By the way I'm Mindy, and this is my twin sister Cindy."

I don't know what to say to all of this chatter. "I'm sorry. Did you say your mom had a stroke?"

A veil of sadness crosses over Cindy's face. "Yeah, she can't eat or anything, but she can smell and hear. If that's the only joy we can bring her this holiday, so be it. She'll know her family is with her."

"Mindy and I aren't married, and we don't have kids, so we volunteered to do all the cookin' for the bunch. We're using all of Mama's Thanksgiving recipes. We always helped out but never made the whole dinner ourselves. It won't be as good as Mama's, I'm sure of that. We just hope we don't disappoint her. It's really about family not the food. Right, Mindy?"

If food is not so important, why did they fill the overhead compartment with an entire Thanksgiving feast? I volunteer to change seats with one of them so they can sit together and talk, but my request is dismissed. Unfortunately they like to talk around me. I feel like I'm in the middle of some weird verbal Ping-Pong match, and the distance between lobes is the space above my head.

"No, thanks," Cindy explains. "We like meeting new people and would prefer to share you."

With me in the middle, it gives them an opportunity to hit me with both barrels. I put up my best defense, silence, but it was not good enough. A nap is the only other option I have to making this flight not a total disaster, so I close my eyes hoping to at least rest if I cannot work.

"Sweetie, do you want some cornbread?"

Out of my half-sleeping haze, I open my eyes to see a big piece of cornbread in front of me. Did Grandma just show up on the plane? Am I dreaming?

"We're keeping the cornbread right here on the floor in the special bag. It's probably still a little warm," Mindy chimes in. "By the way what's your name, honey?"

Finally I give up and decide to join in their conversation about holidays and family. "Jo," I volunteer.

Quickly I grab the piece of cornbread Mindy offers to
me before one of them changes her mind. This is going to be
a long trip, I'm starving, and I might as well make the best of
it. Grandma would be proud.

Cindy jabs me in the side. "Jo, what's your favorite
Thanksgiving story?"

For some reason I am quick to respond with the flour
angel story and give them the highlights. What I thought
was going to be the plane ride from hell actually turns out to
be a fun respite.

"Josie Beth, just give people a chance," I hear
Grandma's words in my head. "Don't be so quick to react to
what you see. You can't always judge a book by its cover."

As usual, and way too often, Grandma was right.
Cindy and Mindy are funny, generous, and joyful,
reminding me of Grandma. Their warmth passes through
me. The squeezing that I first felt was oppressive now feels
like a blanket of kindness. I realize I now have something
else to be thankful for, Cindy and Mindy taking my mind off
my career and relationship troubles.

The flight attendant announces that it is time to put
back our tray table and seats to their upright positions to get
ready for the descent. I chuckle as another attendant starts
walking up the aisle to collect cups and pretzel bags. Once
Cindy and Mindy broke out the cornbread they couldn't
stop there and brought out what amounted to a full course
meal. We hurry to straighten up the mess and laugh as the
flight attendant says, "I didn't realize they catered meals on
this flight."

As the plane finally lands, a cheer erupts from the
crowd. Was it for Thanksgiving, for a safe flight, or maybe
because they, too, were on their way home? Miraculously,
the flight attendant brings my luggage to me. I can add that
one to my thankful list as well. The sisters tell me to go
ahead of them. I'm not sure how they carried all of this food
on the plane, but I will trust they can get it back off. I wish
them both a happy Thanksgiving and thank them for their

hospitality. I don't know why, since it is totally out of character, I reach down and give them both a hug and a kiss on the cheek. Pulling my laptop from under the seat, I follow the parade of passengers off the plane.

With the crowds getting denser, I can't get to the rental terminal fast enough. It's already 12:30, and I want to get on the road and out of here. Thankfully, they have my car. Maybe there's hope for this holiday. Maybe, just maybe, I will get some of what I need. The peace I was hoping for this morning, some relaxation, laughs, and a dose of Grandma's love.

After the cramped plane ride, I'm eager to have the car to myself. Speed is one thing that can always clear my mind. The back roads home are great to drive on, no cops, just the open road and the radio. Finally I will have time to do some serious thinking, like why I don't appreciate Grandma. How would I feel, if like Cindy and Mindy, I was visiting her in a nursing home today? Or even worse, not having Grandma at all, like the little boy in the airport. I should have a grateful heart, but I don't anymore.

The ride to Grandma's is a blur; I must have been on autopilot. My mind is still racing, running all these scenarios through my head trying to finalize how best to write this article. There is a fine line that I'm trying not to cross, but with all the information that Bob, Liz, and Nicole provided I'm starting to see abortion in a whole different light. I know that my readers are a little more liberal than religious, so how do I strike the balance in being truthful without alienating the audience I worked so hard to build?

The ringing of my cell phone startles me back to the present. I forgot to turn it off after I called Grandma to tell her I landed safely. The ID shows Earl's name. I'll let it go to voicemail; I'm not ready to talk to him. Glancing at the missed calls I realize there were three from Pete. In the mountains, reception is iffy; I'll call Pete back when I get a chance. I turn off the phone, toss it onto the passenger seat, and turn up the radio to my favorite local station. Peace, I just want a little peace, and it's a guarantee I won't get it anytime soon.

Dusk settles around me, and I turn on the headlights. I can't believe how early it starts to get dark. I hate it when we lose the light during the winter. Those long, now lonely, winter nights will come upon me fast. No more romantic nights by the fireplace, sipping wine, and eating Earl's wonderful soups. A wave of conviction comes over me, warning me not to go down that road; it's too dark and lonely.

Chapter 12
Warm Welcome Home

"So he got up and went back to his father. While he was still a long way off, his father caught sight of him, and was filled with compassion. He ran to his son, embraced him and kissed him."
Luke 15:20 (NAB)

Pulling into the gravel driveway, I take a precious moment to sit and gaze at Grandma's warm and cozy little house; a direct contrast to the one I just left. Turning off the ignition, a quiet stillness surrounds me. It is both a welcome relief to the frenetic way this day began and a peaceful distraction to all the decisions pressing upon me. The porch light beckons me closer to the safe harbor of home. My life has always been this dichotomy of happy/sad, frantic/peaceful, my way/Grandma's way, truth/ignorance. The magnet of love and laughter that filled Grandma's home draws me here, and then, at the same time pushes me away. There is some comfort from the comments I receive from my followers each week that I am not alone in living this tug-of-war life. Maybe that is why my column is resonating with my generation. I'm speaking the truth and shedding light on the pain of this constant push and pull.

My foot barely hits the ground before the front door flies open. Grandma walks out into the darkness. "Welcome home, Josie Beth," she shouts at the top of her lungs. If I only had a dimmer switch to turn her down to a tolerable energy level, these visits home might not be so few and far between.

In all her glory, Grandma stands waiting. The sigh of relief that escapes from my lips will likely mirror the one Grandma is releasing as well; she is able to relax now that her baby is home. Picking up her apron, she wipes her hands, and then extends her arms in anticipation. Open, waiting, and praying, I'm sure, for me to fold into her embrace. Grabbing my bags I walk slowly up the driveway,

relishing the peace that I know will not be permanent.
My heart thumps in my chest as I pick up the pace, take two
steps at a time, and reach the landing. Resignation takes
over as I drop my bags onto the porch, freeing my hands so I
can settle into her loving arms.

"Josie Beth, I am so glad to see you," she whispers
into my ear. At that very moment I surrender to the power
of her embrace. How can a hug have such transformational
powers? Her warm touch has taken my troubles, tied them
to the end of a balloon, and released them to the heavens.
My jaw unclenches and my shoulders relax for the first time
in months. Desperate not to lose this feeling of love, I tighten
my grasp and hold on to her embrace longer than usual.

Reluctantly I let go, knowing that I need to break the
spell before my resolve is broken. I got what I needed, a
booster shot of love, maybe I should just turn around and
go. As though sensing my tentativeness, Grandma swoops
up my laptop bag and heads toward the open door not
giving me a chance to retreat. Having no choice, I grab my
suitcase and follow her. Not wanting to lose this moment, I
pick up her empty hand, grasp it tightly, and together we
stroll into the house hand in hand.

Glorious smells overpower me with loving, joy-filled
memories as I cross the threshold. Pumpkin spice,
cinnamon, sweet potatoes, apple - it all starts a whirlwind of
down home memories that have always included fun, food,
and laughter. Too often I try to distance myself from these
memories, this place, but I am not always sure why. Is it
because I'm a grown woman, because I'm a different woman
than the Josie Beth who left for college over ten years ago or
is it this town shrinks me back to believing I'm not good
enough?

What I do know is that every time I come home, I
lose my competitive, driving edge. Grandma's way of living
is like sandpaper. It mysteriously smoothes down the rough
edges that this new phase of my career has given me.
Coming home takes me one step back for each two steps I've
taken toward my goal of becoming a syndicated columnist

by thirty-five. Maybe that's why these homecomings are harder and harder to bear. What once was a dance for fun has now become a dance of determination not to lose ground. This distance I have created is much more than physical; it has reached philosophical and spiritual levels. Each time I see and speak to Grandma, the gap widens and I fear one day it will be impossible to get back across.

Grandma pushes me up the stairs with an order to unpack and come down "right quick" because we have work to do. She can't be serious. How foolish of me to think I could come here to relax. I'll get caught up in Grandma's holiday frenzy. I always do; it's impossible to resist. Knowing Grandma, she's been cooking for days, which means the kitchen will have the disastrous aftershocks of Hurricane Esther.

"You never know who will stop by or who needs a dinner, Josie Beth," she always says. It's how she "planned" for the holidays and her excuse for the abundance of food. She definitely walked her talk. The door was always open, and the house was always full. But the toll that these monster holidays are taking on her physically, and me mentally, might be too high a price to pay. For once in my life, just once, I would love to experience a quiet, peaceful holiday with just Grandma and me. Was that too much to ask?

Knowing what lies ahead of me, I take the steps slower than I need to. I step into the shrine I once called my bedroom, place my laptop on the desk, and make room on the bed for my suitcase. I've heard of parents putting the rooms of deceased children into a time capsule, but I'm still alive. Looking around the room for any subtle changes, curiosity overcomes me and draws me to the closet. Slowly I open the door. Disappointment settles in as I see the shelves still covered with memorabilia highlighting my life in this small town. There were no sports trophies, homecoming crowns, or cheerleader pompoms, but I did have my fair share of debate and writing ribbons. *The geek awards*, I say to myself. Boxes of old essays, term papers, and journals take up the top two shelves of the closet. They are proof, I guess, to Grandma, that I have achieved something meaningful in my life. I use to write about faith, family, and even some funny things. Grandma had been my most fervent fan and encourager, ensuring me that God had plans for me, big ones. If that's true, what is taking Him so long? Finally I realized I had to take my career into my own hands if I was going to reach my dream.

Standing on my tiptoes, I reach up to pull something with legs off the top shelf. I extract the old china doll that I hated from the moment she was given to me. Why does she keep it? If she only knew the unpleasant memories, memories that I have not and will never share with Grandma, and the emotional eruption that occurs each time I see this doll, she would have burned it. Throwing the doll down in disgust, I remember how this ugly, old thing was Grandma's excuse for not being able to get me that special doll every other girl was getting for Christmas.

That particular Christmas Day was when I first became aware of the painful truth that we were poor folks. That day I made a vow to myself: I would make my mark so I will never have to suffer the pain and humiliation of being poor again. I refuse to let this place, or Grandma's antiquated values, sway me from honoring that commitment.

This room gives me the same eerie feeling as my basement, something or someone is lurking in the closet, under the bed, or behind the ruffled curtains looking for the right opportunity to attack and transport me back in time to the poor little girl named Josie Beth. Seeing everything I have worked so hard to leave behind so blatantly displayed makes me want to tear up the room and scream "I am Jo!" at the top of my lungs. I want to open the window and throw all the reminders of my childhood out the window. Maybe they too could float up to heaven to never be remembered again.

Is there any place that I can just be me; not Grandma's little girl, not Pete's writer, not Earl's girlfriend, just Jo? When did life get so difficult? How many times do I ask myself that question? Picking the awful doll up from the floor, I fling her across the room with more force than I intended. Crashing against the wall, her china face in now split in two. Now what? Should I stuff her in my suitcase and throw her into the woods on my way back to the airport, like some secret mob burial? Do I tell Grandma the truth about this doll's ugly history or just shove her back into her hiding place?

"You okay, Josie Beth? Are you coming down soon?"

"Yeah Grandma, just dropped something. I'll be right down." I just need to find somewhere to bury the evidence of my rage. My last choice is the best option. Walking back to the closet, I once again stand on my tiptoes to return the nameless, now faceless doll to her shelf.

Stumbling into the kitchen I am faced with dishes, plates, bowls, and pots piled precariously high on every possible inch of counter space. How does she cook like this? My look of disapproval does not get this visit off to a good start. With a sly shrug of her shoulders, she once again pleads for kitchen disaster forgiveness. I shake my head, give into her and push up my sleeves to start working on the mess. Hopefully I'll be done before midnight.

Moving from the sink to the cabinets to return the cooking pans to their proper home I notice a small handprint turkey on the refrigerator. Faded, curled at the edges almost not recognizable. What is that doing there? She probably pulled it out of the shrine upstairs just trying to rattle my memories. And it works the magic she was clearly planning. Removing the magnet and placing my young handprint turkey into my adult hands, I remember the day I brought it home from school.

"Grandma, Grandma," I yelled waving my turkey in the air as I jumped off the bus. "Look what I made for you today."

Grandma took my hand as we walked toward the house together. She was always there waiting at the bus for me with a smile and a willingness to hear the events of the day.

"We had a big Thanksgiving feast, and I got to be an Indian," I told her. "It was so much fun. Miss Betty told us the story of the first Thanksgiving with the Pilgrims and Indians. She was teaching us to share and why we should be nice to our neighbors just like you always tell me Grandma."

The smile on her face from that remark let me know what was important and valuable in this house, kindness, sharing, and making a difference. Nothing has changed.

"Then the kids were all saying what they were thankful for, and I told them I was thankful for you. All the other kids were thankful for their mommies and daddies. I was the only one who didn't have a mommy or a daddy," I said. "They started laughing at me and calling me Little Orphan Josie Beth. Miss Betty made them all stop and apologize to me."

"Oh, sweetie, you're not an orphan, you have me and you are a daughter of God. Remember the Bible stories and how Jesus was made fun of, too. Each time they say something mean, remember how much Jesus loves you and how proud He is that you're not being mean back." This was her way of handling each taunt I received, asking me to suffer in silence for Jesus. No wonder I don't know how to face bullies, I just retreat.

It's interesting that I now remember a different expression covering Grandma's face. One I did not recognize as a child, but can now see it for what it was – panic. Before that day I didn't realize how different my family was from my classmates. Curiosity always got the best of me so I asked what I now call "the big question."

"Where are my mommy and daddy? I forgot what you told me, Grandma. Can you please tell me again what happened to them?" I asked.

I'll always remember the look in Grandma's eyes. Her mind would travel to some faraway place where I was never invited. The pain and hurt in her eyes were evident, even to a five-year-old. This was obviously not an easy topic, so I said nothing else.

It felt like forever before she finally spoke. "Josie Beth, your mommy and daddy are in heaven looking over you. Okay, sweetie? Always remember that you are loved. Nothing will ever happen to you because I am here for you. I promised your mother that I would take care of you, and I never break my promises."

"Can I talk to them?" I asked.

"Well, yes. Sure you can talk to them whenever you pray for them," she replied.

"Can we pray that they will come back?" I pleaded.

"We can pray for whatever you want, Josie Beth. God always wants to hear from us and knows what is in our hearts."

In my innocence, I thought people could come back to life. Wasn't that what I was taught about Jesus and Lazarus from the Bible stories?

"Would you like to pray for them now?" she asked.

Grandma and I got down on our knees right there in the kitchen and prayed a heartfelt prayer. Grandma always knew the words to say to comfort me and strengthen my faith in God. Now, I wonder where that childlike faith went to. I can't remember the last time I really prayed, or when I did pray, believe that God heard me.

"Let's hang up your beautiful turkey on the refrigerator. Do you want to help me bake pies? We need quite a few since our whole family will be coming over for Thanksgiving. Our church family, our neighborhood family, and anyone else who walks through the front door is part of our family. We are so blessed, aren't we, Josie Beth?"

And as the singing, flour skating, dancing, and cooking started, my curiosity about my parents stopped. Grandma was right; we were so blessed. What happened to us, *to me*, that I no longer see the blessings, only the mess? I place the old handprint turkey back on the fridge and return to work.

After hours of clearing and cleaning, our conversation moves backward in time, as it always does, recalling the holiday stories of the past. We feed off of each other's stories, laughing, teasing, and crying at some of the incidents and antics that happened during those holiday dinners. This material is so great, maybe the two of us should write a book, our own little down-home holiday story. It would definitely be put in the fiction section, because no one would believe all the craziness that came through that door and into our house.

My favorite story was the time Grandma forgot to cook the turkey. The best part is how she keeps, until this day, trying to pretend it did not happen. This year she takes a new approach.

"Josie Beth, I remember clearly that I assigned you turkey duty that year," she says with a sly smile.

"Don't even go there. How can you blame a twelve-year-old for not cooking the turkey?" I ask her. "You won't even trust me now to be anything more than kitchen assistant and dishwasher."

She shakes her head. "I know. I should have taught you how to cook, not just help. Well, it's never too late to learn?"

"I'm tired, but there is no way I am falling into that trap. I know everything I need to know about feeding myself. It's called dialing and ordering."

Grandma's turkeys are always so big that it required the two of us to lift the heavy pan with the thirty-five-pound turkey and the fixings out of the oven. That day we were armed with hot pads. Together we slowly opened the oven door and peered into the cold, empty space. With shocked expressions, we looked at one another. Grandma gets down on her knees, sticks her head far into the oven to make sure the turkey, though dead, had not escaped through some secret trapdoor.

The hunt for the missing turkey began as we looked around the kitchen, hoping that the turkey had scampered away, or that we just forgot to put it into the oven. The search for Tom Turkey ended when I opened the freezer and there he was, hard as a rock, and three days away from thawing.

That day I learned in the midst of a crisis comes the best traditions: we served dessert first. Everyone was so stuffed from the pies, cakes, and breads that no one even noticed until later that night that the turkey was never served. When our guests finally realized there was no turkey, the laughter and teasing got so bad that it was hard to tell the difference between the real and the made-up scenarios that were unfolding.

Grandma doubled over laughing so hard. "Volcano, the volcano," she said, reaching up to touch her eyebrows. While stirring the turkey gravy one year, it bubbled up, erupted, and exploded right in her face, singeing off her eyebrows. Grandma was spraying cold water all over her face and asking me to run for ice and an eyeliner pencil at the same time. I wasn't sure which way to go. That was the first, and maybe only time, I saw Grandma with a touch of vanity.

"Josie Beth, steady your hands, and stop that laughing. I'm going to have four sets of eyebrows by the time you're done. I'm not hosting dinner without eyebrows, do you hear me?"

Watching these long ago memory movies with a new, adult perspective makes me realize there were so many things that I did not see. Grandma's diligence in making the holidays a big, almost theatrical presentation was so opposite from her day-to-day approach to life. How hard she worked in providing for the two of us, and how no matter what, she wanted my life to be filled with fun and laughter. The year of the missing turkey Grandma had started working part time as a nurse in our local clinic. Two jobs and raising a granddaughter on her own, she obviously was being stretched far beyond her capacity. She was depending on me more to take care of some things around the house. Maybe, just maybe, it was my responsibility to take care of the turkey after all.

The kitchen is now in the orderly state that I prefer. It has taken hours, but worth the effort. Grandma heads up to bed reluctantly, but willingly. She thrives in this self-made chaos where I go to extremes trying to keep everything from spinning out of control. Grandma gives everything, even her problems to the Lord. I, on the other hand, would snatch every bit of control I could from Him to redirect traffic, reset clocks, and change people's minds to think my way, not theirs.

Walking through the house, I shut off the lights before heading up the stairs to the shrine. How did I go from wanting to scream this morning to laughing so hard that my face actually hurts? So what is the better place to be, screaming or laughing, crazy deadlines or crazy people, alone or home with Grandma? Again I see the two polarizing sides of my life, and I wonder why I want to scream.

Goals, deadlines, and personal recognition fuels and fires my life. Grandma's life always has and always will have a purpose, serving people. She knows exactly who she is and why she is here. She doesn't let anyone or anything, even me, take her off that purposeful path. Maybe there is a clue to my life in all of this. Is the work I'm doing purposeful? Somehow I know something is off track, but how do I diagnose this pain, this emptiness I am feeling? I know it's not just from Earl leaving me; it was there before him. This pain is deeply rooted, somewhere so deep inside of me it might reach into my soul, if I still have one.

Chapter 13
Turkey Time

"Stop judging and you will not be judged."
Luke 6:37a (NAB)

The smell of turkey permeating through the air is my signal to get up and get back to work. Glancing over at my iPhone to check the time, I rub my eyes in disbelief. It's already 6:00 a.m. Since the sun wasn't even up, I wonder if this woman ever rests. Taking a good long stretch to relieve the sleep from my body, I feel small shockwaves of pain in my neck and shoulders, reminders of the hours spent over the kitchen sink. Maybe today is going to be a good day, the best holiday ever. Well, it is off to a good start. After recounting so many Thanksgiving disasters last night, the smell of turkey is a good sign that this might be the good day I need.

If I'm tired, how does Grandma feel? She's at least forty years my senior. Compassion sweeps over me and pushes me out of bed. If age were measured by energy levels, it would be the reverse. Grandma's bottomless source of energy should be studied by the Department of Energy. If there was a renewable energy source, it is certainly Esther Reynolds.

Longing for a long hot shower after missing one altogether yesterday, I know I will again have to get ready quickly before she comes looking for me. The shower will have to wait until later. I grab my sweat pants and sweater and pull on my knock-off boots as I head on down to the kitchen.

"What time did you get up?" I ask, while grabbing the hot cup of coffee and homemade sticky bun she hands to me. My eyes glaze over as I observe the new chaos that's taken over the kitchen counters.

"Happy Thanksgiving!" she cheerfully chimes and rattles off the list of "must do's" before the hour is up.

Shaking my head, and this time with a little laughter, I push up my sleeves as I prepare for round two of the Hurricane Esther cleanup. Before I know it, we are in our old rhythm. The kitchen is alive with sound from the humming of the refrigerator to the clanging of the pans and utensils in the sink and the sharp cuts as Grandma's knife hits the old wood cutting board. "Kitchen Music" is what we've always called it. A rhythm that beats in the core of our souls, where our toes are tapping, dishtowels are swirling, and flour floor dancing occurs.

"Do you hear music?" she asks.

The kitchen music stops, interrupted by a sound that is from a different time and era, the present. It's my cell; I thought I'd turned it off. Before I even pull the phone from my pants' pocket, I know who it is. Why didn't I change the ringtone or shut the phone off before coming downstairs?

"No, Gram, it's just the ring tone on my phone."

"Ringtone, how funny is that. I thought I was losing my mind. Who's calling you down here?" Her senses are on high alert. "It's probably Earl just wanting to apologize for not coming down for a visit, huh? Are you going to get it, or keep looking at it like you don't know what to do with it? By the way, how do you answer that phone?"

Thankfully the phone stops ringing. "We've got too much to do," I say as I put the phone back in my pocket. "He'll call back later." He calls more now that we're apart than he did when we were together. And he wonders why I can't make sense of our relationship.

＊＊＊

Today is about the same as any other holiday at our house; lots of people, old "family" members, and a few new faces. There is a quantity of food that would feed a small third-world country. Grandma asks who would like to say grace. No one responds, and Grandma is clearly disappointed. If this is her flock, why are so few following her? She looks over at me, and I find a way to hustle myself back into the kitchen "right quick" to avoid taking over the sacred ritual of grace.

From the kitchen I can recount every gesture she will make, every word that she will speak. She clears her throat. "All right, looks like both the cooking and praying are up to me. If you could all bow your heads . . . Dear Father God, the Creator of all things, we thank You for this bountiful blessing of food, family, friends, and forgiveness. Lord, we are most thankful for the gift of Your Son in whose holy name we pray. Amen."

Is she afraid to say anything else, or does she not know any other way to pray? Maybe she is looking for a change, someone to pass the rituals to, but no one, including me, is willing to pick up the prayer baton.

A tapping of a water glass stops the sound of silverware hitting plates. I peek my head back into the dining room to see who is causing the commotion; it's Grandma. What is she going to say next?

"If you could all raise your glasses, I would like to offer a toast to my precious Josie Beth. She has been the biggest blessing in my life, and I want to acknowledge her for all the help she given me in preparing this meal and for rescuing me from another kitchen disaster or inspection by the Board of Health." That one got some laughs; her messes are legendary.

Thinking she was done, I open the door to come back in but she continues. "Her warm heart, passion, and desire for truth have brought her the recognition she has so desired as a writer."

She then holds up my column in the *Philadelphia Daily Bulletin*. "*Two Sides to Every Story* is raising some eyebrows, even mine, but I know she will follow the path that the Lord is setting in front of her. I want to honor her tonight in her hometown for making it in the big city and for following her dreams."

The group claps and our neighbor, Babs, pushes me

all the way into the dining room. The applause does not outweigh the embarrassment that I feel from Grandma's heartfelt, yet, backhanded compliment. I regret today ever drawing eyebrows back on her face. *Breathe Jo, breathe.*

Stepping into the arena of applause, I thank everyone and ask them all to sit down and eat before their meal gets cold. For these dinners I should have a starting gun, because it's a food race: a race to see how much food they can jam down their throats in the shortest amount of time. Three days of chopping, cooking, and cleaning for twenty minutes, tops, of chow downs.

Tryptophan, or turkey coma, has set in. The room quiets down to a din clatter as the last eater in the race sets down his fork in defeat. Deep sighs escape from the mouths of our guests as they desperately try to find room, even a centimeter of space within their bodies through the release of their sighs. Breathing becomes labored. Squirming occurs as they try to find a comfortable position in their chairs. Some were almost ready to get up and move, but they stop. Rosalie, one of Grandma's church ladies, stands up. "Let's all give a round of applause to the Reynolds ladies for bringing this fabulous dinner to the table," she says. "We can't always guarantee that there will be turkey, but we know there will always be a warm welcome and plenty to eat."

I shake my head and laugh in agreement. Rosalie takes center stage to usher in the next phase of the holiday, stories, which are always at the Reynolds ladies' expense. You would think after last night that I could not laugh anymore at these lame old stories, but coming out of the mouth of Rosalie, our great story teller, we are there enjoying her rendition of the stories one more time. My stomach and sides hurt so much from laughing that I then remember why all the preparation was worthwhile. It was for the joy and laughter. Every once in a while Grandma and I would make eye contact and a silent message passed between us; this is what holidays are all about family, friends, and making memories.

By the time Rosalie retells the story of the year there was a turkey-nabbing, I could not take much more. The embellished details of how this man in a cloak and fedora swept in through the front door and left through the back with our turkey hidden under his cape are hysterical. Mr. McCurry had to stand up and lean against the wall for support, tears flow out of his eyes, as he tries desperately to speak.

"How can you have no turkey at Thanksgiving two years in a row?" he finally utters.

"Esther ran after him trying to give him a pie for his meal," Mrs. Howell, our backyard neighbor, chimes in. "It was not an act of charity; to this day, Esther, you can't convince me of that. It was all a sinister plan to slow him down to get the turkey back."

Maybe there are two sides to Grandma as well.

"All she could wrestle away was the turkey leg. She ran back to her house waving the leg over her head and doing a victory dance. She was at least satisfied to have some proof that she did in fact have a turkey. Pride won out that time."

Maybe Grandma had more pride than I thought. She is so happy that for the twentieth year in a row Mrs. Howell corroborated her story, even if she did not like the dig about pride.

"Can I tell one more story, please?" Rosalie asks. We were all begging for mercy and hoping for dessert, but there was no stopping her.

"Remember the time that Sister Francis, who was old as Moses, fell asleep in the living room? Josie Beth was probably only around seven, and the kids organized a plan to recreate the Pilgrims and Indian theme. Joey Banner, whatever happened to that devil of a child who tied Sister Francis up in the chair? We were all so noisy eating dinner we did not hear her cries. By the time that poor woman was untied there wasn't much left to eat. Sister Francis had to settle for a peanut butter and cranberry sandwich and a sliver of pumpkin pie for dinner."

How many families have stories like this to tell? Lost in the stories and friendly banter I'm suddenly jerked back into reality. The first question about my personal life rang through the air, a warning shot, that the next phase in our holiday meals, the interrogation phase, was about to begin.

How's work, Josie Beth? Is that all you do, write one column a week? How to you like living in the big city? Where is your boyfriend? Do you still have a boyfriend? Where did you get such a pretty car? Didn't you fly down? How long are you staying? And on, and on, and on! I try to dance around as many questions as I can, because I wasn't even sure of the answers myself. The more questions the more I feel my jaws clench and shoulders tighten. "Get out of here!" my brain finally screams.

I bang the table as I quickly jump up. The water glasses are doing their own little dance. Grabbing as many plates as I can, I start clearing the table. My mind is racing, my blood is boiling; how dare they ask such personal questions! Am I mad at their questions or because I don't necessarily like the answers?

How dare these losers have the audacity to ask me all these questions when they don't even care about the true answers or me? It's none of their business! Most of them don't even have jobs. They belong in a shelter; Grandma picks up stray people like other people pick up cats and dogs. These people can't even take care of themselves. They're always at Grandma's begging for handouts. Now they even bring their bratty kids with them. They're a bunch of blood-sucking idiots. Grandma can hardly make ends meet, and she's got to feed everyone that comes into her path.

"Do not judge others, and you will not be judged." On no, another one of those Bible verses Grandma is always using. These Bible verses have been jumping out of my head a whole lot lately. Why now? One will come out of nowhere, and then wham, another one slams against my head. "Feed my sheep!" That's Grandma's job. I don't want to feed anyone, especially this hungry crowd.

Grabbing the last plate I can put into my arms, I retreat into the kitchen to get away from their questions and to find some peace. Surprisingly I find it within the chaos of the kitchen where I can create personal space, order, and time to calm down so I can bear what is left of this holiday dinner. Each time someone enters the kitchen wanting to help I politely, but emphatically chase them away with a bit of reassurance that I have it all under control.

"Go, enjoy yourself. It's no bother," I say, hating the lie but not willing to tell them what I really think. "Sure, there're plenty of leftovers for everyone. Go ahead; pick every last piece of meat and every crumb of bread that you can find."

They never surprise me with what they will do and the demands they will make while they're here. They are never satisfied.

Are you? Are you satisfied with yourself, Jo? A persistent voice in my head asks.

"I will find you one day, and silence you forever," I say out loud. Now I remember why I did not want to be here; communing with those who take more than give brings out the worst in me.

Kitchen music, the rhythmic movement of washing and drying dishes, brings about the much needed silencing of my mind. "Peace at last," I say breathing a deep sigh of relief. The noise from the dining room has quieted down enough for me to hear Grandma saying goodbye to the last of her guests. The kitchen door swings open. I am relieved to see only Grandma standing there.

"Everyone's left. What a night! These are such joyous times, aren't they, Josie Beth?"

She stands there waiting for my answer giving me that worried look she's been giving me a lot lately. "What's wrong, Josie Beth? What's bothering you? You look so tired."

"Yes, Grandma. I'm tired. I'm tired of all the

questions. Why all the questions? Everyone wants answers. I can't handle that and the judgment from you about everything that I do, say, and think."

I raise the turkey carcass that is sitting on the sideboard into the air. "Don't you see? All these demands make me feel picked apart like this turkey. Everyone wants a piece of me until there is nothing left over." I have no idea where this anger is coming from, or why it is directed at Grandma.

"That's all right, Josie Beth. I know you're feeling overwhelmed." Her calmness and the love and kindness in her voice does not put my emotions under control, it catapults me to a place I do not want to be.

"You call it overwhelmed; I call it trying to make something of myself. Why aren't you feeling overwhelmed with all of these people that you insist in taking care of? Aren't you tired of taking care of everyone? Don't you ever want to be taken care of or do something more meaningful with your life? Is this all you want?"

Grandma limps over and puts her old, wrinkly hands in mine. She looks deeply in my eyes. "Josie Beth, I've told you many times that I made a promise to the Lord. The promise was that I would take care of anyone He put in my path."

"Break the promise! You already fulfilled it a hundred times over. You're getting up in years and the burden on you now is too much. You can hardly make ends meet. What has God done for you lately? I don't see you rolling in riches."

"God has given to me abundantly. He has never failed me. He is my Rock and my Salvation."

The conviction in her voice reassures me that what she says, she believes, but it is not convincing me.

"Josie Beth, when I was your age I took on more burden and troubles trying to do it my way. And along the path all that I had to show were the sins and failures I had accumulated. It was only when I turned my life, my whole

life, over to Him was I set free. I never, ever, want to be
a prisoner of my way again. Now that was a price too high
to pay."

"What have you ever done wrong? When have you
ever failed God? You're a friggin' saint. God should be
showering you with . . ."

"Josie Beth, you only know one side to my story, the
one that you want to see, your loving Grandma. Thank you
for the vote of confidence, but I sin every day in my mind, in
my heart, in my words and my actions. I keep asking for
forgiveness and pray to live God's way and to stay on this
path that He has placed me on."

"Sin? There's no such thing as sin. That's what the
church keeps telling you to keep you down. It makes you a
slave to charity and hopeless people."

"Josie Beth, you . . ."

"Grandma, you've never had to deal with today's
challenges. You have no idea what it feels like to deal with
all the pressure, decisions, and deadlines. It's difficult today.
The world's different. The world doesn't fit into the God-
box you believe in. Wake up, Grandma! It's the twenty-first
century. The rules have changed!"

"Nothing has changed, Josie Beth. The world is the
same. We have the same challenges, choices, and dilemmas
since the beginning of time. Do we place God first or
ourselves first? The faces have changed, that's all. I do agree
with you that we have more choices than we've ever had
before, which makes it even more difficult to do the right
thing."

How does she keep so calm even through my rage?
The calm veneer cracks as Grandma's eyes start to fill up.
I'm disgusted with myself for bringing Grandma to tears and
disgusted with her for pushing me to do it. Why is she on
everyone's side but mine? She defends the drug addicts,
alcoholics, thieves, and probably a murderer or two in the
bunch. But me, I just get her chastisement for wanting to be
a successful. What is the sin in that?

Exhausted we retreat upstairs. I immediately fall asleep, too tired for thoughts or worries.

Chapter 14
Time to Go

"Desire without knowledge is not good; and whoever act hastily, blunders."
Proverbs 19:2 (NAB)

I wake with a start. The sun is up, but I don't smell any of the usual morning smells. "Oh my God, I've killed her!"

I quickly jump out of bed and race across the hall to check on Grandma. Quietly, tentatively I open her door. Relief rushes through my veins as I see her chest rise and fall. Thank You, Lord, she's breathing. Gazing down at her well-worn face, I marvel at the peace and beauty that shines through. Backing out of her bedroom, I close the door making sure the usual click from the lock does not disturb her slumber. I hustle into the shower knowing today I can take the long hot shower my body has been craving. If nothing else, this house has awesome water pressure. The power and heat of the water beating down on me gives me the courage to make the call to Pete that I've delayed for two days. I know he won't be happy with me not responding immediately, but I think he will be pleased with how I intend to write the third article.

What I realized is that it doesn't matter; last night was proof of that. No matter what I do, what I write about, or how I live, unless I become Grandma and give my life over to the poor and downtrodden, she will never be satisfied.

Pete lets me know how disappointed he is about the second article. I thought he wanted to hear two sides to the discussion. Apparently the pro-life research and data I cited had readers a little outraged. I thought that conflict sold newspapers, maybe not. He's adamant that the third article needs to be less graphic. I remind him that the third article was going to be from my perspective and why I believe this debate won't go away. To get him off the phone I reassure him that I realize how important this third article is to him, the paper, and my career.

I dress, pack my bag, and head on downstairs to face Grandma and her disapproval. The smell of coffee reaches me, and I know Grandma's in the kitchen. I kiss her good morning and grab a cup of coffee before settling into a chair opposite her.

"Grandma, I'm leaving," I whisper. I'm sure she assumed I was staying until Sunday, because I really didn't tell her any different. Last night sealed the deal and confirmed what I've known to be true for too long, her life is not the life for me.

"Josie Beth, we really need to talk. I'm so concerned about the decisions you've been making. These articles that you're writing, well, it just about broke my heart. How can you take positions like that? Do you have any idea what you are doing to women by sending messages that living together and abortion are okay? This is what happens when you put God in a box; you start see things from the world's perspective, not His. He has plans for you Josie Beth and this isn't it."

"What do you want from me?" She won't give up, so I must leave before I say or do anything that we will both regret.

"I want you to live the life God has planned for you, to not toss away our values, and to not forget who you are in Christ. Please stay, you've just got here and we hardly had time to talk," she says in her last attempt to get me to stay.

"Grandma, how many times do I have to tell you? *Two Sides to Every Story* is my byline. I'm giving perspective on current topics, opposing views, and I'm opening up dialogue. It's a good thing. Did you even read my second article from the pro-life standpoint? Why is everything an argument with you? Please understand, I need to live my life my way, and that's why I need to leave today."

Her hurting eyes, the pain on her face causes me to

make a promise I don't believe I want to make, or will be able to keep. "I'll be back in a few weeks for Christmas. I promise I'll stay longer." The lie makes me sick to my stomach. It adds another link in the chain that binds me to a place I no longer belong.

Reluctantly, we say our goodbyes on the porch. *Run, Jo! Run before you get into another argument.* Closing the car door, I find my sanctuary of peace. I hit the gas hard, wanting to get away as fast as I can before I change my mind. Glancing back I realize Grandma looks so old. Her eyes are tired and heavy. There is more to her look than the normal post-holiday exhaustion.

Her words are ringing through my head. "Josie Beth, we need to talk. You don't know my whole story, I'm a sinner." In my verbal competition to shut her down and not listen to her insults on my lifestyle and choices, I wonder if there's something Grandma wanted to tell me, but I wouldn't let her. The way she held my hands in hers on the porch, it was almost a plea. Is she sick? Is she dying? Is she losing her house? I can't think of this. Now that the pressure is really on, I need to focus on the work I have to do and the next impossible deadline to meet.

I'll have more time at Christmas. We'll talk then I try to convince myself, knowing that we won't. We never do. Our relationship has become a tug of war with her trying to force me to live her way, in some ancient construct of how women should live, and me tugging from the opposite direction, trying desperately to pull her into the twenty-first century way of life, into my way of living.

Looking back one last time, I blow her a kiss and sign "I love you" as I peel out of the driveway. This rash decision of mine to leave early will keep me waiting in the airport longer than I want, but I need to get out of here before Grandma smothers Jo to death. She's hell-bent on resurrecting her little Josie Beth. Why won't she let her die like I did? If I wait till Sunday, Grandma could've broken my resolve, changed my mind, asked another question, and this time I might have to tell her the truth.

Esther - Chapter 15
The Peace after the Feast

"Golden apples in silver settings are words spoken at the proper time."
Proverbs 25:11 (NAB)

There is something so peaceful about the day after Thanksgiving, even in the midst of turmoil. The baking, shopping, rushing, and socializing allow me little time for prayer and quiet reflection. Just sitting looking out at the quiet winter day gives me strength to move forward.

"Lord, I'm so grateful to have had Josie Beth back home, even if for such a short time. There was a feeling of normalcy in those two days reminding us what we need to focus on love, laughter and togetherness, instead of the confrontations and disagreements that have divided us.

After Josie Beth's abrupt and angry departure, I'm fearful that I might not see her again. "Lord, I trust that Your mighty hand will be involved in the changing of her heart. Please bring her back to me, at least one more time, for Christmas. What did my Papa always say, 'No matter what troubles the world - Christmas cures everything.' I hope that holds true this Christmas. We both need to be cured of our selfishness and aching hearts.

"Lord, I'm so amazed that You saved a wretch like me. My unworthiness and Your abundant grace mystifies me each day. I sit here wondering why You love me when I've sinned so deeply against You. That's why Christmas is such a precious gift to me. The depth and breadth of Your awesome love and mercy is demonstrated through the gift of Your beloved Son. Why did You choose a baby to transform and heal this sinful world? Why did You redeem me not once, but twice, through a precious baby? Lord, my heart swells with love for You knowing Your plans are for my good and Your glory.

"Today I thank You for the gift of free will, even

though You knew, from the beginning of time, the mistakes I would make by choosing my way not Yours. With the magnitude and gravity of all my shameful sins, You not only forgave me, You trusted me with the precious life of Josie Beth, my redemption child. Lord, I've been fighting to bring her back to You, but most days I feel like I've lost the battle and I'm losing her."

She is mine. This is not your battle to fight, His gentle voice reminds me.

"But Lord," I whisper. "With so little time with her I need to take advantage when we're together to change her mind, to help her see the wrong path she is on."

She is mine. I have her in the palm of My hand. Free her with the truth.

"Why now are You prompting me to let her know my truth, her truth? Maybe the truth will set us both free. The well weaved story of deception is what I wanted her to believe, and more so than that, is what I wish were true. She will finally know how I've used delay and diversion tactics to keep the truth from her. Not giving her this gift of truth would be an injustice that I can no longer defend."

She needs to know. She needs to know the truth you've dreaded telling her.

I nod my head in understanding. Yes, she needs to know how sick it makes me feel that I lied to her and how I convinced her to believe my lies.

Remember that she needs to know how she saved your life that fateful day.

"Yes, Lord, she needs to know how she changed my life and brought me such joy. She needs to know so much, how every day I thank You Lord for the gift of her. She needs to know that she is Your sign of redemption. She needs to know that You love her. She needs to know how much Earl loves her."

She needs to know that she is already significant in My eyes. She needs to know the truth that I brought her into this world to tell.

"Yes, Lord, she needs to know all of this, or I will go

to my grave with so many regrets."

Esther, she needs to know that she is My beloved daughter.

"Lord, please give me the grace and strength to tell Josie Beth the truth, because she does need to know. I'm afraid, Lord. Josie Beth and I have been fighting so much lately. This truth could put more strain on our relationship and make the rift so deep between us that it might be impossible to repair.

"Lord, I know I can't do this without You. Please give me Your words. I've waited so long for Your perfect timing. I know Your timing is now. In Your Son Jesus Christ's precious name I pray."

Jo - Chapter 16
The Pressure's On

"Therefore, do not make any judgment before the appointed time."
1 Corinthians 4:5 (NAB)

Reaching the airport in record time allows me an opportunity to relax, grab a cup of much needed coffee, and get started on my work. Pete said that if I nail this third article and get it in on time for the anniversary of *Roe v. Wade*, he would recommend me for additional feature articles. That means I need to have my first draft to him by January 2nd. That will give us two weeks for rewrites and edits. Being featured is a powerful incentive, and it definitely gives me the motivation to make this last article my best. What it doesn't do is give me the much-needed breathing space.

Pete also made sure that I understood that the publisher is pressuring him to get these articles in line with the paper's views. I thought we were in the business of reporting the truth, that's why I got into journalism. Views and opinions are for the editorial pages. Maybe I need to revisit what I wrote to see what's out of line. Let's add another layer of pressure, writing within invisible lines. I'm still feeling the flack from the second article and remembering the accolades from the first. I guess I do know where the paper stands, and what the readers want. But where do I stand? What do I want? Do I choose truth or acceptance, truth or significance, truth or my career?

The whole point in me taking these articles was to do research and present facts. I guess it is my time to make the decision. What is the truth? Is every life precious and deserving of a chance to be born? Or is it a woman's right to decide since it is her body? After talking to Nicole and reading all the information that Liz had given me, I now know why this fight continues.

Like everything else, I over think this article to the

point of exhaustion. Pulling out my laptop I decide to table that discussion and work on something light and easy, my weekly column. What idea should I start with first? Should it be the Hallgivingmas holiday, why people are so mean during the holidays, or is small talk really worth the time? One thing I am very thankful for this wonderful day after Thanksgiving is that my only seatmate slept the whole trip home, which allowed me time to do some great work on the flight home. The words were flowing out like the Focus Fairy had cast a magic spell on my fingers. I was able to write two articles. I decided to write about the pros and cons of spending the holidays with family and the idea of one big mega holiday. Pete will get a kick out of that one. Maybe I need to throw Hanukah into the mix making it Hallgivingkahmas. We were both complaining how we would rather work than be at these large family gatherings. Both of these articles should get some great feedback from our readers, who love to share their opinions. Hopefully they will share some of their holiday stories, but none of them will top mine.

With the quiet of the flight and getting so much of my work done, I find myself missing the cast of characters to observe. I can picture Grandma doing a Mindy/Cindy and carrying our Thanksgiving dinner onto the plane. One difference, she would have fed and served everyone. Air marshals would have had to pull her away from the cockpit door as she attempted to feed the pilots. Grandma is probably the biggest character of all. What happened to us? There was once so much joy and laughter, even during my difficult teen years. Grandma was always so supportive; she always helped me through my hard times. Now something has changed with her, what is it?

Stop the ruminating, Jo, it gets you nowhere. That's why Grandma always tells me to stop thinking so much; it ruins your day. I go from thankful to remorseful, from making progress to being stuck as I try to rewrite the outline for the last abortion article.

"Enjoy what you've got, where you're at, and who

you're with, and you'll always be happy." Another Estherism plays with my mind.

Happiness seems so elusive to me. Why is it always so easy for Grandma? Maybe I have overextended myself. With the lack of sleep, the work piling up, deadline pressures, and problems with my relationships, how can I be happy? Running away seems to be the answer. Not returning Earl's calls and leaving Grandma's early is the only way I know how to stop the bickering, which definitely doesn't make me happy. I couldn't take another round of judgment from her on what I'm doing with my life and career. They both want me to play it safe and small, but I want to be large and loud. I want to prove to the world and myself that I'm here for a reason. Now that will make me happy!

Chapter 17
Grandma's Sick!

"Give her the fruit of her hands; and let her own works praise her in the gates."
Proverbs 31:31 (KJV)

The icy roads are making my second trip back home in two weeks very stressful. When I ran out on Thanksgiving, my gut told me Grandma wasn't feeling well, that something was wrong. She just has not been herself over the last couple of weeks. Whenever we talk, our conversations are short and strained. If I didn't know better, it feels like she doesn't want to talk to me. Is she mad? She's never reacted to me this way before. Selfishly I believed her when she told me, "I'm fine." I was only worried about Pete's demands and his precious article.

Yesterday one of Grandma's neighbors called to tell me that Grandma isn't doing too well. I couldn't believe what Babs told me. Grandma hardly comes out of the house and hasn't been to church since before Thanksgiving. Why has Grandma been telling me a far different story? Silent suffering servant, that's what she has always been, and it's going to be the death of both of us. Why does she still treat me like I'm twelve? She has always tried to sugarcoat what's going on as if the truth will kill me. She'll probably kill me for worrying about her. Then the lecture will start because I drove down in these unsafe conditions; I'm not ready to hear that one.

With the icy conditions, I didn't even bother trying to fly down. With my luck and how my life has been going lately I would be waiting in the airport for hours only to have the flight cancelled. Today I need to feel in control of some aspect of my life and being in the car driving, even if I can't drive fast, at least I'm moving and making progress.

Headed south I thought the roads would be clearer; unfortunately that's not the case. This storm is making the ride longer, the night darker, and my anxiety rise through the roof. The constant sloshing of the windshield wipers is fraying my nerves with each squeaky sweep. The radio offers no reassurance. Every channel only informs me of the steadily dropping temperatures and that the icy roads are slippery. "If you don't have to be outside in this, stay home and keep safe," is the advice of a motherly DJ. As if I and all the other fools on the road just decided to venture out into a storm for the fun and danger of it all.

Attempting to keep what little strength and sanity I have left, I turn my mind to prayer. When was the last time I even prayed? Will God even answer? Maybe that's why I've lost so much of my faith; I have been living not knowing if my prayers are being heard. My prayers start with gentle requests, move quickly to pleading and begging, which leads to hysterical crying. "I can't lose her, Lord. She's all I've got. I'm sorry. I'll be a better granddaughter. You can't take her now."

Not only have I lost emotional control, I've hit a patch of ice and my car is spinning out of control. Swerving to miss the car coming in the opposite direction takes my car for another unplanned and very scary spin. In my feeble attempts to get the car back into control the song "Jesus Take the Wheel" echoes in my head. "This is not good advice," I scream to no one but myself. Either instinct, or maybe God, is paying attention. I remember what to do. Reluctantly I steer into the skid and thankfully make it to the side of the road unharmed.

Trying to gain my composure seems impossible. My heart is beating way too fast, my head is pounding, and my stomach retching. I wonder if I can drive the last hour of this trip. Two weeks ago I was running away from Grandma, now I can't get to her side fast enough. *Please Grandma. Don't leave me now.* My desire to see her gives me the strength and courage to get back on the road knowing home is only thirty miles away.

Was this out-of-control spin a sign? When will I ever admit I can't do it alone? After texting Earl to let him know what was going on, he immediately called to let me know he would drive down with me. Why did I decline his offer? Right now I would be relaxing in the passenger seat knowing that the driving tasks were in his capable hands. I must be crazy because the real reason I said no was that I don't want him thinking I need him.

Ten exhausting hours after leaving my house I finally reach the safety of Grandma's driveway. Panic sets in as I look ahead and see the house is dark, not a light on anywhere. Grandma always leaves on a light just in case some vagrant might come down from the mountains or out of the woods and need a place to stay; she sometimes forgets she's not Motel 6. My feet can't seem to move fast enough, as I fly up the front steps, open the door, and take two steps at a time to reach her bedroom door. Fear stops me; what if I'm too late?

Please, God, I will treat her better. I promise. I'll call her every day if that's what it takes. Just give me more time with her. Slowly I open the door and gratefulness sweeps over me as I hear her gentle breathing. Approaching her bed, she appears to be a mere shadow of the person I saw only two weeks ago. If it weren't for the breathing, it would be hard to find her buried under at least three of her handmade quilts.

She stirs and looks up at me. "Josie Beth, is that you sweetie? What are you doing here? Is something wrong? What time is it?"

"Yes, there's something wrong–you. I came down after getting a call from Babs yesterday. She said you've been having these spells lately. I know I should have stayed with you. I knew something was wrong when I came home for Thanksgiving. When did all this start and don't try lying to me!"

"Josie Beth, I didn't want to add any more pressure on you. I know you're busy, and it's just the flu. There was nothing you, or anyone else, could do. It's just going to take some time."

She motions me to come and sit down on her bed.

"Why didn't you tell me?" Why didn't I hear it in her voice when we talked? Have we talked in the last two weeks? I don't even know. She looks so frail. *God please don't let me lose her.* Anger rises up for her not calling me and telling me. I realize I'm not angry with her, but at myself for letting myself get so immersed in my career.

I bend down to kiss her forehead and touch her cheek. "Grandma, please stop trying to protect me." Softening my voice, I stroke her cheek. "I'm a grown woman, a woman who you raised to be strong and independent. Why can't I take care of you, love you, just like you have done for me?"

As my head rests against her face, I feel a trickle of her tears.

"Josie Beth, I don't deserve you, never have. You've been God's greatest gift to me. You should not have the burden of taking care of me; you didn't sign up for that."

Her tears are met by mine. "Grandma, you're all mixed up. I don't deserve you. You're the only one who has loved me for my entire life. Even when I drive you crazy and disappoint you, you're still here waiting and loving me. Don't leave me now, I'm not ready."

Her face softens. Her breath is relaxed. She takes my hand from her face and squeezes it with a renewed strength. *Lord, please give me a chance to show Grandma how much I love and appreciate her. I've been running away from home since I was eighteen*, I silently pray.

"Now let's get to the important topic. When did you start feeling sick?"

"I'm not exactly sure when it started. I just began feeling tired and needed to take little rests now and then. I'm over seventy, you know. I've been to two doctors, and they just attribute it to the flu."

"Grandma, you need to go to real doctors, not the ones in this one horse or should I say one-red-light town."

"Josie Beth, they are real doctors. One is even from up north and trained at Johns Hopkins."

"You know what they call the person who graduated last in their medical school class? Doctor. That doesn't prove anything."

"Josie Beth, I've been in the medical field for a long time, and I know it's just the flu. When you get my age, it really can knock you down. I'll be better for Christmas; that I can promise you. I can't promise what will happen after that. It's all in God's timing, not mine. Stop your worrying."

"No! Don't go talking like that. You're going to live to be a hundred."

"Please don't wish that on me."

I begin to shiver and try to wrap my coat tighter around me.

"Josie Beth, take off your shoes, come under the covers with me and get yourself warm."

Will I ever grow up? Before she has the words out, my shoes are off, and I'm under the blankets with her. The warmth of her bed, the weight of her quilts, and the closeness to her brings back wonderful memories.

"Sundays are for snuggling," she would always say. We would cuddle together while Grandma would read or tell me endless stories. Those were the days when sleep came so easily.

Esther - Chapter 18
Just Listen!

"Stop condemning and you will not be condemned."
Luke 6:37b (NAB)

Josie Beth arriving last night, concerned about my health and showing her love for me was a miracle. But one of those miracles that I wish could've been delayed. This flu bug has taken every bit of my energy. She's here now, and I can't let this wait any longer. Today is our day of truth. I wish I could delay this day, because all the love I received from her last night could be erased like letters on a chalkboard by this truth.

As Josie Beth opens the front door, she drops the grocery bags and immediately comes over to me. "Grandma, you must be sick! You're usually on the front porch as soon as my tires hit the driveway. I've got the medicine from the pharmacy and stopped to pick up some additional food."

"Sorry, Josie Beth. I was deep in thought. Do you need help? Were you able to find everything that you needed?"

"Yes, Martin's was surprisingly well stocked for this time of year."

"That's good, Josie Beth," I reply with a deep sigh.

"Sorry I took so long. Mr. Ferguson actually recognized me at the pharmacy and asked me how you were doing. Grandma, why does everyone else but me know that you are sick? You still don't look well."

The concern in her voice is obvious as she kisses me on the forehead. "You feel a little warm. There's perspiration on your forehead, and you look a little flushed. Should I call your doctor?"

"Do you have anything that needs to go in the fridge?" I ask, ignoring her question.

"Just a few things. It can wait. Do you want me to

call your doctor?"

"I'm fine. Please put them away and then come right back. I'd like to tell you something."

Josie Beth does what I ask of her, but not before giving me a concerned look. She has no idea what I'm about to reveal to her, and it breaks my heart having to tell her the truth. My heart is thumping loud, and I pray that it stops. I can hardly hear myself think, let alone hear the quiet voice of the Lord.

The room goes quiet. Panic sets in again. I pray silently, pleading for courage and strength. *Please Lord, I can't do this without You. Please let me hear Your words. Get me through this without breaking down, or backing out*, I pray.

Josie Beth is back in the room. Truth time has come.

Patting the chair next to me, I motion for her to sit down. "We need to have a serious talk."

"I knew something was wrong. Mr. Ferguson's question was more than a question, wasn't it? Something has been wrong for weeks, and you're afraid to tell me. You haven't been yourself since Thanksgiving. What's wrong? Is it more than the flu? Is it something more serious like cancer or heart problems? Oh no, are you loosing the house? Tell me. I need to know!"

"Josie Beth, how do you jump to such conclusions? Stop worrying about me. I've only got the flu. My finances are fine. I just need to talk to you and tell you a story, my story."

She gives me that knowing look. How many times have I talked to her about controlling that overactive mind of hers? Then the expression on her face changes, as she teasingly says, "Aren't I a little big for stories? What do you mean your story?"

"This story is age appropriate. I've waited so long for you to be ready to hear it, and I believe its time. I want to tell you how I grew up and share some of the poor choices that I've made." The smile disappears from her face, and her brow is creased with intensity and curiosity. "It will help you understand why I get so upset with what you've been writing about in your articles."

Josie Beth fidgets in the chair, showing she is uncomfortable with my comment. Maybe I should have skipped the part about her articles and let the story paint the picture.

"What do you mean the truth? What's this all about? I come back home to help you and this is the thanks I get? Are you going to use this as an opportunity to put me down again? Trust me, I can do that task myself."

Her face tells me she wants to bolt, but I can no longer let her run away when the truth becomes too uncomfortable. *Please, Lord, give me the words*, I silently pray.

"Josie, this has nothing to do with you, and yet it has everything to do with you. As much as you don't believe it, I'm not trying to condemn you. You're getting me so rattled I can't even think or speak. Please relax so I can gather my thoughts. I need to tell you something that's very painful for me before it's too late."

Josie Beth eyes open wide and begin to fill with tears. "What do you mean 'too late'? You are dying, aren't you? Grandma . . ."

"Josie Beth, stop! Please stop. You're right; I'm sick and I'm dying; we're all dying. But right now, we're both here and my soul is aching to tell the truth before it's too late. My lies are too heavy to bear. I've withheld the truth from you, and I need to tell you my story."

"Truth about what?"

"If you would just sit still and let me talk I'll tell you the truth that you have been seeking your whole life. Are you willing to listen?"

The tears stop, and I can now see anger well up within her. "You've been lying to me my whole life, and now you want me to listen? What's this all about? You're not making any sense."

"I'm doing this all wrong. Josie Beth, you always think I'm condemning you and maybe it appears that way because I question your choices. I only have the best intentions. I don't want you to make the same horrible mistakes that I've made. It's out of love that I say these things, not out of condemnation."

"It sure doesn't feel like love."

"I'm sorry about that, but we talk to each other so infrequently."

"See? Condemnation."

Taking a breath, I try to get this conversation back on the right track. "My heart breaks when I read some of your articles."

"Condemnation," Josie Beth says again.

I can see that she wants to say more, so I beg the Lord to take over my mouth and close hers.

"I know it's about two sides to every story. It hurts me to see you write about a side that is so against everything that I believe in and I tried to instill in you as well. I'm afraid, that's all. I've never meant to condemn you or drive you away."

"I'm glad that issue has been cleared up," she says with an edge of sarcasm that shows me how much I have hurt her with my judgment.

Laying my hand on hers, I start again. "Josie Beth, back to the truth I've withheld. Please understand it was to protect you and not hurt you. I thought the truth would do more harm than good, so I lied. I was wrong, so wrong. Please forgive me."

"Okay, I forgive you," she responds. "What's this truth that you're so desperate to tell?"

Now I know I piqued her curiosity. I squeeze her hand gently. "Wait until I tell the story and then decide if you can forgive me or not."

"Are you going to tell me, or leave me in suspense for another thirty-three years?"

"Josie Beth, I want to tell you my whole story and not leave anything out. This is our story, and it needs to be told before it's too late."

"Why do you keep saying, 'before it's too late'? Is this some sordid pre-death confession? Well, if so, I don't want to hear it."

Lord, why is she making this so hard? I pray to myself. *Are you there? Are You listening to this? Where are You? I need You now before the damage I do is unforgivable.*

Taking a deep breath, I try again. "I don't mean that kind of too late, Josie Beth. Wait until you hear the whole story, then you can decide. I just need you to hear me out. It's not about condemning you. It's about me telling you the truth of who I am."

"What do you mean, who you are? You're my grandmother, and that is all I need to know. Please, is this really necessary? If you want someone to hear your confession, shouldn't you being telling your pastor!"

I can hear the squirm in Josie Beth's voice. She wants to run. I can hear it, feel it, and see it. "Josie Beth, please listen. Just listen to what I have to tell you and please with no interruptions. Can you do that for me? Please understand I need to tell *you* this now. I know your mind. Please, for once, hear me out and then I will answer any questions you have, that much I can promise you."

"I'll listen. You actually have my curiosity piqued. And I will try my best not to interrupt. I'm sorry how I'm responding to you, but you're making me very nervous with how you're acting. I've never seen you so upset."

Finally I can feel Josie Beth settle down. Her usual diversion tactics are not working. I know her so well. She seeks but does not always want to know the truth.

Open her ears, Lord.

Chapter 19
The Truth is so hard to Tell

"And will know the truth, and the truth will set you free."
John 8:32 (NAB)

Josie Beth remains silent, but her face is already telling me that this is going to be painful, very painful. She is so fragile. I'm not sure if I can go through with this. The tension in the room is too much to bear, and I am sweating like it's August, not December. Needing some relief from the heat and another precious moment to plead with God for strength, I get up to crack the window. Josie Beth starts to stand up to help me, but I motion her to stay seated. *Please, Lord, give me Your strength. I can't do this on my own*, I pray.

Sitting back down I pick up my Bible. To avoid Josie Beth's watchful eyes, I look straight ahead and not at her. Her impatience is urging me to move on. "Josie Beth, I'm not sure where to start, so maybe I need to start from the point of truth that you know, the death of my parents. I told you I was an only child and both my parents died when I was a teenager. That's true. That's all I ever shared with you and for good reason. Some things are too painful to put into words."

Glancing over at Josie Beth I see she's finally paying attention. It gives me the strength I need to continue.

"Things really changed when my father died. Not so much his death, but all the decisions I made trying to fill the hole in my heart. I loved my Papa. He was my hero. He was more than just my hero; he was a war hero as well. My father took his American citizenship very seriously. His family emigrated from Poland when he was eight. His parents and grandparents shared stories of the Polish people's persecution and oppression throughout the ages. Papa enlisted in the army to fight in WWII. The Nazis had taken over his family's beloved Poland, and he wanted to help stop the evil from invading our borders. Papa survived the Battle of Normandy and was awarded a Purple Heart. I was three or four when he enlisted. Fortunately I don't remember too much about the war. I only remember missing him desperately."

The next part is so easy to tell and brought back such happy memories. "When Papa got back we were two peas in a pod. I stuck right close to him to make sure he would never leave me again. I would go anywhere and everywhere with him. Papa was the heart and soul of my family and our neighborhood. He was that special kind of person that everyone wanted as a friend. He did everything with such joy and love."

Josie Beth is looking at me with such compassionate intensity. She knows the power of loss. "Just like you, Grandma. Now I understand why you work so hard," she says.

"Maybe you're right, Josie Beth. Thanks for saying that. It means more to me than you know."

"Go ahead," she prompts. "I want to know more."

"One of my fondest memories was Papa's love for storytelling. He read me mostly Bible stories about Joseph and his brothers, of Moses and David. Along with all the men in the Bible, Dad told me about his favorite Biblical hero, Queen Esther."

Looking over, I see Josie Beth's reaction to my name. "Yep, that's where I got my name. He insisted. He hoped that I would follow Esther's example by standing up for my people and having the courage to tell the truth, even at personal risk."

I feel a tear of disappoint trickle down my face. Have I disappointed both of my fathers by this lie?

"I think your father chose the perfect name for you, Grandma. I see you every day standing up for your people."

She will not feel that way after I tell her the rest of our story. *Do not be discouraged, I am here with you,* I hear a quiet, still voice tell me.

Sitting up a little taller now, brushing the invisible

crumbs off of my sweater, I lean forward to tell her my favorite part of my story. "I can't tell you who many times my father read the story of Esther to me. And like you, I always wanted to know more. Who are my people, Papa? Who am I supposed to save?"

"'The Lord will reveal who they are when you are ready,' he would say. 'Always be willing to take risks, open your heart, and work to ensure their freedom.'"

I'm astonished that Josie Beth is sitting still, even though I know her mind is working. There is a question on her face. Dare I ask her?

"But what about your mother? Where was she in your story?" she asks before I can continue.

I take a deep breath. "I wish I had some wonderful memories of my mother, but I don't. She was always sickly, confined to bed with the lights out and curtains drawn most of the time. My Papa waited on my mother hand and foot. He did everything for her. What I remember most was the amount of love in which he cared for her, always calling her his princess. I never heard my Papa complain. Never. He just showered her with love. I guess he thought if he loved her enough she would heal. Being little, I didn't understand what was wrong with her."

"Grandma . . ."

I hold up my hand, silently begging her to be patient. "Papa would always fix her up by combing her hair, putting on makeup, and dressing her ensuring she looked pretty before he left for work. He was hopeful that one day she would leave her room. On Sundays, if the weather permitted, Papa would sit with her on the front porch. He was a big believer in the healing power of fresh air. But even those short outings from the bed to the porch exhausted her. She said that she needed to be alone most of the time. Papa talked to my mom as if she were a child. I even talked to her the same way. She felt more like a sickly sister than my mother."

"What was wrong with her? Did she have an

accident?"

"Even though no one ever said it, I knew she suffered from severe depression. From what I can gather it started after she lost a baby. I was about six at the time so I don't remember much about the miscarriage, only that she never was the same.

"I knew Mama loved me, and she tried to take an interest in what I was doing. My mother would ask the right questions about school, but I knew when she had enough. So I would leave her room to start my homework or dinner. That's all I knew of my mother, in bed with the lights out. That's just how it was; it was normal for me and taught me how to care for others."

"Grandma, I'm so sorry to hear this. I can see why it's so painful for you to tell your story and why you've kept it a secret from me."

She has no idea the secrets I've been keeping, but if it helps her to still see me as Saint Esther for a while longer, so be it.

"A freak accident sadly took away the little joy we had." I again wipe a tear from my eye realizing that the pain from my loss still exists. "I was in high school at the time. Papa was helping a neighbor with his car. Why Papa was helping is beyond me. We didn't own a car, and he didn't know the first thing about them. But that was Papa, always helping. The story is that they had the car up on a makeshift lift of cinder blocks. They were out on the street; we didn't have driveways in the city. Papa was under the car when a drunk driver barreled down the road, hit the car, knocked it off the cinder blocks, and crushed Papa. He was pinned under the car and was killed instantly."

Tears pour down my face. Through watery eyes, I can see Josie Beth is also crying. I thought I was over the pain, over the loss, but here it is. She stands up, comes over, and throws her arms around my neck. Maybe the compassion she feels will stay. Maybe she will understand. Her care gives me hope; hope that this is God's perfect timing.

Josie Beth sits back down and is listening so intently that I proceed with caution. I've opened up old wounds of mine and given her fresh ones that will not heal before the end of this story.

"When Papa was killed my whole world fell apart. He was the loving center of our lives, my best friend, and our sole supporter. The devastation, the abandonment, I felt from losing Papa finally helped me realize how loss could cause my mother to be so depressed."

"So at sixteen I became the caregiver for my mother. She could do nothing without my father, and now it was all up to me. He was her lifeline, her reason to stay alive even through the hell of depression. To this day I still can't believe he left her and left me. I knew it wasn't his choice, so I blamed God for taking my Papa away. That decision to blame God, to walk away from the faith my father had instilled in me, was the worse decision I ever made. The world told me my anger at God was okay."

I take a tissue from my pocket, which gives me time to pause and pray that Josie Beth will hear God's love and redemption through this story and not just the ugly sinful parts. Josie Beth allows this pause, sensing how deep my hurt is. *Keep going*, I prompt myself. So I continue.

"It didn't help matters that Mama sank deeper and deeper into depression. I always wondered why didn't God take her and let my precious Papa live. The sicker she got, the more I resented her. During the few years I cared for her, I took all my resentment, all my pain, and all my anger, and directed it towards her. I had somehow blamed her for something that she had no power over and distorted the truth. I started to see her as weak and needy. It was through this distortion that I made the decision that I would always be able to take care of myself and never depend on anyone to take care of me. Somewhere within my grief I forgot my father's love for my mother. Instead I fed myself with bitterness and resentment from his abandonment."

"You were only sixteen. I would be resentful now!" Josie Beth says these words and her face tells me she regrets saying them.

"Are you trying to tell me something?" I say with lightness knowing the truth about how much Josie Beth loves me.

"Oh Grandma, that's not what I meant. It's just that you had too much to handle at any age. At sixteen it's just inconceivable to me. You're an amazing woman. I'm so glad you finally told me your story."

"Hold tight, Josie Beth, I've only just begun. Can I continue or do you need a break?"

"No, please, tell me. I want and need to know. I just assumed your life was easy since you're always so happy. Guess that's why you need to tell me the truth."

"This story only gets harder, so if you need a break, let's take it now. Can I make you some tea? I need to stand up and stretch. Whenever I sit for too long my bones begin to ache."

Josie Beth agrees to the tea and runs off to the kitchen to start the kettle. I head to the bathroom and take these few minutes to gather my thoughts.

Closing the bathroom door, I stand against it and weep. "Thank you Father for opening her ears and for giving me the words that she will be able to hear," I pray aloud. "Yes, Lord, yes, let my story glorify Your goodness in the midst of my sins." Gratefulness fills my heart. Looking in the mirror I can see the toll this story has already taken. Truth might set you free, but lifting the burden of it is very hard work.

Josie Beth comes back into the living room with a tea tray, some cookies, and my favorite tea mug. The serenity prayer wraps around the cup, and my hands hold onto the words and the warmth.

"Thank you, Grandma, for insisting that you tell your story. You're right. It needs to be told. I would love to write about it someday -- that's if you'll trust me with it."

"Let me finish the story before you decide."

Josie Beth nods in agreement and settles into the sofa providing some welcomed distance from one another. Her face is reading love, compassion, and understanding. How long will that last?

"The hardest part of resenting my mother was forgetting the lessons of my Papa to be loving and taking care of people. Papa was love in action. Grief, resentment, and anger created a powerful combination that distorts the truth about God, who He is, and what He has called us to do. It also gives Satan a foothold in your life that can be hard to regain."

Josie Beth shifts her position and grabs an afghan from the back of the sofa. She layers it on as though protecting herself from the subject of God's love, which has become very difficult for her to accept. I will not let it deter me from telling her the truth.

"Papa left us with a small insurance policy. It wouldn't last forever so I needed to find some way to earn money. Both time and money were running out. The crazy part is that I didn't want to take care of my mother, yet I chose to go to nursing school."

"At that time your options were really limited," Josie Beth chimes in. "You know you made the right choice, don't you?"

"Yes, it was the right choice, and nursing has served me well. My classes in nursing school helped me understand and take better care of Mama. So I am grateful for that as well. This information, learning the truth about her disease helped me see her through Papa's eyes. I know that's what my Papa would have wanted, and I finally felt like I was starting to heal."

"Grandma, you're being a little hard on yourself. You beat yourself up because you weren't perfect after all you went through. Maybe your standards are too high."

"Yes, they are high standards. Standards set by God and confirmed by Jesus to love unconditionally. I could only think about how I was hurting, and not thinking of my mother's needs or her loss. I will give myself a pass on being a teenager, but this bad behavior lasted for too many years causing me to make some horrible choices."

"Grandma, your idea of horrible is not putting away the shopping cart, or holding a door open," she says with a laugh.

She has no idea what I've done or am capable of doing. "Josie Beth, let's see how you feel when I finish. After graduation I took a job as an OB nurse. Maybe it was because of my mom losing a child, or because I just fell in love with the babies. Whatever the reason, it was a great fit, and I loved my work. At the hospital I could actually see the impact of my care. It gave me strength to continue to care for my mother even when she felt like she was a hopeless cause."

I take a small sip of tea. I know how the next chapter in my story is going to change how Josie Beth feels about me, possibly forever. Can I just stop here, Lord, before I lose her?

"Just when things started to improve, my mother passed away. The feeling I had when she died was so different, so revealing of how my heart had turned hard in only a few years. I did not feel the grief, sorrow, or pain that I did when Papa died. When Mama died I finally felt free, and it was intoxicating. I could now live life on my own terms, nothing and no one holding me back and dragging me down."

Josie Beth is still listening, and I think she is starting to see me in a different light because the story is becoming so dark. I pray for His light to shine through my story.

"Without Mama, I was all alone, which left me vulnerable. Desperately wanting to be independent, but also hungering for love, I made the second biggest mistake of my life, I became involved with an older doctor at the hospital."

Why did the thought of Charles, not bring sadness, but a sickness to my stomach? Did I ever really love him? I know he never loved me.

My silent reflection opens the door for Josie Beth to comment. "Why was that such a mistake? Oh no, he was married? Grandma no. No, that can't be true! You would never, ever do something like that."

She believes in my lie of being a saint. I'm not and never have been. The truth of Jesus' words brings me much needed comfort. *Whoever has not sinned, pick up your stone.*

"Josie Beth, I can and I did. You're right. He was married. And I was young and foolish looking desperately for someone to love, protect, and care for me. He filled the hole in my heart that my Papa had left. Obviously, we had to keep our relationship a secret. But that did not stop me from romanticizing about him and lying to myself about what this relationship really was. I was hopelessly in love with Dr. Charles, and I thought he was in love with me."

I didn't want to look at Josie Beth, but her silent stillness is speaking loudly. Is this what it takes, sordid details to keep Josie Beth quiet? She is pushed so far back and deep into the sofa as if she is attempting to disappear from the room. If she was handling this part of the story with such difficulty, what will she do when I get to the end? *Lord Jesus, please give me strength to go on.*

"Josie Beth, I'm so sorry that I have disappointed you, but there is so much more I need to tell you."

I look at her hoping for an answer, anything because the silence is too hard to bear.

"Why? Why are you telling me this now? If you're trying to make me feel bad, it's working, but not for the reasons you're thinking. If you're trying to convince me that you're some awful woman, I'm not buying it, but good try."

In a hundred years I never would have imagined this reaction. She thinks I am making this up. How did we get here?

"Josie Beth, you don't believe my story?"

"I believe the first part, yes. The second part, about your being involved with a married doctor, no. It's all fiction. It's taken right off the pages of a *General Hospital* script. Next thing you'll be telling me is that he knocked you up and you had an abortion. Don't bother I've already seen it."

I try to capture the gasp of air that escapes from my mouth before it's released. Josie Beth looks over at me. The shock on my face is telling her the truth that she did not want to believe. This story is true.

Josie Beth is now pacing the room. She is screaming something, waving her hands, but I cannot hear her. I feel like I am going to faint. *Lord, set me free*, I silently plead. *Let me say the truth You have been prompting me to tell. Give me Your strength, Your Words, Your love. I take a deep breath before I can continue.*

"Josie Beth, I'm sorry. This is why it's so hard to tell you. Please realize I am not the same woman I was back then. It's only through the grace of God that I have been redeemed."

"*Redeemed* is that what you call it? I have another name - you're a hypocrite. You know that, don't you? You're condemning me for living with Earl. He's not married, I haven't gotten pregnant, and most definitely, I have not had an abortion. And you sit in judgment of how I'm living my life? How dare you!"

She is so hurt, so angry that she is screaming at the top of her lungs. Do I stop or go on?

"Josie, Josie Beth," I say quietly. "Please forgive me. I have never claimed to be without sin in my life. Because I'm such a sinner I know the pain of sin. That's why I've tried so desperately to show you where the path of sin can lead you, to do the unthinkable."

"Part of me wants to leave now and never come back. The other part wants to hear the end of the story so I know everything about you." The venom pouring from Josie Beth's mouth is frightening. She has run the gamut of her emotions.

"Josie Beth, there is nothing you can do or say that I

have not already done or said to myself. I wish I could tell you that the rest of the story gets better, it doesn't. It was all downhill until you."

Josie Beth still paces the room like a caged animal. My truth seeker is, in truth, a scaredy cat, which is why I have waited so long to tell her. But now that I've opened the vault of truth, she needs to know all the truth.

"Josie Beth, please sit down. Please." Reluctantly she returns to the place on the couch. Her look has now turned to disgust. What will be her next reaction? Not wanting to think about it, I just carry on with my story.

"I can't believe I was involved with a married man. Even after fifty years, I still can't believe what I did. I was lost, confused, being led by lust and a lack of God in my life. Like all sin, it started so innocently. It was just the first step on a path of sin leading me in the wrong direction. When I became pregnant, everything changed."

Josie Beth's mouth drops open, but she refrains from saying anything. She closes her mouth, shuts her eyes, and I'm sure somehow she's willing her ears to close as well.

"I was so happy when I found out I was pregnant. Charles and his wife didn't have any children. This would give him the opportunity to leave his wife, and we could be together. I believed he would be delighted, especially if it were a boy, but that wasn't the case. Instead he became angry. This once handsome man turned ugly and mean right before my eyes. The passion and love I thought we had instantly died. I can still hear him shout at me.

"'You're NOT keeping this baby, Esther. Do you understand? I do not want your bastard child, and I don't want you. Do you understand? You're a little piece of trash I picked up that's all.'"

Josie Beth stands up again and walks over. "He didn't say that, did he?" How quickly her anger has turned back to compassion. *Lord*, I pray, *I am hopeful she will understand the whole story.*

"Yes, I wish that was all that he said. His words were

finally speaking the truth that I refused to see.

"'Don't you think that if I wanted a child I would have had one with my own wife not a slut like you?' he had yelled. "'Wake up. You're getting rid of that baby.'"

"It was the truth, and I had known it for some time. I was nothing to him; I never was. But I refused to listen because I was so broken. That's why I tried to protect you from living with Earl. I know Earl is a good man, but I thought Charles was as well. It was not to judge you, Josie Beth. It was always to protect you."

"So why did you have the abortion? That part will never make sense to me."

"I wanted the baby and at first refused the abortion because I believed he couldn't make me. But when you're all alone in the world, and desperately trying to hold onto something you love, you make really, really bad choices."

"Where were your friends? You had no one to go to?"

"No one. He had all the power. The one thing I vowed I would not let happen to me did, being dependent on someone. It sickens me to this day when I can now see so clearly how I got to this place. Part of me believed I deserved everything that he was saying about me, and even worse I started believing it to be true."

Josie Beth sits back down. Her eyes lock on me.

"It got ugly, really ugly." The shame of it is still there. Why? I don't know. I know the Lord has forgiven me.

But have your forgiven yourself? His quiet voice asks. The truth of God's word stops me, is that true? It can't be, of course, I've forgiven myself. Shaking off the thought, I continue.

"He told me, 'If you think you're going to entrap me by having this baby, it's not going to happen.' He grabbed me by my hair and forced me to look in his face. I can still see the ugliness and the desperation. He was as scared as I was. How did we get to this place?

"He was adamant about the abortion. 'Tomorrow, tomorrow morning I will pick you up here at 6:30. You will be ready. I will take you to a doctor, and you will get rid of it. Do you understand?'"

Putting my face into my hands I weep for me, for Charles, our child and mostly for Josie Beth having to hear this ugly story. Josie Beth again comes over to comfort me.

"Grandma, how could something this awful happen to you? Why do you want me to know this? Look what it's doing to you. Stop, stop, I get the picture. I don't want to know anymore."

Pulling myself together I thank her for her kindness. "Josie Beth, I wish I could stop, but you need to know the whole truth. If I believed I didn't have to tell you, I would not have said a word. I would have taken it to my grave, but this truth needs to be told."

Reluctantly she agrees to allow me to continue. Do I tell her how he pulled my hair, slammed me against a wall, and threatened to ruin me, or do I remove these details? Am I trying to paint a picture of me being helpless and him evil? *She needs to know the truth, the whole truth.*

Taking a breath, I continue. "Pulling my hair harder and pulling me closer to his face, he threatened me. 'If you do not do this, I will make sure that you never, and I mean ever, work in the medical field again. Is that understood?' he had yelled.

"Shaking my head yes, he finally let go of my hair and stormed out of the apartment. Even though abortion was illegal, he had connections and I was not given a choice, or at least, I thought I didn't have any. He coerced me into having an abortion. He threatened to have me fired and make sure I would never work in a hospital again. I believed in him and his power to ruin my life. He was never going to leave his wife; he had a reputation to uphold. I was devastated. I wanted Charles and his baby in the worse way."

Josie Beth kneels down beside me, places her head in

my lap, and quietly sobs. *God, thank You for the blessing of my Josie Beth*, I pray.

"My life was crashing around me and I had no one, absolutely no one I could turn to. I had filled most of my free hours and all my thoughts with Charles. My friends were shocked by my behavior and had stopped talking to me. I didn't care. I believed they were jealous. I even stopped going to church, because I knew what I was doing was wrong."

This statement brings Josie Beth's head up, and she looks right in my eyes. "You stopped going to church?"

She says it with such unbelief, like all the rest were possible, except for that.

"Not just church, I stopped praying altogether."

"Sorry I'm not buying this story."

"Josie Beth, I abandoned anything and anybody that got in the way of Charles and me. In my absolute sinful nature, I believed that if I had the abortion, I would not lose Charles. Sin is powerful. It separates us from God and impacts our ability to hear and live the truth. Thankfully, God did not leave me. He was waiting around the corner for my return."

"That's why you're so hard on me. You don't want me to get hurt. For that I thank you. For not trusting me, I'm still working on that."

"I will not lie to you. The abortion was a horrible experience. I felt like I had traveled to hell and back again. This was no back alley abortion. Charles knew the right people. However, I bled for days and developed an infection. I thought I was going to die; maybe it was my only hope. I was all alone and afraid. The isolation, the regret, the pain, the loss were all so unbearable. The condemnation I felt was suffocating. If I had just kept God close, none of this would have happened. I could only hope that maybe God was still leading the way."

"How can you believe that God had a hand in any of this?" she asks me is if I've lost my mind.

"Josie Beth, sweetie, God had nothing to do with tempting me to sleep with Charles or any of the rest of my sins. He just takes the mess, cleans it, up and gives us another chance, a chance to do it His way. He never gives up; He never gives up on His children. I gave up on Him."

"I'm having a real hard time seeing God in any of this. I'm sorry, but it's the truth!"

"Josie Beth, for a long time neither could I. I know this is hard for you to hear. And it's equally hard for me to tell. So please let me finish before I lose the little courage I have left. I promise to answer all of your questions. Just please let me get through this."

Josie Beth nods in agreement. I fortify myself by pouring us both another cup of tea.

"When I was finally able to go back to work, I was treated differently. Charles wouldn't talk to me, look at me, and had me moved to another floor. Everyone knew. Gossip runs through hospitals like infections with killing speed. I knew I needed to leave and find a place that I could start over. So when abortions became legal, I moved to New York City and was the first in line to save what I thought were 'my people.'"

"Is that when you became pro-life?"

"Sadly, no. Bitterness had set in and again clouded the truth. My belief was that if I supported woman's right to choose, no one would ever have to go through what I went through, the pain, shame, and isolation. I believed the shame from the abortion had caused me to isolate, but that wasn't true. The isolation started with my yes to Charles, and no to God. I know that now, but not then. So I was determined to make a difference by caring for women seeking abortions in their time of need. I knew what it felt like when I thought that no one was there for me. I honestly believed I had found my people, just like Papa said I would."

Josie Beth pushes away from me and begins pacing back and forth across the living room floor once again.

"You started working in an abortion clinic?" she

yells at me. "Who are you? Where is my grandmother, because I want her back? Not this sick lie your telling me about her."

"Josie Beth, I wish these were the lies; I do. I'm trying to tell you who I was, no, who I am. Don't you think I know this is difficult for you? But God has a plan in all of this, even if you can't see it today or anytime soon. On this, I am asking you to trust me."

"How can it get any worse?"

I will not answer that question, so I continue. "Shortly after I started working for the abortion clinic, I began having episodes of depression that I could not kick. My greatest fear was coming true; I was turning into my mother. I would not give into the depression and forced myself to go to work every day. I tried medication, therapy, even self-medicated with alcohol, but nothing helped. The psychologist and psychiatrists told me I had delayed grieving for my father. Yes, that was part of the problem. I didn't have time, or even know how to grieve for my father or my mother."

"So the doctors were telling you it was grief? This was the reason for all of your bad choices. Sounds like an excuse, and I expected more from you," Josie Beth says.

"Josie Beth, I am not making excuses for any of my choices. I made them, each and every one of them. The interesting part is that my abortion, well, I never allowed it to enter into the discussion with my doctors. My guilt had turned the truth inside out and the legalization of abortion in some way made me feel it was okay, but it did not stop my depression. No one can help you if you don't give them all your symptoms. I was just dealing with the socially acceptable ones."

"Why didn't you just quit? Why did you stay?"

"I'm not sure. When you think you're right, it is very painful to look yourself in the mirror and see the truth. But the truth was coming at me almost every day when I came to work and had to deal with protesters against abortion. They would block the driveway and beg me not to go in there, not to be part of the slaughter of innocent children. I fought back telling them women deserved the right to choose and to make these very private decisions without judgment. No women should be forced to go to back alley doctors to have an abortion."

"You were saying that? How did all of this change?"

"Yes, I was judging what I thought were the religious fanatics who needed to move the church into the twentieth century. Day after day, week after week they were outside the clinic. Most of the protesters were peaceful, others spoke their disdain by holding up signs saying, 'Stop Killing Babies' or 'Stop Abortion.' Some were kneeling and praying on their beads."

"No matter what you say, or how much you try to paint this picture, I can't see you doing any of this."

"For that, Josie Beth, I'm grateful, but that was who I was. It's interesting that their protests would not dissuade me from saving my people. I knew I was doing the right thing, even though they didn't think so. I believed if abortion was safe and legal, women could then openly talk about it. I wanted to stop feeling like a criminal, and I thought this was how to stop the pain and guilt I was feeling."

Josie Beth's expression changes again; this time she is nodding in agreement. "You did what you had to do, Grandma, but what changed? Why are you giving me such a hard time when I'm only writing about abortion? You not only had an abortion, you were helping other women have them. Do you see the hypocrisy in all of this?"

"Of course I do. Josie Beth, the whole story needs to be told, and then you will agree with me. Abortion is not a solution."

"Right now, you're not changing my mind. At least I'm hearing the perspective of someone who lived it and worked in it. Maybe I do need to hear the whole story."

"You do, Josie Beth, you really do. Day after day, week after week, I got to know most of the faces of the people that showed up to protest. Some of them were there every week. There was this one man that especially attracted my attention because he wore a medical lab coat. What really stood out is that he would sometimes bring his wife and children with him. I called him the "mailman," because he would be there every Saturday rain, sleet, or snow. One particular Saturday in May the "mailman" was standing alone with a bouquet of flowers right by the driveway. As I entered the parking lot, he looked at me with such pleading eyes that I felt compelled to stop. When I rolled down the car window, he handed me the flowers and a business card and said that he was praying for me. They all were praying for me, as he gestured to the crowd on the sidewalk.

"What compelled me to roll down the car window and accept his flowers, I have no idea. For some reason he looked so alone without his wife and family. I know what that feels like. I was curious where the rest of his family was and asked him. He reassured me that they were all fine, it just that baseball season had started. He showed kindness and respect for me, even though he did not respect or approve of what I was doing. Oddly, there was something about him that reminded me of my father.

"Pulling into my reserved parking spot, I took a moment to look at the card. Oddly, it was a Mother's Day card and he had signed it Doctor Jeffers. I don't know if it was because he was a doctor, or that he assumed I was a mother, or that he was praying for me. But all these various emotions collided inside of me, and an explosion happened. How dare he! What a self-righteous bastard coming on to me when his wife and kids are away!"

Josie Beth lets out a gasp. "What did you call him? I can't believe my ears."

"I'm not sugarcoating any part of this story. I want you to know where I was, how I felt, and how I was finally set free. Can you bear with me for a few more minutes?"

Josie Beth nods in agreement so I continue.

"The part I hated worse, where did they get off praying for me? I didn't need their prayers. Then it hit me. He wanted to remind me that these women were all mothers. How insensitive could he be? And then I thought of my baby. It was not a memory that I wanted to remember and had pushed it deep down inside. How old would he be now? I always thought that baby was a boy."

The pain in my heart was almost unbearable. Why after over fifty years can I not lift this burden? "Lord, please forgive me."

Forgive yourself. I already have.

Is that true?

I could see that Josie Beth senses my sadness. Taking my hands into hers, she looks me in the face. "When are you going to forgive yourself? Maybe after telling me and knowing I forgive you, you can forgive yourself. I forgive you, Grandma, I do. You don't need to tell me anymore. You've said enough. I understand why you're against abortions now. You're done talking. Look at you. You look like you're going to have a heart attack."

"Josie Beth, I wish I could stop here, but I can't. You need and deserve to hear the whole story. I'll be okay; let me finish. I'm almost done."

"Let me get you a glass a water first."

"That would be nice. No ice, please, just from the tap."

The few seconds of silence provides me with the energy to finish this, to tell the hardest part of this story. *Lord, please let her know she is loved. Let her feel the overwhelming presence of Your love. I'm so afraid of how she will react to the hardest part of this story*, I pray.

Josie Beth hands me the glass of water and sits back on the couch. Again, I welcome the physical separation, providing a barrier to the words I need to finally utter out loud for the first time in over thirty-three years.

"Right around that time the clinic started doing some later-term abortions. I didn't agree with this procedure at all, and it was illegal. Even when they told me it was for the mother's health, something did not sit right with me. I believed in a women's right to have an abortion, but I hated the final outcome, ending a life."

Tears stream down my face. Silently I plead, "Where is Your strength, Lord? I need a massive dose of it now."

"No one likes the outcome. That's why it's such a difficult choice to make," she says simply.

"Josie Beth, it's worse than you could ever imagine. After each abortion I was asked to count body parts to make sure nothing was left inside the mother, which is a major factor causing infections. With the late-term abortions, there were times the whole fetus would be disposed. I no longer felt I was saving my people. I was tearing them apart and throwing them away."

"Baby parts? I can't listen to this."

"Josie Beth, it still sickens me to think of it today. I remember the day, the day I hit my all time low. Lower than the day I buried my Papa. Lower than the day I buried my mother, and even lower than the day I aborted my own baby. There was this darkness that I had never experienced before, and it was all around me. So dark that I did something I had not done in years, I prayed."

Josie Beth starts to cry again. Hopefully it will place a layer of protection on her. *Please, Lord, hold her close. Give the comfort only You can give*, I plead to the Lord.

"I prayed not to God my Father, but to my earthly father. I begged him to help me. I desperately needed his help and guidance. His words rang in my heart, to save your people. 'Papa,' I cried. 'I thought these women were my people. I thought I was fighting for their freedom from oppression, to make their own decisions, to help them through this difficult time. If these are not my people then who are they?' Then in a voice, an audible voice as if he was in the room with me, I heard his voice again tell me. 'You'll know Esther, you'll know.'"

"You prayed to your Papa? That doesn't make any

sense."

"When you've turned your back on God, when you have shut Him out of your life, you believe the lie that He no longer cares or will listen to you. And that's how low I had gotten. Like I've said before, God was there waiting for my return. That dark dreadful morning a very nicely dressed young woman came in for a late-term abortion. I couldn't help but notice her wedding ring. Why was a married woman of some means having an abortion, a late-term abortion? She was different. She was scared, most of the patients are, but something wasn't sitting right with me about this lady.

It's amazing how someone who hated the judgment from the people I worked with at the hospital, the judgment from the protestors, that I was so quick to judge this woman. My initial guess was that she probably had an affair and was trying to hide it from her husband, but the belly bump was obvious. No, I think her husband would have noticed since she was visibly pregnant. Maybe she had an amniocentesis test showing the possibility of Down syndrome? I looked at her with disdain. What kind of person was she?"

"What made you upset with her and not the others?"

"She looked like she should have known better. The doctor came in, gave her the injection, and hours later I was there when she delivered the fetus. I was sickened by how many times you could see a perfect baby, just needing a little more time to develop, being aborted. How could it be that just ten years before I was trying to save babies, now I was part of destroying these little lives? How did I get here?"

"They were babies that were viable, they could have lived?"

"Yes, but the mother made a choice to have an abortion, and that superseded any other right. But something was different this time with the baby. When this fetus was delivered, it cried, a soft weak cry. We were all startled, especially the mother. The mother asked what we were going to do. One of my colleagues said we would take care of it, meaning dispose of it. I don't know what possessed me to jump in, but I did and told her 'I would take care of her.'"

"Don't!" Josie Beth yells. "Please don't tell me anymore. I've got to get out of here." She stands up, looks around for her purse, grabs a jacket from the closet, and heads for the door. "I can't listen to this anymore. If you are trying to shock me into seeing your abortion conversion story, it's worked. But if you took that live baby and disposed of it, I don't ever, ever want to hear about it. Do you hear me? Take that one to the grave." Josie Beth did what I knew she was going to do all along, she ran from the truth.

I try to stand up to catch her, to let her know I didn't hurt that baby, but it was too late. My legs would not cooperate and the toll of telling this story had on my heart, mind, body, and spirit was just too much to take, for me and for Josie Beth.

Jo - Chapter 20
Ugliness Surrounds Me

"And coming to her, the angel said, Hail, favored one!
The Lord is with you."
Luke 1:28 (NAB)

I stop to throw up in Grandma's hedges. The thought of baby parts, abortions, and her affair has made me sick. Ugly images of her life's events run through my head and surround me like a cloak of darkness. Her story has permanently destroyed everything I believed about her. Was this some plot that Babs and Grandma concocted to get me down here? Would Grandma stoop so low by letting me believe she was sick? Well, she's sick, really sick; she's sure proved that today.

The desire to get as far away from her as possible propels me out of the driveway and onto the highway. Driving down here all I could think about was what my life would be like if she were dying. Now I have no idea what to do. Who do I call, who do I turn to? That list is very short: Earl or Grandma. There's no way I'm going to call my friends from work. After all I've told them about Grandma, they will think I lost my mind. Maybe I did. Maybe it's hereditary. My great grandmother had some obvious mental health issues. Grandma sure does, and I wonder if my mother suffered from the same problems? Why is Grandma telling me all these ugly stories about herself? What is she hoping to gain?

The roads are still a mess from last night's storm. I slow down and take a deep breath trying to erase the ugly images that are flooding my brain. If this is finally truth time, then let it be the whole truth. Maybe, just maybe, I will finally hear about my parents and what happened to them. Not wanting to give her any sense of satisfaction by returning too early, I decide to take a slow ride, look at the snow, and enjoy the Christmas decorations in these small, one-stop-light towns.

Christmas was always the best time of year for me. What changed about this season, I don't know. Maybe to enjoy it, you have to believe it. Santa Claus disappeared for me in the third grade. I hated to see him go, but it felt better realizing that there is no Santa Claus than believing you were less worthy of great gifts than your classmates. Maybe it's the same with God. It's easier to not believe, because when I was doing it His way, as Grandma likes to say, I was getting nowhere with my career. Now I'm finally making some headway, getting the recognition I've worked so hard for, yet my personal life is falling apart.

Two hours into what I thought was going to be a short drive, I realize I'm starving. The stress of hearing Grandma's sordid life story has given me a headache, and the hunger is making me feel worse. Hopefully something will be open in one of these small towns. My head is pounding, and I am not sure what will cure it - food, coffee, or both. With a sudden chill in the air, a nice mocha latte would sure hit the spot, and the caffeine would help me to think straight.

In the next town, I stop at the only eating spot on Main Street. I notice the name of the diner in bright neon lights over the door, Room at the Inn. You've got to be kidding me. Did they change the name just for me? This is reminiscent of those *Touched by an Angel*™ episodes that Grandma would religiously watch. Every part of me wants to turn right back around, leave the parking lot and keep driving back to civilization. My stomach growls again, and I know the fight is already over.

Lucky for me, there is a parking spot on the street right in front of the diner. Is that a good or bad sign? At this point, hunger is winning over my concern for taste and quality. As I slowly get out of my car, I notice the back parking lot is full of old cars and semis. This place is probably a hangout for Grandma's cast of characters. I read the sign taped to the door as I enter the small establishment. "We're closed today between 3:00 and 4:00 for Christmas

Pageant." My head wants to turn away and run before some angel in human form, shows up to tell me how I need to reconcile with Grandma, and by the way, God loves you.

I've got an hour to get something to eat before they close up, so I decide to go in and face whatever miracle is awaiting me. Funny, "Room at the Inn" was what Grandma always said about our house during the holidays. What are the chances that I'd pick a place with this name today?

The place is full of dollar store decorations and country western Christmas carols. Inside is more packed than the parking lot. Every booth and table is full, so I sit at the counter. At least I won't be sitting alone. I'll be with the two truck drivers at the end of the counter who are flirting with the waitress. After a quick assessment, I realize mocha latte will not be served here. They probably serve coffee from percolators poured into tin cups.

To keep with the whole bad TV script scenario going, the frizzy-haired waitress approaches me. "Sugar, can I get you something?" Does every diner waitress call you *sugar?* I ask for a cup of coffee and a club sandwich with fries. Finally catching my breath after my escape, I realize the life I once knew has disappeared. I'm disappointed in everyone. Grandma and Earl are at the top of the list. Lost in my angry thoughts, I'm startled back to reality.

"Can I get you something for your coffee. Cream or sugar, Sugar?" she asks with a laugh.

"Sorry, I was lost in thought. What I really want is a chocolate mocha latte with whipped cream?"

"Sugar, we just have straight coffee. I can get you a scoop of Ovaltine with some whipped cream if you'd like."

"That's all right. Skim milk and a yellow sweetener will be fine."

"No skim milk. There's not much call for it around here. We have regular milk or cream. I do have a variety of sweeteners. I'll bring them right over."

Even though this place looks like it has seen better days there is actually an air of excitement as people chat

with their tablemates. More than one family is decked
out in their Christmas finery. A pang of jealousy wells up as
I see parents, two kids, and a grandmother. They look
happy, almost like they are waiting for something special to
happen. It's that special look of anticipation on kids' faces
this time of year with thoughts of Santa and the gifts they
will be getting.

Next I notice an older couple in the corner booth.
They are all starry-eyed, holding hands, and deep in
conversation. I wonder what their story is. Did they just
escape from the nursing home? Is that why at their age they
look so darn happy?

The waitress puts the coffee in front of me. "That's
Marie and Jerry. Cute, aren't they? Legend has it that they
come here every year around Christmas and sit in the same
booth for dinner. The first time they ate here, they thought it
might be their last. Jerry was being shipped out to Germany
during World War II. They were recently married and
vowed if he made it home that they would return here each
Christmas to celebrate. What's even more amazing is that
they've kept their promise for over sixty years! I've been
here for over ten, and they haven't missed one Christmas
season, not one. I'm so sorry for rambling on. They're just so
cute they make me gush! I hope to find myself someone like
that who keeps his promises. I'm not sure guys like Jerry
are even out there anymore. Do you know what I
mean? Your sandwich will be right up. By the way my name
is Peg. We don't get many strangers in here, just our
regulars and those waiting to attend the pageant. Are you
just passing through?"

"Yes, no, I'm not sure. I've just left my grandma's,
and I'm not sure which way to go."

"It looks to me like you've just lost your best friend?
Need someone to talk to?"

"Thanks, but no. It's something I need to work out
myself." I feel the weight of the world. Realization sweeps
over me. I didn't lose just a best friend. I've lost both of
them, Earl and Grandma. I now have no one. Then I quietly

added, "My Grandma and I haven't been getting along lately. She shared something with me today from her past and it really, really upset me. So I left before anymore damage could be done."

"Oh, sugar, I'm so sorry to hear that. We've all got baggage. Sometimes it's best just to leave it buried, because it's too ugly and smelly when brought to the surface. Is she sick or dying? Truth seems to come out at crisis times. But trust that she knows best."

A bell rings. "Another angel got its wings," everyone says in unison.

Peg reassures me it really means an order is up. "We've all watched *It's a Wonderful Life* one too many times, and this is the most Christmassy place I've ever been. That's why I decided to stay here when I ran away from home. If you think it's crowded now, you should see this place after the pageant. Everyone comes back for dinner. Why don't you come to the pageant with me? It's just at the VFW hall across the street."

"Oh, I don't think I can. I should get back on the road."

"Sugar, this pageant comes just once a year, and you really should come along. You can think about it while you eat your sandwich, which I need to be getting before another angel gets its wings. I'll be right back."

This place does have the Christmas spirit. I can sense their joy even if I don't want to and don't feel it myself. When was the last time I felt excited, happy, or full of joy? I can't remember, and I don't want to think about how long it will be with this newest bit of family news.

"Here you go, sugar. Did I get your name?"

"It's Jo."

"Hello, Jo. If you don't mind my asking, what was your tiff about that made you want to escape?"

"Thanks, but really I can't talk about it right now. I just learned some information about my grandma's past, which like you said, should have been kept buried." I am not going there with this lady, no matter how nice she seems.

"I found that right now is always the best time before
you bury that bit of evidence. Take care of it now before it
starts rotting inside of you, or festers. Bring it to the Great
Healer. Trust me on that one!"

I give Peg the eye roll. I didn't mean to but it
happens whenever so-called godly people start telling me
how to run my life. I put my head down to take a bite of my
sandwich and also to signal to her the conversation has
ended. Peg gets the message and turns to walk away, but
then comes right back.

"It's Christmas, and I know you're hurting. I can see
it all over your face. You can try anything else you want to
try and stop the pain. It won't work. Turn around and look
at these faces; everyone has a sad story to tell, a broken
heart, some lie that is killing them, some brokenness that
needs a Savior. You think you're special. You can roll your
eyes at me, but it won't change the truth. I've tried it all and
when I reached my end is when I looked up, and there He
was waiting for me. Don't let this day pass you without
finding time to remember what the reason for this season is,"
she walks away over to the front window.

I want to shout, "How dare you!" How dare she
dismiss my pain! She has no idea what I've heard, how
disgusted I am, and how confused I am. Grabbing my purse
I am ready to run again, run from Grandma, run from Peg,
and run from this place of too much joy, too much cheer, too
much Christmas. As I begin to rise I feel a hand on my
shoulder, pushing me back onto the stool. I turn around just
in time to see my car being towed away and Peg holding
onto me.

"Your car was parked in front of the fire hydrant.
Floyd is a stickler about parking, especially with the pageant
tonight. We had a near miss two years ago when one of the
little ones dropped their candle in the manger peering in to
find Jesus. Fortunately someone found the fire extinguisher
in the dark and got the fire out right quick."

Could this day get any worse? "Where did he tow my car to, and how do I get it back?" One parking mistake has turned this awful day into a disaster. I look over at Peg and she has this smirk on her face as if she's saying to me "told you so." Why didn't she tell me about the hydrant? Was she too busy getting into my business and delivering her sermon to notice, or is she spiteful to out-of-state drivers? Tears start flowing as though a dam of emotion burst inside of me. Deep, pathetic, uncontrollable sobs escape from my mouth. Now I have the full attention of the entire inn. Every eye was on me, even the old couple in the back stopped staring at one another long enough to stare at me.

Someone is pushing a tissue into my hand, and someone else is patting my back. "Guess you've got no excuse about attending the pageant," Peg whispers. "Floyd will be directing traffic for the next two hours. Sit down, I'll grab you a hot Ovaltine and then you can tell me what is really troubling you."

Peg grabs my sandwich and walks me over to a hidden booth in the back corner. "I'll be right back, now don't go running off," she says with a little chuckle. Her sense of humor is grating on my nerves, but right now she is all that I have so I stay put.

As promised, Peg is back with a steaming cup of hot chocolate with big dollop of whip cream on top. She sets it in front of me and the tears start back up again. All I can think of is Grandma and how she always solved my problems with hot chocolate. Grandma always knew what to say to calm my fears, dry my tears, and cure my broken heart. How in just a few short hours could she be the one responsible for breaking my heart?

"Okay, sugar. I know a runner when I see one. I've been a runner for most of my life. Whenever the emotions got too raw, the truth too difficult to bear, I ran. Who or what are you running away from today?"

Between the snot and tears I am a watery, snotty mess. Peg grabs a tissue box from the back of the booth and hands it to me. "I'm going to have to call Bo from the back to get the mop and bucket. What could be so bad, Jo? What could be so bad?"

"I told you already," I say between sobs. "My grandmother just dumped her entire sordid life on my lap, a pre-Christmas present."

"Jo, we all have these stories in our heads about the people we love. We are all sinners, but we just have our own rating scale."

Peg's accusations stop the tears and turns on another emotion, anger. "How dare you judge me! You have no idea who I am, and what I'm dealing with right now. Who do you think you are, condemning me?"

"I'm nobody from nowhere, that's for sure. But right now, I'm the one sitting in front of you watching your heart break and wanting to know what caused it."

"Why do you even care?"

"Why do I care? Because I showed up at this place ten years ago with my own sad story. We're all hurting. Someone sat me down, told me the truth, and literally saved my life. That day I made a promise to do the same, or as they like to say, pay it forward."

Taking a sip of the hot chocolate gives me some time to think. Who is Peg, and why did I show up here? Don't even call it another "Godincidence." I can't take anymore God stories. What I do know is I need to tell someone, and Peg is right, she is right here.

"Where do I begin? This could take days to tell."

"Let's start with the condensed version, and we can chat more after the pageant. I've only got about ten minutes before the stampede across the street occurs."

Recounting the high points to this low story, I watch Peg's face, and she doesn't even flinch like she's already read the book, seen the movie, and now it's just another rerun playing on TV. Maybe Grandma was right about one thing: this world has become all so sordid that the really sordid doesn't even faze anyone anymore.

"Sounds like you've got every right to be upset," she says, grabbing my hand. "Secrets are painful, and some should stay buried. But why did your Grandma tell you now, what's going on?"

"I wish I knew. Grandma has not been herself lately. We've been fighting so much about my choices. I don't know maybe this was a ploy to let me know how low I could go, too."

Peg shakes her head and takes a deep breath. "It only takes one step, Jo, just one. We make a choice and down we fall. That's the lesson from the beginning of time. None of us feel we are capable, and we all are. Sounds like your grandma has spent an entire life trying to redeem herself."

"Redeem herself! That's all you can say?"

"No, I can say a whole lot more, but I have a pageant to attend. And you do, too. So finish your fake mocha latte, and let's get over to the hall. Seems to me you need a good dose of Christmas. I don't know much, but what I do know is that Christmas cures everything."

Peg grabs me by the arm, helps me put on my coat, and grabs my purse while ushering me right out the door and across the street. I'm not sure if she is the shepherd leading me to slaughter, but I just know I have nowhere else to go.

What do I have to lose? Reluctantly I follow the parade to the hall. We find a seat near the front, and Peg nudges two people in so that we can fit. They happily move in and whisper a Merry Christmas.

My mind starts to wander again, and it is almost impossible to believe that I'll be spending Christmas alone this year. Maybe this is more telling of the pathetic life I am living than I want to admit; no friends to call and invite myself over. Maybe that's why I allowed myself to be hijacked by some crazy waitress into attending a Christmas pageant; I am in need of a friend. Sitting with a hundred strangers who all have such looks of anticipation on their faces, I was almost expecting some famous country singers to show up on to this little stage.

The lights are shut off, and I am poised to bolt when I feel Peg's hand on my arm. She whispers to me to wait because the pageant is about to start. There is a faint flicker of light that grows as I see a procession of young children dressed like angels holding candles and singing "Silent Night" so sweetly.

As they approach the stage, the spotlight comes on and I see a motley crew of slightly older children squirming on the stage. They look as excited to be here as I am. The song finishes, and there is this solemn quietness that fills the air. An older, scruffy looking gentleman comes onto the stage and starts telling the story of Jesus' birth. Not the Bible version, or a version I have ever heard before, but a version that has me sitting upright and interested. Maybe it's his voice that had a tenor and tone to it that drew you in closer and closer. Maybe it's the rawness in which the story is told, not all neat and tidy, but the rawness of the sacrifices and mysteries, the humble beginnings, and hardships endured so that we could be free from sin.

How did I miss it, or did I just choose to forget it? Mary was a woman with a whopper of a story. She was pregnant by the Holy Spirit. It sounds almost comical when you think about anyone trying that stunt now with ultrasounds and DNA testing. I also forgot that Joseph stuck with her when he could have left her or had her stoned to death for the infidelity. Jesus was born into such a humble beginnings, it makes my life seem extravagant by comparison. He did not have handmade clothes. He had filthy, dirty rags that were torn and tattered swaddling Him in a manger.

The tear trickling down my face is not for the pageant. It's for me. In my push for significance, I pushed every thread of Jesus' story from my memory. How could I be so blind that in my pursuit of truth, I stopped believing the real truth? And that truth is being told to me right now, on this stage, in this small town by a gentle man who has a voice of an angel.

Where did it all unravel, Lord? I pray. *When did I forget this story and start believing only in the stories that fit my choices? Lord, you give us all the right to choose: to choose You or to choose the world. When Mary chose You, she chose the more difficult path. Not seeking success or significance, Mary only wanted to honor Your will for her life. How distorted my views have become!"*

Now, as I hear her words, I know Mary is just stating the truth. "He has regarded the lowliness of His handmaid; for behold, henceforth all generations shall call me blessed." Mary will be known forever for her *yes*, her beautiful resounding *yes* that was the first step in transforming this world.

Just when I think I can't take the power of these remembered truths, the storyteller turns into a singer and "Oh Holy Night" is sung powerfully and beautifully. The words of the song feel like they are being imprinted on my heart. As he sings, "fall on your knees" everyone around me does as the song commands. I drop down not in obedience, but in reverence, in awe of this special day and awesome miracle.

My tiny trickle of tears, turn into sobs. I can either choose to believe or run away. Straddling the Word of God with the word of the world has left me alone and lonely. Earl's honor and respect for me as a woman has been viewed as outdated, not an act of love. Grandma's constant prayers and guidance were not condemnation or rejection; it was out of love for me. The worst part is the truths that Nicole, Bob, and Liz were desperately trying to tell me, I rejected as another one of my right-to-choose moments. I did not make the choice that Mary did, to say *yes* to her Son. It cannot be coincidental that God choose for His Son to be born of a young virgin woman. As with all His plans, they are for our good, not our restriction.

The song ends, and I feel so sad. My heart is actually begging for it to be sung again, and it is, this time by the little children as they walk down the aisle and out into the now dark street. Looking out the window, I see the procession headed into the direction of the Room at the Inn.

Maybe this is all a dream. Maybe I am in some coma after I ran myself off the road yesterday, or maybe this is God looking down on His daughter and saying, *I have plans for you, plans to prosper not harm you.* I just need to choose which path I will take, His or mine.

Chapter 21
On Angel's Wings

"But the path of the just is like shining light, That grows in brilliance till perfect day".
Proverbs 4:18 (NAB)

By some Christmas miracle, my car is waiting for me in the parking lot. Attached to the windshield wiper is a piece of paper. Well, I guess a ticket is the least of my troubles today. Snatching the paper I look in disbelief. It is a ticket with a very kind message. A big *X* and the words, "Merry Christmas" is written across the front of the ticket. I turn it over and on the back another handwritten message, "Your debt is paid in full." Kissing the ticket I place it into my purse for safekeeping. With renewed energy I hop into my car to drive to Grandma's. I opt to take the highway and not the back roads that brought me to the Room at the Inn.

Surprisingly the trip back flies by, almost like I'm traveling on the wings of angels. It sounds so corny, but I feel a lightness and a hopefulness I haven't felt in a long time. Even if it only lasts for the ride home, I will remember it forever. Because I've been touched by an angel. And that touch is warm, gentle, and beautiful, not the thump over the head from God's messenger that I deserve.

The night is clear, and the stars are out in full force. I almost believe I could see that star of Bethlehem. That is one of the things I do love about this area of the country; there is no light pollution out here. The roads are virtually empty and when a car does pass by, I feel they are reassuring me that the road ahead is safe and welcoming. I had started to believe that the hustle and bustle brought the spirit of Christmas. Now I know the calmness, peace, and silence is where the true spirit of Christmas resides; it's in the place that we can hear the voice of truth. And my being able to hear that voice again, well, that is a miracle in itself.

Slowly I pull down the drive and look at the home I

grew up in. It's nothing much to look at to the untrained eye or one who has been blinded by the pursuit of success. Oh Grandma, how can I have been so blind to all that you have been teaching me? Why am I blinded by the glitter and glitz of the other side and miss the glow and goodness that is on your side?

Why have I never looked at our life from her vantage point and how hard it must have been for her to raise me alone? How often have I seen the frazzled look of moms with their children and never once stopped to appreciate how she was raising me all alone.

I didn't realize how much older she was than these moms, and she did it by herself. Never a day off, I was hers 24/7. From a child's eyes, blinded by selfishness, I didn't always see that I had her unconditional love. I only saw what I was missing, my mother and father.

The lights were on, as expected, but Grandma was not waiting at the door when my car pulled up. My hope was that she would be on the porch waiting for her prodigal daughter to return and welcoming me back with open arms. How many times can I run away from her and still expect forgiveness? Even as a child I pushed her, pushed her to see if one day she too would abandon me like my parents did. But she was steady, consistent, and true. She was always dependable and loving. I can't remember her ever not keeping a promise. Why did I always doubt her love?

Uneasily I walk in the front door not sure what will await me. There has to be a point that Grandma will no longer accept my tantrums against her. Sadly, even the kitchen is quiet. I tentatively push open the kitchen door, and there she is sitting at the table, hands folded in the midst of a beautifully prepared dinner. Candles are aglow on the table, soup in the urn, holiday napkins are in place, and the only thing missing - me at the other end of the table. The clock chimes seven, the appointed time of our usual dinner. I take my place. We then hold hands across the table and pray.

"Grandma, what were you thinking?" is the only

thing I could say

"Just waiting for my Josie Beth to join me, so we could say grace.'

"How did you know I was coming back?"

"I didn't. I just thanked God for your return, that's all. Just a little prayer with a lot of hope sprinkled in that you would open your heart to forgive me."

"Grandma, how do you make faith seem so easy?"

"It is easy. Just keep looking up when you get down."

Grandma ladles out the hot soup and places a biscuit on my plate. The subject of my leaving never came up, and I did not want to bring up her story again. I just want to enjoy this wonderful dinner. The urge to be close to Grandma is overwhelming, so I get up and pull out Grandma's chair, put my arms around her and say, "I love you, Grandma. Thank you for all that you have done for me, and all that I know you will continue to do for me. Don't give up on me, Grandma, please."

By the look on Grandma's face, I have just given her an early Christmas present: hope that her wayward granddaughter has finally turned the corner and is coming back home for good. But another look comes over her face, one of hurt and pain. I know that telling me the truth hurt her. I hope my forgiveness will open up our hearts to healing.

Esther - Chapter 22
She's Alive!

"Therefore they took away the stone. Then lifting up His eyes, Jesus said, 'Father, I give thanks to you because You have heard Me.'"
John 11:41 (CPDV)

"Lord," I pray under my breath, "Thank You for delivering Josie Beth safely back to me. She seems so at peace. Do I finish telling her the story now, or do I wait?"

You've waited long enough. She needs to know the whole truth.

"Are you okay, Grandma? I realize now how hard your story was to tell. It definitely took a toll on me. Why don't you go upstairs and rest? I'll clean up the kitchen; it actually looks surprisingly tidy. Did you cook or just defrost?"

I know she's trying to make light of the situation, and I am grateful. "Josie Beth, I had nothing else to do so I cleaned while I was cooking. It wasn't as hard as I thought it would be. You can clean up these dishes, but when you're done come sit with me for a while in the living room. I still want to talk. So much has been said, but I'm sure you have questions, and I have more to tell."

My legs are weary as I walk into the living room. My heart is heavy. I have no idea what to expect. This first part has been a miracle. *I can see Your work all over her face. Lord, is this some cruel joke to make her next exit out that door her final time? Please give me strength.* I close my eyes for a few minutes, but it must have been longer than that. I feel a warm blanket over my legs, and my beautiful Josie Beth is sitting across from me.

"You took a little catnap. You needed it. Kitchen is clean, and I have the tea tray on the table. Would you like a cup? I made chamomile."

The cheerfulness in her voice has me more scared

than her anger. How can I break her heart again, when it seems that something has cured it?

"That would be great, Josie Beth. Thanks for letting me rest; I did need it. You left before I could finish the story. The ending is not what you were thinking. I did not harm that baby. Those days were behind me. That baby was a miracle child."

She nods her head in agreement, and I pick up where I left off early today. "None of us were sure what to do with the baby. At that point I wasn't sure of anything in my life. But I was positive that I was destined to save this innocent baby girl. Our normal procedure was to take the dead baby to the waste disposal area, but I did not dispose of her. I wrapped her in towels, placed her in a box, and called the front desk telling them I needed to leave. I was sick. No one questioned me, because I looked like hell that morning, and I still looked like hell when I left out the back door with the little girl."

"If I were going to save her I needed to get her help right away. She was so tiny, maybe only two pounds. Where was I to go? I prayed to Papa again for guidance. Doctor Jeffers, the doctor who was always praying at the clinic, came to my mind. Where did I throw his card? I was operating in panic mode. What if the baby died before I could get her help? I couldn't go to the hospital. How would I explain the baby? They might take her away from me, and that was not going to happen. This precious gift was mine.

"Looking into the box I saw she was barely breathing. 'Be strong,' I tell her, 'I'm going to save you.' Where is that card? Pulling over to the side of the road I stopped my car, got in the back seat, and by the grace of God I found the doctor's card. Wednesdays, back in the day, were doctor's days off. There was no other alternative so I kept driving to the pediatrician's office.

"That day I did more praying than I did in the previous ten years combined. When I finally pulled up to his office, there was only one car in the back of the parking lot. 'Please God, let it be Dr. Jeffers, please God,' I remember praying. Taking the box out of the front seat, I ran to the office door. It was locked. I banged and banged. Please, please I begged, please answer the door. Nothing. My heart sank. I began to cry, really cry. Cry for the death of my father, cry for the death of my mother, and finally I allowed myself to cry for the death of my baby. Looking up to heaven I said, 'Papa, I tried. I tried to save her.'

"'Can I help you, miss?' a voice asked. I looked up and there was Dr. Jeffers in his white lab coat. Our eyes met, and I knew he recognized me. Again he asked if he could help. I showed him the box. He came over to take a look. I'm not sure what went running through his mind when he saw the little baby barely breathing. 'Where did you get the baby?' he whispered.

"'She was born at the clinic. Her mother aborted her, but she was born alive. She cried, and I needed to save her. Please help me save her.'

"He opened the door and led me into the examining room. He looked over her and asked me what type of abortion method was used. I told him prostaglandin. He asked if the baby was injected with any other drugs. I said I didn't know. I begged him to please help her.

"He wrapped her up again. He told me to hold her and keep her warm. If she stops breathing try to resuscitate her, and he left the room. What is he doing? Is he calling the police? Somewhere I found courage, the courage to stay. It felt like hours, it was probably only a minute when he came back with a needle. He gave the baby an injection, of what I wasn't sure of at the time. I didn't even ask what it was; I was so distraught. He told me to keep an eye on her and make sure she's breathing. Yell if something changes, I need to make some phone calls.

"I sat holding this baby like it was the only baby ever born. Thankfully, there were no sirens, no cop cars. The doctor came back in about ten minutes later, but again it felt like hours. He put his hands on my shoulder and asked me to trust him. He was going to take me to the hospital and say that I had the baby at home and brought her to his office.

"'Do you have insurance?' he asked, and then immediately changed his mind. 'No, on second thought, I'll put you in as a charity case. That way this won't get tangled up with your insurance company and your employer having access to your records. You'll need to claim her as your child for the time being until we find her a home. Do you understand?'

"'No!' I screamed. 'She's my baby. I saved her; she's mine. I beg you, please don't take her away.'

"'First things first,' he tried to soothe me. 'We'll work it out. Now we both need to pray for guidance. Come on, we need to go; I already told the hospital that I was bringing you in. God help us both.' As he puts us in the car, the doctor asked me, 'Do you have a name for your little girl?'

"'Yes, I do, I will call her Josephine Elizabeth after my Papa and Mama.'"

The gasp that came out of Josie Beth's mouth is the sound I have dreaded for so long; it was the sound of truth ringing through this home. Quickly I move out of my chair and try to hold her. The look of contempt she gives me lets me know she wants no part of me. The truth is more painful for her than I anticipated.

"Josie Beth, you are so loved. You're my most precious gift."

"Are you sick? Did you think that this information would somehow beholden me to you? I thought I came from nothing, but now I know I'm less than nothing. I'm trash, and you're a trash collector."

"Josie Beth, Josie, calm down. What are you saying? You're getting it all wrong. Don't you see that God gave me you as a gift? You saved my life."

"You lied to me. Everything about my life is a lie. My mommy and daddy didn't love me. They wanted to get rid of me."

I tried to have her understand what a miracle she was by how she came into this world and into my life. What other words could I have chosen but the truth? I never wanted to hurt her. She's God's perfect example of why each life is precious.

She runs, as I knew she would. I try to grab a hold of her sweater as she slows down to grab her purse. "Please, Josie Beth, please let me finish," I beg, but I can't stop her. She runs so fast out the door and down the steps. I wait to hear the slam of her car door and for her to race down the drive. There is nothing but silence. I get down on my worn out knees and pray out loud like I never prayed before.

"Please Lord, have her come back to me again. Can I please have two miracles this day? Was I wrong to tell her?"

Trust in me.

Minutes pass, and I continue to pray and hope that she'll come back. I'm frozen in place, petrified to go out to her and face her wrath. Did she need some time alone? She hasn't left yet, maybe there is still hope she will come back in the house and talk. "Lord, let her know I love her."

Finally I find the strength to rise from my knees, only to hear the sound of the car starting. From the window, I watch Josie Beth's car charging down the drive. Each stone from the gravel driveway hits her car is a stone being thrown at me in condemnation. You're a liar, an adulterer, and a baby killer; you're a trash collector, you're nothing. For each of the babies I helped destroy, for each of the lies I have told, for each of the lives I have ruined through my sinful selfishness, am I now paying the price? The thought sickens me, but I know it is true; I'm being stoned by my own daughter. Where is Jesus in all of this?

What was I expecting? Was I expecting Josie Beth to accept this information, this revelation about her true self, with an open heart and mind? I did expect her to be upset or confused, but to run away? Not when she came back tonight with such peace on her face. I was not expecting her to storm out of the house without a word, a glance, or even a fight. This is not what I had been praying for since the day I brought her home. What happened to all the years of love and devotion? How could we have eaten dinner with such joy, and now it has turned to anger? There were no tears, no yelling; she just ran away without a word.

"Lord, was this Your prompting me, or was it my own fear that somehow in Josie Beth's investigation about abortion she would uncover the truth about her birth? I wanted to own our story, not have her discover it through her own research. Lord, was I being selfish or faithful? I feel so alone, Lord, so brokenhearted. I thought this was what You wanted. I just never imagined that You would lead me to revealing the truth only to abandon me."

I will never leave or abandon you.

"Then why now? She obviously was not ready to hear the truth."

This was my perfect timing. She is one of my sheep, and she will hear and know my voice.

"Lord, you are paying attention to my prayers. I felt that Josie Beth has been moving away from You. She has become so enamored with her career that Your truth no longer was important to her. Now I realize this conversation was to lead her toward You, not away from me.

"O Lord, my heart swells with love for Your awesome mercy and love. And how blessed I feel to be part of Your plan for Josie Beth. Lord, no matter what it is, it is good if it is in Your hands. I will sit and wait for her return, trusting and resting in You."

Peace settles into my heart, and the fear washes away. I will rest in the Lord and believe that His plans for both Josie Beth and I will be fulfilled. My hope is that through her pain, Josie Beth will see the truth that I now know about abortion: it destroys lives.

Jo - Chapter 23
Run, Jo, Run

"But Jonah made ready to flee to Tarshish, away from the Lord."
Jonah 1:3a (NAB)

Get out of here. Run. Run as fast and far away from her as you can. Get out of this house and as far away from her as possible; get away from her and this awful truth. My life is spiraling out of control, and I have no way to stop it. How can I feel this lost in my own front yard? I keep turning in circles looking for answers. Begging and pleading to God for relief from the pain, from the hurt, and from this ugly truth.

Everything that I believed to be true is all a lie. Who am I, who do I belong to? How could she lie to me for all these years? How could she put on such a charade and then talk about God and truth when our life was nothing but a big lie?

Finally, I get in the car and lock the doors. I'm in no condition to drive, but that is the only way to get out of this mess. Turning the key, I pray that it will start on this cold night. I step on the gas and gun it down the driveway. Grandma always hated me driving fast out of the driveway. Well, too bad. I hope she hears every angry stone pounding against my car; each one I hurl is meant for her.

By the time I come to the road, I'm crying uncontrollably. I can't stop the tears, and I can't seem to catch my breath. The loneliness is pressing down so deeply on me. The pressure on my chest feels like it will crush me, but who would even care? I have no one. For my own safety and the safety on any other poor loser on the road, I pull the car over to the shoulder. My tears have blinded me, and my racing mind has caused everything to blur.

Turning off the engine, I wish I could turn off my emotions and these pummeling thoughts. Who am I? Why did my mother not want me? Who are my parents? Do they know I'm alive? Everything I thought I knew about myself is a lie. I'm not an orphan whose parents died in a car crash. The truth is my mother aborted me, wanted me dead, and for some bizarre twist of fate, I was born alive. I wasn't loved or even wanted. I was thrown away, discarded as nothing. She didn't even care when she heard me cry. What kind of woman delivers a living baby and allows it to just die? I am the child of a monster. That truth was too hard to bear.

All along I thought I was loved. How could she lie to me like that? What kind of sick person is she to pull this off for so many years? She then expects me to understand and forgive. I wish I hadn't survive the abortion. I can't take this pain. God help me. Where can I go, who can I turn to?

❊ ❊ ❊

I wake up not knowing where I am. My hands are numb from gripping the steering wheel so tightly. My neck and head hurt, almost as if I've been run over. Then I remember. I have been run over, run over by truth. Lifting my head up, the freezing cold darkness of the car matches my dark, cold thoughts. How long have I been sitting here?

Now I remember why I fell asleep. I had to quiet the thoughts and words that keep running through my head in an endless loop. Now another loop is playing, saying something very different, yet very familiar.

You are loved. I am with you. I will never leave or forsake you.

Where have I heard those words? Why do these words keep running through my head? In some strange way, it's giving me comfort, but why? Why am I loved? Who would even care if I die? What I do know is that I hate the world and all its lies.

Love rejoices in the truth!

Stop! Stop it! Almost hysterically, I start singing "Grandma Got Run Over by a Reindeer" to put the other words out of my head.

These words are relentless and start playing again in my head. *You are loved. My love bears all things, believes all things, hopes all things, endures all things.* These words are just another cruel, sick lie because I am not loved. I was discarded like garbage. How could she? How could she lie to me? Why does this hurt so much? What was she hoping to achieve from this disclosure, to punish me, to let me know how unworthy and unlovable I am? If she is not my grandmother, then who is she?

Get out of here and go as far away as possible. My body aches with physical and emotional pain. Grandma tried to convince me that she rescued me from that horrible woman, from that horrible place. Right! I heard her story. Grandma isn't the saint I thought she was. More lies, more deceptions. All that I ever wanted was the truth. All that I've ever gotten have been her lies.

I vow to never look back, or go back. That chapter of my life is closed. And it will never be revisited. She was wrong not telling me the truth years ago. Where does she get off playing God, deciding who should live or die?

My love never fails.

I start the car. Not knowing where else to go, I head north. God help anyone that gets in my way. Anger, hurt, and pain are my driving forces. Speeding along this very open highway is the only thing that clears my mind. I don't want to stop. At the speed I'm going I'll probably end up in Canada by morning. Maybe that's not such a bad idea; I have nothing to lose. Today is the first day of my real life.

No matter what, these remain: faith, hope, and love. But the greatest of these is love.

"Stop preaching to me! You're making me crazy," I yell.

Gracious words are a honeycomb, sweet to the soul and healing to the bones.

Eight hours and four states later, I end up at Earl's front door. Why here? Why now? Is he even home? And if he is, will he even answer the door? I haven't seen him in weeks. I bang and bang hoping he answers. Thankfully I hear shuffling and the lock turning. The door opens, and I wearily stumble into his arms.

Earl - Chapter 24
With Open Arms
"Lord, You have probed me, You known me."
Psalm 139:1 (NAB)

What in heaven's name in going on? Who's banging on my door like a lunatic at four in the morning? It sounds like Jo's voice, but it can't be; she texted me yesterday that she'd be spending this week at her grandmother's. Why would she be here now? Silently I pray nothing has happened to Esther. Esther is the only family Jo has. Why didn't she call me, or text me first?

I stumble toward the door. "I'm coming, Jo, I coming," I yell. Throwing open the door, Jo collapses in my arms. What is going on? Has Jo been in some kind of an accident, a fight? She's disheveled with black streaks of mascara running down her cheeks. I've never seen her like this. Bending down I pick her up and gather her into my arms. She rests her head on my chest, and I draw her closer into me, never wanting to let her go again. Whatever brought her to me, even in this distressed state; I am grateful that she is back in my arms.

Gently I settle her on the couch, cover her with a blanket, and sit down next to her. She molds herself into my chest. Racking sobs escape from her mouth and echo through the room. Stroking her hair, I wait for the explanation to her sudden appearance.

Tears finally spent, Jo lifts her head. "I probably look a wreck, don't I? I am a wreck. Please hold me. Tell me that you love me. I need to know that someone loves me."

"Jo, of course, I love you. What's going on?" There is no response to my question. She just clings to me desperately as if she's making sure I won't leave her.

For what seems like hours, I hold her. So many concerns run through my mind, but I let them all go so I can sit and hold her in silence. Finally I feel her release her hold, letting me go as she falls into a deeper sleep. If there were something life threatening about her visit, she'd have told me by now. Gently I pick her up from the couch, and I carry her into the bedroom. "Please stay," she whispers as I put her on my bed.

What could have caused all this pain and sorrow? "Jo, is Grandma okay?" I finally ask.

"She's as good as dead to me," she spits out.

The tone of her voice warns me that her answer is final. Her response is so cruel, so out of character for Jo, I don't think I could have asked the next question even if I wanted to. Maybe I misheard her, or in her exhaustion, maybe she's confused.

I do as she asks and lay down next to her. I wait and listen for her breathing to become the natural rhythm of sleep. Whatever trauma she has suffered, she continues to play out in her sleep as sobs still escape from her lips. Holding her tightly, I hope and pray that she will feel and know my love. In the stillness of the morning, with her curled in my arms, I remember the first time I met Jo.

After I abruptly left the law practice in Texas, Deb, my sister, had been drumming up work for me by leaving flyers in the local supermarkets. Jo found one of them and called me to ask my advice. She was interested in buying this older house and wanted a professional's opinion on the viability of bringing an old Victorian back to life. She wasn't even sure if it was worth the effort. Jo had already done her research on me by asking around town. She was told I was an expert in fixing up older homes. Older houses do have an amazing draw for me since I restored my ranch house. Something about that old house was calling Jo to buy it; she even referred to it as her dream home.

When I saw the house I knew immediately what it was that attracted her; it had the most the beautiful wraparound porch. At first glance, I thought the house was a prop for horror films with the peeling paint, broken windows, shutters hanging at precarious angles, porch boards missing, and sagging porch roof. Jo had fallen in love and wanted to restore the house to its former beauty. The draw was further understood when I walked inside and saw the amazing walnut staircase in the foyer. Jo was able to see past the aging to find the hidden gem. I had to admit, it had possibilities. As I walked around the house, I noted that the foundation looked solid; it probably could last another hundred years.

After my assessment, we went into town to her favorite restaurant to talk about the house and if it could be saved. 'If you have a solid foundation, everything else can be fixed,' I said. Jo wanted to make sure she wasn't making a mistake. Since she put in a very low bid on the house Jo wasn't even sure if it would be accepted.

The delight in her face surprised me; she really did love this rundown house. We discussed getting an estimate together and how long it would take to make it habitable. There was something about her, and her house, that drew me to help both of them. Even with other jobs already lined up for the next couple of months, I decided to find time for Jo's project. I asked if it would be okay if I worked nights and weekends. It was summer and the long days would give me an opportunity to help her. She immediately said yes.

After working on the house for about a month I was surprised one Saturday when Jo invited me to join her for lunch. That day is when I got to meet the real Jo. Not the all business, life-is-so-serious, talk-so-fast-she-hardly-breathes Jo. I finally met the down-home, warm, friendly, and loving Jo. It was that Jo that I instantly fell in love with that day.

Jo's painful cries break my reminiscing, yet thankfully she is still asleep. Drawing her closer to me, I hold her tight hoping to make her pain go away and for this moment of closeness to last.

The sun peeking through the window prompts me to quietly sneak out of bed. Hoping I'm making the right decision, I call Esther. The sound of Esther's voice startles me. Not just because it sounds worn out and tired, part of me thought she really was dead. Jo just couldn't bear to tell me the truth.

"Esther, it's Earl. Is everything all right?"

"Earl, have you heard from Josie Beth?"

"Yes, she's here. She arrived at my door this morning."

Esther exhales a huge sigh of relief. "Thank You, Lord Jesus. Is she okay?"

"No, she's not. She looked like she was crying the entire drive up and hasn't stopped yet. She's even crying in her sleep. What's going on?"

"Didn't Josie Beth tell you?"

"Tell me what? She just showed up. She didn't tell me anything. Do you want to tell me what happened?"

"No, Earl, I can't. It's Josie Beth's place to tell you. Thank you for calling and letting me know. I've been up all night waiting and worrying. Now, I need to sleep. I'm even too exhausted to talk."

With that remark, I know Esther will be okay. Now I hope Jo will survive this as well.

"Earl, my prayer's been answered, Josie Beth is safe. If she's with you, she's right where she should be. Take care of her Earl. Tell her I love her. Hopefully one day she'll be willing to believe it again."

"Esther, I will. Whatever this is, I know God has His hand in it."

"I hope He does, because this is such a mess, only He can clean it up. I know you're a godly man, so please pray for us. I need every prayer I can get. God help me, Earl; I think I've lost my little girl."

Esther starts to sob and before I can say anything or ask what this mess is, she hangs up. I keep staring at the phone in disbelief: disbelief that Esther doubts God, disbelief that Esther believes she's lost Jo, disbelief that Jo came back to me. Before today I wouldn't have believed any of these situations were possible. I'm more confused now than when I made the call. Whatever transpired between Esther and Jo has a potential to destroy them both. What could it be? *Lord, whatever is going on, please help them*, I silently pray. *Give them the grace to believe that with You all things are possible.*

The sound of the bathroom door closing lets me know Jo is awake. Did she overhear me talking to Esther? I hope not. I don't get a chance to ask her because the next thing I hear is the bedroom slamming shut. That signal is loud and clear, she needs to be left alone.

Thankfully today was a light day with only one customer meeting that I'll be able to reschedule until after the New Year. There is no way I am going to leave Jo today. Moving into the den I do the only thing that I know that stops my worrying. I grab my Bible from the shelf and open it to the prayerful Psalms. The best place to start in times of trouble for me is Psalm 139, "You have searched me O Lord and You know me."

Peace still eludes me. Aloud I pray, "Lord, I don't know what to pray for, so I pray for Your grace, for Your healing forgiveness to wash over Esther and Jo. Bind them with Your love. Only You, Lord, know what they need. I know what I need now is Your wisdom."

It's late afternoon when I finally hear Jo again. This time she's in the shower. Hopefully I have enough hot water. When Jo has something on her mind, she takes long, hot-water-emptying showers. The interesting part is they work. She'll come out all red and wrinkly, and usually with a solution to whatever problem has been troubling her.

Jo finally emerges into the kitchen with a sheepish grin that almost begs forgiveness for the long shower and the fright she gave me. She likes to solve her own problems. I know to keep quiet and wait for her to talk. While she was showering, I made a fresh pot of coffee. A toasted and buttered bagel is waiting for her. No matter what time of day it may be, Jo still wants breakfast when she wakes up. Maybe it's her way to reset her clock after a long night.

Jo sits down across from me, clean faced, wet hair and in my embarrassingly tattered blue terry cloth robe.

Boy, she looks beautiful.

"Do you want to talk?" I ask tentatively.

"Not yet."

Jo eats in silence. She gets another cup of coffee, refills mine, and walks to the den. Wrapping herself tightly in a quilt, she motions for me to sit next to her. Laying her head on my chest, we sit in silence.

After a few minutes, Jo lifts her head and faces me. "Earl before I tell you anything, promise me, promise me that what I say will not change how you feel about me. Do you promise no matter what I say that you'll still love me? Because if you can't then . . ."

My silence was a moment too long.

Jo bursts into tears. "I knew it. I knew that you couldn't love me."

"Jo, please wait. I'm trying to understand you. Trying to comprehend what has happened in the last few hours. My silence has nothing to do with my lack of love for you. Something has hurt you deeply, and I want to watch each word I say. So, yes, no matter what you tell me, I will never stop loving you. Nothing could change that, nothing."

"I've been living a lie. Grandma's well constructed lie. No wait; she's not even my grandmother! She stole me. No, she saved me from the trash is what I really should say."

"Jo, you're not making any sense. Trash... stole you? What are you talking about?"

"Yes, Esther trash picked me from an abortion clinic. Do you know where my high and mighty, all-righteous grandmother worked when she was younger? An abortion clinic! What a hypocrite! All her preaching about the sanctity of human life, and that woman worked in an abortion clinic. Isn't that a revelation?"

I sit in stunned silence. This can't be true. How can it be true? How can a baby be stolen from an abortion clinic? Jo doesn't give me time to even ask her a question.

"I've been a failure from the beginning of my life.

My mother had an abortion, and I was born alive, so I am a failed abortion. I couldn't even do that right. Grandma said she heard me cry and couldn't put me in the trash, so she stole me and ran away. My mother didn't want me, and my grandma is a liar."

"Jo, this can't be true. Who told you this?"

"Esther did. Esther has been waiting, waiting to tell me this sick truth my whole life."

"Why would she say this? Jo, she loves you too much to hurt you. I know that to be true. But why now, why did she tell you?"

Jo's voice rises with each unbelievable word she says. "She told me I needed to know the truth: that I needed to know it now. Even that long shower didn't wash away the disgust I'm feeling. My whole life has been one big, contrived lie, but why? Who am I but a piece of trash that was thrown away? Was I so unworthy that my mother wouldn't keep me? How could she hear me cry and walk away? Did she care that I was alive? Why would she just leave me there to die? Did she not see me as a real person, a living and breathing person? Do you know what it feels like to know you're a throwaway child? Do you know how my heart was screaming all the way here? Do you have any idea the pain and disgust I am feeling? I can't even put words on these feelings."

I didn't know what to say. The story is so hard to comprehend. I again pray for words of wisdom. "Jo, you are loved. You're hurt, justifiably so. Who wouldn't feel lost and confused? Please don't forget you are loved and have always been loved. Maybe not by your natural mother, but you sure are loved by Esther. I called your grandmother's house this morning when you were asleep."

"Stop calling her that. She's not my grandmother."

"I was surprised when Esther answered the phone. I thought something dreadful had happened to her, what else could have caused such a reaction from you? I just assumed she died. I felt relieved to know she was okay. Jo, her last words to me were to tell you that she loved you."

"Do you call that love, lying year after year? You don't lie to people you love."

"Jo, I don't know why Esther said she stole you, or if she did. If all of this is true, I can only guess why she lied about your parentage. When did you want her to tell you the truth? When you were five, ten, fifteen, or twenty? You're not taking the truth very well now at thirty-three. How would you have taken it at a younger age? I can't even imagine how much this truth hurts. Is there something really wrong with Esther? Maybe that's why she thought you needed to know the truth now?"

"I don't know. Right now I don't even care. She just dropped this truth bomb on me, and I ran. I couldn't stand to be with her a moment longer. Nothing feels real right now, nothing."

"You are loved, Jo."

"Why do you keep saying that? I kept hearing those words in my head all the way up here. *You are loved.* It's creepy, you using the same words."

"Maybe they're the words you are supposed to hear right now."

"Earl, I've got to go. I need to think things through and want to go home. Can I borrow some sweats? I left my bags at her house."

"Sure, they're in the bottom drawer. But don't you think you would be better staying here a little longer until you do think things through? I'll stay out of your way; I don't want you to leave."

"I need to leave. I'll be okay, honest. I need to get in my own clothes and be in my own house. I can think better there. Sorry, don't put that worried look on your face. You know I'll be okay."

I watch as she heads for my bedroom to change. Again I pray for words of wisdom. I don't seem to know what to say. Jo came out looking beautiful even in my ragged old sweats. How I love this woman. I just wish she would stop over thinking all her feelings. Time and patience is all I can give her.

As Jo comes over to me, I hold her and bury my face in that curly hair of hers. I love every strand. Then suddenly the words of wisdom came to me.

"Jo, I want you to think about two things while you're alone. One, think about life without Grandma; not Grandma dead, but Grandma alive and you never seeing her again. And the second thing, don't you find it miraculous that your cry saved your life and transformed Esther's?"

"What do you mean transformed?"

"You said Esther worked in an abortion clinic. Because of your faint cry, she now knows that all life is precious. Look at how she treats everyone with so much love. Don't you find that to be miraculous, or at least transformational? Something changed within Esther, and it started with you."

"Stop trying to make this into some kind of Christmas miracle. Christmas miracles cannot cure everything. I didn't change Esther. I didn't, I couldn't have. I was only a baby."

"What about Liz Betts? Didn't you tell me that she also heard her baby cry? Do you think Esther and Elizabeth would be doing what they were doing, if it wasn't for the power of a baby's cry? Don't you feel that it's an odd coincidence?"

Jo starts to turn away, but I hold onto her. Needing to let her know the truth, the truth she needs to know, that she is loved.

She bristles.

"You are loved," I say again before letting her go.

Out the door she runs.

"Lord, it's all in Your capable hands. Please let Jo see the light of the truth that she is loved. Let her know Your love. Because Your redeeming love is what she needs to feel. No matter what her mother or Esther did, You have always been there. Somewhere deep inside, she knows this. If she would only remember the most important truth, she is loved by You."

Jo - Chapter 25
By the Light of the Moon
"As face mirrors face, so the reflects the person."
Proverbs 27:19 (NAB)

Sitting in my driveway, I'm paralyzed with fear and unable to go inside my house, my dream house. Everything looks the same. The rockers on my porch gently move in the breeze, beckoning me to come sit and sip some chamomile tea. But I'm not the same. Maybe this dream house is a lie, too. All I have ever dreamed, worked, and hoped for has come tumbling down by the wrecking ball of truth.

My life now feels like this house the first time I saw it abandoned, tossed aside, and left to perish. This dark empty house mirrors how I feel right now. Warmth and love are all gone destroyed by a horrible truth. This powerful truth has caused a whirlpool of emotion that is sucking me into blackness; pulling me down, down, down. I am pulled down into the realization of what I really am; I am nothing but trash. These thoughts are impossible to stop. I know if I don't stop them they will crush me. The Jo I believed I was, the Jo I worked so hard to become; I don't know how to save her, or even if I want to anymore. Is she a lie as well?

Sitting in my car, I wait for these feelings to pass, to free me, to give me strength so I can move forward. Not knowing what else to do, I pray out loud. "Dear Lord, I'm so lost and confused. Help me."

My mind instantly quiets.

Maybe my prayer is answered. Gaining some strength, I get out of the car, but I'm not ready to go inside. I decide to take a walk on this beautiful, but cold, moonlit night. I grab my jacket from the back seat and head down to the path by the river.

The fresh air and this momentary peace allow me the space to replay all that has transpired in the last twenty-four hours. One thing I'm sure of, I need to block any concerns that I have for Esther. How can I ever look her in the face again knowing what she has done, realizing who she really is, a hypocritical liar, and what I am, someone's trash?

Shivering at the thought, or at the truth, I pull my jacket tighter across my body. The coldness will not stop me. I am determined to reach my destination. Fear takes over that I will not make it in time. Time for what, I'm not sure. My feet pick up a pace, trying to match the pounding of my heart and head. I begin to run. Run to escape the pain, run to escape these horrible thoughts, and run toward my place of refuge, the river.

Maybe I've been drawn to this town for a reason. The river beckons me to come in and wash away my pain. The moon glistens on the water inviting me to walk across the moonbeam, but this too is a lie.

Keep going and you'll find relief, a strange and scary voice vibrates inside my head; prompting me to do the unthinkable. Is that the only way to escape the torments of truth?

Wash yourself clean of the lies and half truths, the strange, scary voice again prompts me again to move into the water.

"Should I jump in and end it all? Will that stop the pain?" I shout.

Slowly, tentatively I walk into the water but the coldness stops me, cuts right through me, and forces me back to the safety of the shore.

You are loved. This time the voice is loving, tender and welcoming.

"Loved by whom?" I scream.

By Me. Again the loving voice encourages me.

"It's another lie. No one loves me. How could they? I'm discarded, wretched waste. I am no one, and no one loves me. I have no mother, no father, and even my grandmother is a lie. I belong to no one."

You are mine. I was there when you were knitted in your

mother's womb.

"Yeah, you saw how that turned out. She aborted me. Who are you, anyway?"

I am the Way, the Truth, and the Life. Whoever comes to Me . . .

Pushing these words away I wonder, should I end it all like my mother wanted? It would only take me moving into the center of the river and letting go. The current will float me away, away from the pain, away from the lies, and away from this horrible truth. The battle continues to rage inside of me. Maybe I'm losing my mind, or maybe this is just a bad dream. If only I could wake up and go back to yesterday, go back to being Josephine Elizabeth Reynolds before the ugly truth was revealed.

The sound of that name makes me retch into the water, throwing up the little that is left of her. What is the truth? Who am I really? I don't know anymore. I just want to make all this horrible pain stop.

A gentle force holds me, stopping me from moving into the water. I glance around to see if anyone is with me, but I am alone. Instead of jumping into the water I feel compelled to look down into the river. The water magically presents a storyboard of my life showing me long forgotten scenes. Maybe I am hallucinating, maybe this in only a nightmare and I will awake whole and maybe even happy again.

What I see are all the hours each summer Grandma and I spent at the creek near our home. We would dance, sing, swim, and picnic until dark and the fireflies guided us home. In these memories, I see myself smile and laugh. These are wonderful memories that somehow I had distorted in my mind as not being good enough.

Grandma spent hours that day trying to teach me to swim. The picture in front of me is of a middle-aged woman wearing a housedress and holding me, protecting me, and coaxing me to kick in the water. With all the splashing and flaying of arms and legs, you would have thought one of us was drowning. Through my struggles not to let go of her, I drank a gallon of water that day. She never gave up on me. Another picture flashes before me and I see myself swimming, laughing, and loving the freedom of the water. A bubble of laughter rises up inside me, but I push it down. I will not release her; I will not forgive her from the hurt she has caused me.

But the happy memories continue to flow in an unending loop as more times with Grandma are revealed. Grandma was always finding ways for me to have fun, to test my strength and my faith. Whether putting a tire swing in our yard, climbing up a tree, or swinging into the creek from a rope; I was always afraid to try, to let go. Then I see her, always waiting, with open arms to catch me, encouraging me to try, to take a chance, to soar.

What these memories reveal to me is how she has been nurturing and coaxing me to be my best since I was a child. Is that what she was doing all along, preparing me for the truth? To give me the strength and faith I needed to survive the lies? Tears continue to flow as more of my story is revealed.

I was loved.

Then I see different times. Times when I knew deep down inside of me that Grandma wasn't telling the whole truth. When she was hesitant to provide details by reminding me how painful they were to tell. I knew one day I would finally hear the whole truth, just not this truth. Did I like my story, the story of a poor little orphan girl being raised by her loving grandmother? Is that why I never pushed her to tell me the whole truth?

The lies had worked for me then, but the truth slaps me now. It reminds me that I'm smarter than that. I should've known something wasn't right. There is nothing about me that looks like Grandma, not one little thing. Why were there never any pictures of my parents? Whenever I asked, the pat answer was when we moved from New York we only took what we could fit into the car.

Now I realize that part was true. Grandma always said the memories caused too much pain, and that part is also true. Why now, why did she tell me now?

"Lord, for once can you answer my prayer? Just tell me what I need to do to take away the pain."

Forgive, Jo. Forgive.

"I can't. I won't forgive her; I won't forgive any of them. How can You ask me to do this? You know what they did to me."

Forgive them their trespasses as I've forgiven you. Release them all into My hands.

Somewhere deep inside of me, I know this is the Lord's truth spoken through His prayer. That if I did not release them, forgive them, I would be in bondage forever, never being able to escape the pain of this truth. But how can I? I don't know how I can forgive them after all that they have done to me.

"Teach me, Lord," I plead. "I don't know how."

Chapter 26
Home Alone

"Forgive, and you will be forgiven."
Luke 6:37c (NAB)

Clouds cover the moon making the walk home darker, colder, and wet. Either the weight of my wet pants is slowing me down or all my energy is being drained from my body. The war inside continues to rage, attacking me physically, emotionally, and spiritually. How do I make it stop? Walking out of the woods and onto the street the world is alive with Christmas. Houses wrapped in twinkle lights like lighthouses along the river illuminate a safe path home.

Reaching my house, I hesitate before I open the door. What will I find? I'm surprised by the warmth in the house, reassured by the sight of my fresh garland and the soothing smell of cinnamon pinecones permeating the air. It's a beautiful reminder that Christmas is coming. I slip off my wet shoes and pants, leaving their coldness at the front door. Thankfully the oil boiler, the beast, continues to work. Do I eat, do I sleep, what should I do now? The thought of a warm bath lures me up the stairs. Walking past the hall phone stand, I see Earl's number flashing on the answering machine. Should I call him and tell him I'm okay, or slip into a warm bath?

The bath can wait a few more minutes, I don't know if Earl can. He wanted to come over to comfort and cook for me. "That sounds wonderful. But tonight I need to be home alone, take a warm bath, and go to bed." He reassures me of his love. I hope so, because he's all I have right now.

Lying in the warmth of the bath, more stories are released from the deep recesses of my mind. More stories filled with lies and manipulations, but this time the lies are all told by me. Lies told to Earl and Esther, twisting and shaping the truth to meet my needs. How deeply have I hurt them with my words? Words were always my power source, but how often did I use the truth as a weapon?

Don't be so hard on yourself. She purposefully lied and manipulated the truth for over thirty years. My lies were little lies, childish lies, or lies I used to protect myself. But is that the truth. There was a time in my life when a lie was a lie. Now I have a gradient scale to measure the severity of the lie. Whose measuring stick am I using, mine or God's?

"Josie Beth, who are you trying to hurt or who are you trying to heal?" Grandma's voice plays in my head. 'Remember that's the only two things that generally come out of our mouths, healing words or hurting words. The choice is yours."

Realization of my lies, the misuse of my word power adds an additional layer of new grief; the grief of my own sins. Is this what sin feels like: ugly, heavy and unbearable? If so, how do I get rid of my sins?

Maybe seeking forgiveness is the only way out of this? But how do I learn to forgive, to forget, and to let go of this betrayal?

Start remembering the love.

Remember? Thinking back to Earl's question, how would life be without ever seeing Grandma again? Right now I don't want to see her. I can't. I'm not ready. I don't know what I would say to her. Will facing her again make the pain go away or be irreparable? Is there more to the story that I don't know about? So many questions and yet I have no answers. The thoughts are now coming so fast, pummeling both accusations and attacks at my already fragile mind. Sliding deeper into the now cold tub, I seek relief, but I know I will not find it here. Sleep is my only solution, but will it come?

❈ ❈ ❈

Morning comes too quickly. More rest is needed, but I'm too restless to stay in bed and too exhausted to leave. Reality of the last two days sweeps back into my mind. How can I go on? Why can't life go back to normal? That's what

I'll do–just start today like it was any other day.
Reluctantly I place one leg out of bed. I coax myself, as I do
each winter morning, to leave the warmth and comfort of my
bed. The only difference is I utter out a prayer, "What do I
do first, Lord? What do I do?"

Opening the blinds to face whatever lies before me,
I'm surprised how brightly the sun is shining. Maybe this is
sign.

I put on a pot of coffee. The clock on the oven flashes
8:00. When was the last time I slept this late? Pouring
myself a cup of coffee, I grab a yogurt from the fridge and
walk into my office. So far normal is working. Opening up
the curtains allows the sun to brighten this room as well.

Do I write the newest chapter of my story down?
Looking at years of journals lining my bookcases, I long to
sit in my chair and write to make sense of what I've learned.
Would recording these events be the best thing for me now,
or should I just get down to work? Writing is the only way I
know how to productively control my thoughts. There are
just too many to escort out the door today. Work first,
journal second. With that decision made, I set my coffee cup
on the desk and turn to power up my laptop. It's not there.

Fear enters into me with such a force I'm almost
knocked over by it. Was my laptop stolen? Did I leave it
here or bring it with me to Grandma's? Everything I've
worked on for weeks is on that laptop. My research, my
outlines, my blogs, and the first draft of my third abortion
article are all safely stored on my computer. Turning around
in my office, I start opening desk drawers, pulling cushions
off the couch, searching, hoping by some stroke of luck that
it's here. Maybe, I just forgot to put it on the desk.

Nothing!

Running through the foyer and outside the front door
I stop on the top step. The truth is right there in front of me;
my precious laptop is at Esther's. The sound of my house
phone takes me back to my office to answer the call.

"Jo, I've been trying to reach you for the last two

days. Are you okay? You're usually tied to your cell phone like it's your life line."

Dread washes over me? Did I even give Pete my home number? What does he want, and why did I answer this phone?

Clearing my throat, I try to decide what to say. Truth or lie, do I tell him the truth or a lie?

"Pete, I'm sorry. I've been a little under the weather, too tired to even answer my phone. What's up?" That's pretty much the truth!

"Just checking in, that's all. How's our article's coming along? Sorry to hear you're sick. My kids keep bringing every bug home from school with them. Did you get your flu shot? We've got important work to do, and my butt and yours is on the line. Neither one of us can afford to be sick."

"I've got a solid first draft completed. I'm just waiting to verify the data and research that you had questioned. Once that is done I will send it over to you."

"Great, great, I knew you wouldn't disappoint me. Can you send it over now and let me see where you're going with this?"

What do I tell him? Oh sorry, I went to North Carolina and left my laptop there? I can hear him now. 'You're supposed to log into the paper's server and save it there. How many times do I have to tell you?'

Again I must decide truth or lie, truth or lie. "Pete, I don't have my computer here right now. I need to pick it up and will send it to you by tomorrow."

"Tomorrow, where did you leave it? Didn't you save it to the cloud?"

Here it comes. We've had this discussion weekly over the last six months. "No, I didn't . . ."

"Jo, I feel like I'm talking to one of my kids. How many times do I have to tell you, if you're writing for the paper, all your writing has to be saved on the server? See, this is exactly what I was talking about. Get the first draft to me by tonight, or I'm going to find someone I can depend on to write this last article."

Pete grumbled something about not being able to trust anybody and hung up. Right, I'm sure he's been lied to before, but for every single day over your entire life? I don't think so. I've got you beat there buddy.

"Haven't I had enough?" I shout at the top of my lungs. "I can't do this, I can't go back and face her now, and maybe not ever. This can't be happening to me."

Whenever I think things cannot get any worse, they always do. What next? Will the tax collector start banging on my door wanting to do an audit? Will the doctor call with the bad news from my recent Pap smear, or will Pete call back and just say, "You're fired!" I can't take anymore! Are you listening? I thought I was making progress in the God area.

Panic, stress, fear, disgust, and confusion all fight for first position. Pick one emotion, Jo, and stay with it, I tell myself. You can't do all of them. Panic wins! No job means no house, no car, no food, no life. What do I do now?

Pacing around the house, I try to find an easy solution, but nothing comes to mind. With my concern about my fake grandmother on her fake deathbed, I left without sending the article to myself. My cyber filing cabinet works most days. I just have to put the file in there.

What do I do? The answer is not a simple one, but it's the only one I have left: I call Earl.

Earl - Chapter 27
Old Earl, New Earl

"The crucible for silver, and the furnace for gold, but the tester of hearts is the LORD."
Proverbs 17:3 (NAB)

Seeing Jo squirm so uncomfortably in her seat is painful to watch. Teasingly I ask her if she has to go to the bathroom. She shakes her head no. The mental and spiritual battle is raging deep inside of her; that 's evident. Jo's lips are silent, but her body language is speaking loudly. I watch her desperately try to process and make sense of everything she has learned, about her birth, her life, and how to move forward. She's replaying conversations in her mind trying to put all the pieces together looking for a solution that is not hers to find, it's His.

My only comfort - knowing who ultimately will win this battle. My heart aches to help her, to quiet and calm her fears, and to reassure her of my love even though I know this heartbreak is not mine to fix. With great difficulty, I remain quiet and respect her choice to be silent. I wonder if I were in the same circumstances how would I face Esther?

Please, Lord, help Jo to see Your hand in all of this, I silently pray. *Let her know there is a purpose and plan for her life and her grief. I know you want her to fully forgive Esther. Lord, please show her Your way.*

The swish sloshing of the windshield wipers and the whirl of the car heater's fan are the only sounds within the car. After hours of driving in silence, the quiet becomes harder and harder to bear. I want to talk things out, to help her, but Jo wants to work them out in her head, alone. The lack of conversation is making this ride longer and more challenging with each passing mile. What is on her mind?

Finally, after hours, Jo lets out a deep sigh. Is it a sigh of regret, pain, or fear? Or is it because we crossed over the border into North Carolina and her moment of reckoning is near? Jo finally speaks.

"Earl, can you tell me about the old Earl, the Earl that you don't like to talk about?" she asks. "I want to know about him and the problems you had with your father."

That was not what I was expecting to hear from her. Why now, why in the midst of all of her turmoil does she want to know about this painful part of my life? Maybe it will provide a much needed distraction for her.

"It's a long story, ancient history. I'm not that man anymore."

My unwillingness to share causes Jo to come out of her silence with a roar. "So you're not going to tell me? After all I shared with you last night? I think it's only fair that you tell me your whole story."

"If you want me to tell you, I will. It's not that exciting, and it pales in comparison to your story," I say, hoping to distract her and to make light of her situation.

She reaches over to thump me on the arm, but she will not let go of her curiosity. "What dark secret are you hiding from me? I want to know about your life before I met you, the life you lived as a Texas lawyer. If it wasn't weren't for your sister Deb filling me in, I wouldn't know much beyond your mother dying over five years ago. Both of you rarely mention your father. What's that all about?"

"That's the problem when two ladies get together, they start sharing secrets. You're right. I haven't shared much about my father because whenever I speak or think about him my mood takes a nosedive. I become angry, frustrated, or sad, and then I feel guilty for feeling that way. Jo, he's not a very nice man, and I didn't leave Texas on good terms with him. He felt abandoned; I felt trapped. If it wasn't for Deb's husband being deployed for a year in Afghanistan and her needing help with the boys, I'm not sure where I'd be right now. I'm surprised you haven't read about Harry in the papers. He loves the attention."

"Harry Broden? Your father is *that* Harry Broden? No, he can't be your father. He never misses a photo op or a

chance to sue someone," she says. "I'm sorry, Earl. I
didn't mean it to come out that way."

"Now you know why I don't talk about him. Look at
your response. Do you still want to hear my story?"

"Yes, you're always telling me how you were in the
same position that I am battling with career decisions, and
not always making the best choices. If you want to spare me
the pain of your mistakes, how can I learn if I don't know
what they were?"

"That's true, I'm just not proud of that part of my life.
I wasn't at my best. This story will feel more like a
confession. Even though I'd rather not relive it, if you want
to know . . ."

"Earl, if we're going to have a future together I'd like
to know everything about you. Are you afraid I'll run
away? You've got me captured in your truck, and like you
said, your story will probably pale in comparison to mine.
What's in your past that can teach me how to move forward
with my life?"

She's right. I haven't shared much of my past
because I'm not proud of what I did and who I became while
striving to gain acceptance from my father. But Jo does
have the right to know, and hopefully she will understand
what made me change.

"Where do I start? The first memory I have of myself
is when I was three and our family dog bit me on the nose." I
look over at Jo, and she is glaring at me. "Too far back or
not far enough?"

"Not that far back. Tell me about your adult lawyer
secret life and how you became a carpenter. We can get to
the cute kid stuff later, maybe on the ride back home. What
made you change your career, move, and become the new
Earl? That's the part of your life I need to know about."

"The hard part in telling you my story is to make sure
I'm not bashing or gossiping about my father. I want to
share, and this is difficult, because I also don't want you to
pass judgment on him. But I can't leave him out, because it

just isn't as interesting a story without big Harry Brogan as the main character."

"Is he that bad or that interesting?"

"A little bit of both, but if it weren't for him, I wouldn't be where I am today. It was at the lowest part of my life, when I realized who I had become, that I finally opened my heart and soul to God's truth about life. I can't tell you the story Jo without sharing what God has done in me. That's why it's been hard to share. Does that make sense?"

"Are you telling me that the worst part of your life opened up to a better life? I'm assuming because of me your life's better! Now I definitely need to hear it."

"That's part of it, but not all of it." Even if it only lasts a few seconds, hearing Jo joke with me is reassurance that healing and forgiveness are possible. Now that she's started talking, she won't be satisfied until my story is complete.

"I'm praying that good will come out of my mess also. I know you're a man who loves the Lord, because of how you act. I'm frustrated because Grandma has started acting more like a television preacher, all doom and gloom. She wasn't always like this."

"Jo, your Grandma has a different kind of relationship with the Lord. We all need to have a relationship with Him, and it should look different, because we are different."

"I know. I'm starting to see that now. Earl, something has opened up inside of me, and I'm beginning to understand why I need to forgive, it just seems impossible. It hurts so much."

"And that is why I invited Christ into my life. I learned the hard way. I couldn't do it alone. Without the grace and forgiveness of God, giving me a new start each day, I don't know how I would keep moving forward. And even though I knew better, I kept right on doing it my way and not His. Choosing my way of life has got me into trouble every time."

"Are you talking about me and the choice to live together?"

"That's one part of it. Whenever I went against what I knew was right in God's eyes I made fleshly decisions that hurt those I loved, and me. It was my choice. I don't ever remember you forcing yourself on me. No wait, there was that one time."

"Stop teasing me. I'm starting to understand a little bit better about that slippery slope Grandma, I mean, Esther . . ." she pauses, looking out the window. "I don't even know what to call her. Why does this hurt so much?"

I glance over, and even in the darkness I know there are fresh tears brimming in her eyes. I want desperately to fold her into my arms, to take this pain away from her. *Lord, what do I say to heal and help her?* I plead.

"Jo, you might never get the answer to the reason for your pain, or the answer could be right there in front of you waiting to be discovered. Trust that God has a beautiful ending to this story. As I said before, my challenges pale in comparison to yours, so I'm not even trying to guess your pain. I just know God can and will heal your hurts, just let Him in."

"I believe that's true, but it's still hard . . . Please let's talk about you. It helps distract me, and I want to know about your horrible beginning because I already know your good ending."

That's the warm, sweet Jo I love. I'm so glad she's back. "Okay, where was I? Let's start after law school. I passed the bar exam the first time I took the test, but that still wasn't good enough for my dad. My father deemed me unworthy to work for him until I got some real life experience. So I went to work in the DA's office."

"I can't believe your father wouldn't hire you. Did you have bad grades? Why would he do that?"

"He said I was too green for the work he did, and he wanted me to earn my position, not just be given it on a silver platter. He started the firm from nothing and grew it into the national giant that it is today. He felt it would be good for me to start at the bottom somewhere and work my way up. Finally after five grueling years at the District Attorney's office, and some solid wins, my father deemed me ready, but maybe not worthy, of joining the firm as a partner. To demonstrate what he thought of me, I had to start at the bottom again and do a year of clerking with him."

"That's harsh, but didn't you feel better earning the position rather than it being given to you?"

"In most situations, yes, but the truth is that I will never be able to please my father. Since the time I was a kid I didn't live up to his standards. Whatever I was doing, playing sports or in academics, I just did not measure up to his expectations. It was hard to live under his intense scrutiny."

"What did you do to survive it?"

"I thank God for my mother who balanced it all out. She was always my advocate. She begged me not to go to work for him. She knew the strain it would put on not just me, but the entire family. But I just believed if I worked hard enough I would finally get the acceptance I so desperately craved. Sounds pathetic, doesn't it?"

"Pathetic, no. Sad, yes. I'm sorry your dad didn't appreciate how wonderful you are. Why did you go to work for him then?"

"I thought by working with my dad I could prove to him I was worthy. I also thought it would be a great learning experience and prepare me to open my own practice one day. In my mind it was a compromise to my mother's wishes, since I knew I was only going to work with him for a few years. Unfortunately, she was right; working together did hurt the family. Whenever we got together as a family, Dad always turned the discussions to work and openly criticized what I was doing. The worst part is that working for my dad wasn't that different from the DA's office. I became astute at defending a different kind of criminal."

"Criminals?"

I could hear the shock in her voice that I would stoop so low. "Why did you defend them if you thought they were criminals?"

"Fame, fortune, power, significance, approval, prestige. You name it, and I bought into it, all of the earthly motivators. Five years later I was still there under the control of my father. And as my mother feared, I was following in his workaholic, controlling, money-focused footsteps. My mother begged and pleaded even on her death bed for me to stop working for Dad and start my own practice."

"Why didn't you?"

"Always hearing my father's condemning voice made it very clear that I would never be good enough to have my own practice. I believed him, I hated his motives, yet I wanted him desperately to respect and accept me. Fear of failure is probably the main reason. I didn't want to hear that tape of 'I told you so' being played every day of my life. Working with Dad was also safe. I didn't look for clients; they came to me. What I wanted most, I never got. There was never job satisfaction. What I did get was money that allowed me to buy my ranch. In some ways my ranch made the rest of it bearable."

I glance over to see Jo's reaction. I don't want her to think less of me. "Sounds like I have competition for your affection," she says sweetly.

"Who are you talking about?"

"Not who, what. Your ranch. I can hear the smile in your voice. Do you still own it?"

"Yes. It's leased out for now."

"So why do you love it, and why did you leave it?"

"Being a lawyer left me empty. The ranch is the only place that gave me deep satisfaction, freedom, and a sense of purpose. Out on the ranch I could see the fruit of my labor.

In my office, I was jumping from one mess to another. My father was always down my back trying his hardest to make me into his image and likeness. I just didn't have his killer instinct."

"Is that why you moved away, to get some distance from your father?"

"That was part of it. With equal parts Deb, her boys, and trying to do it God's way, not Harry's or mine."

"Okay. How did you leave the firm and forgive you father? I want every last detail. To think that I've known you for over a year yet I don't know much about your Texas life. I only get the highlights, never the lowlights, from Deb and you."

"The question of when and how to leave the firm was not an easy one for me to resolve. When my mother and uncle died, there was just this emptiness. Both my mom and uncle grounded my father. When they both died, he became a loose cannon. He said he lost it all so nothing mattered to him but winning. The only relationship I had with my father was as an employee. I couldn't do it anymore. Deb was always moving around with Jason in the military, so I felt alone. With my mom gone, there was nothing holding me to Texas."

"Why did you mom want you to leave your father's firm?"

"She knew the kind of law he practiced. I would hear her beg and plead with my father not to take certain clients. Dad always said if their money was good, he was taking it. His choices troubled her. Mom was always worried about our souls, wondering if we were making godly choices or seeking earthly gold."

"You loved your mom, didn't you?"

"Yes, and she would have loved you. Mom was an awesome, loving, caring lady. Why she stayed married to Harry is beyond me. I regret that she can't see me now, happy and successful per her definition. Mom always saw people's hearts. That was how she measured success, not monetarily, but heart and soul success. She would tell me, 'Earn heavenly points by doing God's will, so your life will always be filled with peace and joy. And that is something money can never buy!' Wish I would have paid more attention to how she wanted me to live my life."

"So how did you get the courage to leave?"

"Disgust, despair, depression, and grief are all very powerful catalysts. The real push was after I won a major, high profile court case. Finally, I got what I had always wanted, my father's acceptance, and success. Interesting that when I got my father's respect, I lost all respect for myself. The next morning I looked in the mirror and did not recognize, or like, the person looking back at me."

"Earl, I'm starting to feel that way about the abortion articles I've been writing and some of my columns, like living together before marriage. People like them, I'm finally getting the recognition I have been craving my whole life, and I have never felt more unhappy or unsettled. I've been thinking that a whole lot of sleepless nights started when I joined the Philadelphia paper. Grandma and you both knew it. I just didn't want to believe it. Is that how you felt?"

"Yes, and that is why I ran away to the ranch for my survival. Funny, it was there I had my first real conversation with God."

"Does He talk back to you? I think I heard Him yesterday when I was at the river, and come to think of it most of the way home telling me I was loved. What did He say to you?"

"Lots of things. The first time it happened I thought I was having sunstroke, or was dehydrated from splitting three cords of wood in a matter of hours. Whatever it was I had this desperate need to talk to God, man to Man. I sat down on the nearest log. For the first time in my life, I had nothing to lose, so I just asked, 'Lord, what am I doing with my life? I've been doing everything that is expected of me by my father. I work hard, try to help our clients, I even stop into church from time to time. Why am I so unhappy?

Why?"

"Then what happened?"

"I hear these words resonate through my entire body, 'You're not doing My will; you're doing their will. I have called you too much greater things. Trust in me.'"

"He said that, trust Him? How did you know it was Him?"

"My mom told me that your body knows. There was peace and then a coursing through my body. The words that were spoken I would never have said. Jo, it was both powerful and peaceful at the same time."

"Well, what did you say back to Him?"

"'Who are you and why should I trust you?' is what I shouted back."

"Not the comeback I was expecting. So you didn't know it was God at first, but you're sure now. Why?"

"Did you ever see that movie about the guy who builds the baseball field in his corn field?"

"Of course I did. Do you have a baseball diamond at your ranch? Is that what you're afraid to tell me?"

It's good to hear Jo joke with me. I'm hopeful that telling my story is helping her forget hers, even if for a little while. I can see her shoulders finally relax. Even better is that for the first time in months we're together having a meaningful conversation. I want this moment to last.

I shake my head and take a deep breath. Great now she thinks I'm crazy. If I were sitting in her seat, I would probably respond the same way. "No, I didn't build a baseball diamond, not yet. At first I thought that the heat was playing tricks on me. Did I really hear a voice? I'd really thought I was starting to lose it after only three days at the ranch. Maybe my escape plan wasn't fully thought out. Life on the ranch could be just as dangerous as practicing law."

"You really thought you were going crazy. I can't imagine my level-headed Earl for one minute losing his mind. You're the most logical, even-tempered person I've ever met."

I like it when Jo calls me her Earl; there is hope for us after all. "That was the old Earl. Now you know why I've been hiding him from you. What I did know was that there was a small grain of truth resonating in those words. He spoke the truth, and I knew it. I went into law thinking I could help people. And I did help people. I helped the poor get out of the messes they created. I helped the rich get richer. None of it was really what I had in mind when I went into law school. I don't even know why I went into law school. No, that's not true. It was another attempt to please my father and not knowing what else to do. . . . Funny thing the next time I heard this voice speak, I didn't even ask a question. It just spoke."

"What did He say?"

"He asked, 'When are you most at peace?'"

I glance over to see Jo's face is full of curiosity. I'm thankful that she is responding positively to this story.

"So what did you tell Him?" she asks.

"'Working with my hands and with wood,' was my immediate response. The voice kept asking questions, and I kept answering them. The most astonishing words He spoke were, 'Then trust Me and do it.'"

"God, or this voice, was giving you career coaching; that's a riot. What does God care about what you do for a living?"

"I had that same exact question. That's why I doubted what I was hearing at first. But then I thought, why shouldn't He? My Bible school lessons came back to me, words from the Psalms, from the prophets, and from Christ reminding me of God's plan and purpose for my life. Nothing is random."

Jo shivers in her seat, and I reach over to turn up the heat.

"I'm not cold. I just had this wave, like electricity, run from the top of my head to the bottom of my toes. I don't know if I've ever felt anything like that. Have you?"

"Yes, that's what I was talking about when I was at the ranch talking to God. I've had it several times. It happens whenever I hear or speak God's truth I get that electrically charged feeling."

"So I just heard the truth, is that what you're saying? That maybe this whole horrid story of my birth has a purpose?"

I see her tears start flowing again. I'm ready to pull off the highway so I can hold her. "Why don't we take a break? There's a rest stop about ten miles from here. We can stretch our legs and get something hot to eat and drink."

Jo nods her head. The silence encircles her again as she turns to look out the window. It's as if she believes the snowflakes or the setting sun will hold the answers she is so longing to know.

The short walk, hot chocolate, and candy bar are exactly what I need to continue the drive. Jo slumps back into her seat and shrouds herself again in silence. Some days I would love to know what goes on in that pretty head of hers, other days I'm thankful not to know. For so long Jo has being trying to do it on her own, rarely, if ever, asking for help. She needs it now, and I know that she is turning toward the Lord, which brings me great comfort.

"How did you forgive your father?"

I start to talk, and then stop. Did I forgive him or did I just leave him? How do I know for sure? "That's a tough question to answer. Each day I ask God to heal me, teach me, and release me. By turning to God and reading the Bible, I was learning the truth about forgiveness."

"The truth about forgiveness, I'm not sure what you mean about that."

"Forgiveness is an ongoing process. You just don't forgive and poof the pain goes away. What I finally realized is that I wanted my father to beg for my forgiveness, for what he had done and how he had hurt me. Sadly, he had no idea how much he had hurt me. He was just doing what was done to him."

"So you made an excuse for him. Maybe that works for you, but I don't think I can do that," she says.

The tears start flowing again. How could someone produce that many tears? Through her sobs I know Jo is trying to make sense of all that has happened to her. She is hurt; she is angry; and she has no idea what to do with her feelings, or who to direct her anger toward.

"I had to start somewhere. I started by forgiving him in my heart.

"Your heart? How does that work?"

"Didn't have the courage to go back to Texas to forgive him face to face, so whenever the angry feeling towards him comes up, I say I forgive him."

"That's easy because you don't need to see him face to face. Was he really that bad?"

"I'm not the judge. We're all sinners and have all disappointed one another and God. I had my own sin measuring scale. My sins always seemed to be less grave than others, especially my father's, so I was forgivable and he wasn't. Frankly, The Lord's Prayer scared me straight. Pray that prayer and really listen to what you're saying. It says, 'Forgive us our trespasses as we forgive others.' Jesus did not say, forgive them when they've asked forgiveness, or forgive them only if their sin was a little one. He says forgive."

"I heard the same thing last night. I also remembered how I've put a gradient scale on what I've been doing. If I didn't kill anyone, I was good with God. So you just decided to forgive and forget. That's it? No twelve-step program?"

"There are more, but the first step is making the decision to forgive. I'm not sure if I have steps or a process. When I would go to the Lord in prayer, Jesus was showing me through His Word how His Father is a forgiving God. Christ said on the cross, 'Forgive them, Father, for they know not what they do.' That would be pretty hard after what Christ went through for us. My challenges with my Dad seem petty."

"What do you mean?"

"Jo, I can be kneeling down and putting some varnish on some woodwork and then all of a sudden, I feel tension in my shoulders and anger well up in the pit of my stomach. Out of nowhere I'm reliving some incident with my father. Do I continue playing out this scene, dismiss it, or forgive it?"

"Does it happen often?"

"Unfortunately, yes. That's why I say it's a daily, minute-by-minute decision to forgive. No one said it was easy."

"Have you forgiven me?" Jo asks quietly.

"Jo, there is nothing that I need to forgive you for." This answer seems to settle Jo down, but not me. Because now I start to wonder, have I totally forgiven my father, or just put a safe distance between us?

"Earl, when was the last time you saw your father?"

"It was the day I left. Why?"

"Just wondering, you do talk to him though."

"Yes, I call him once a week. It's a strained conversation, but I do call. He doesn't understand why I didn't come back to Texas and the firm after Jason, Deb's husband, returned from Afghanistan."

"So what did you tell him?"

"I tell him I love where I live, that this is where the woman I love lives, and I love what I'm doing. He just wants to know how much money I'm making. Our values are different and finding safe ground has been impossible. So the conversations are difficult."

"Do you think you'll ever go and see him?"

"Someday I will go. Right now I don't feel ready or, maybe, strong enough to resist his demands."

"At least you have that option. I don't. I'm not ready

to see Grandma either, but I need my computer. My career and livelihood is inside of that thing."

"Do you want me to go inside and get it for you?"

She shakes her head, and we continue in silence. It's now my silence that is so palpable. Jo has given me a lot to think about.

Jo - Chapter 28
Home, Sweet, Home?

"Wisdom builds up her house. But Folly tears hers down with her own hands."
Proverbs 14:1 (NAB)

The closer we get to Grandma's house, the faster my heart beats. Anxiety wells up and is pushed down as anger vies for first position in my mind. A reminder of my abandonment then turns me inside out. What do I say to her, how do I face her? *Lord, if you want me to forgive her, show me a sign. Please let me know that You are with me because this feels impossible.*

It's eerily dark as we pull into the driveway. Where are the lights? Blackness shrouds the house as if death has entered and taken hold. All fear and anger leave me as my concern for Grandma enters in to replace those emotions. Is this Your sign? *Please, no Lord, not this. I'm not ready*, I silently beg. *There is so much more I need to know.*

Before Earl's truck comes to a complete stop; I jump out, fly up the steps, and bolt into the house. My heart stops. I can't breathe, and I'm paralyzed with fear. What do I do, where could she be? Earl comes into the room, and almost as if on cue, the clouds move and light from the moon basks throughout the room with a comforting glow. Calmness cloaks the living room, but why? And then I see her sleeping in her prayer chair. Did she not hear me, why is she so still?

Earl reaches for my hand and together we walk closer. Grandma turns to see me and looks up at Earl. Her face first reads disbelief, then hope and joy. She doesn't speak a word. The gratefulness that rises up inside of me is proof of the love I have for this woman. Whoever she is, it no longer matters. I need her in my life. All the anger and anxiety is pulled from my body, and it feels heavenly. Forgiveness seemed impossible only two short hours ago, because I was not aware of God's healing power through this act of obedience.

Collapsing at her feet, I plead silently for us to withstand the truth after living so long a lie. Grandma runs her fingers through my hair, a calming caress. Love comes through her fingertips, pries open the dam of emotion, and again tears flow, but this time they're tears of hope. Grandma was right, Earl was right. How could I have understood this painful truth as a child, if I'm having such difficulty now?

Sensing our need for privacy, Earl returns to the truck to grab our bags. I read his face looking for signs of what he is thinking. Did the topic of forgiveness open up his wounds as well? He smiles, blows me a kiss, and heads up the stairs for a hot shower and hopefully a restful night's sleep.

Just like in holidays past, Grandma and I stay up after midnight dancing. But this time it is not the jingle bug; it is a different dance, the dance of truth. Whether it was my openness to forgive, or my desire not to let this realization place a wedge between us, something was happening to us. Strong solid walls of protection that we had both built came tumbling down. At first I was afraid this conversation would be too much for her. Yet with each revelation, with each new truth, the stress in her face faded. It was if she were experiencing an emotional face-lift. The burden of the deception she had carried for so long, and so alone, had been given to the Lord. I can't remember feeling this much joy and contentment. Exhausted and knowing we have tomorrow to talk, I recommend that we both head upstairs to bed.

Sleep should come easily tonight with the bed feeling so warm and welcoming. Yet my mind reels, and once again sleep eludes me. Do I get out of bed? Where would I go? There's no TV in this room, no digital clock to focus on, so reluctantly I turn on the light to find something to read. Right there on the bedside table is my old Bible, worn and used with my favorite verses highlighted. This Bible was my constant companion for so many years, even in college.

Psalm 73 opens up before me and like Grandma taught me, I slowly start to pray the words of the Psalmist.

> *"How good God is to the upright,*
> *to those who are pure of heart!."*

That would be Grandma. "Lord, Grandma has been so faithful to You. I know she the truth she carried weighed so heavy in her heart. Release her now, free her from bondage so she can finally feel Your total forgiveness."

> *"But, as for me, my feet had almost stumbled;*
> *my steps had nearly slipped."*

How many times did Grandma warn me of the slippery slope of sin? Ten years of doing everything that I thought was right, hoping, wishing, and pleading for success, a breakthrough had only set me on unstable ground. I still searched for some sign or hint to show me that You cared, that my work mattered. As I continue to read the psalm I'm astonished how true these words are today, as if written just for me and for this exact moment. But how could that be? These words are at least three thousand years old.

> *"Because I was envious of the arrogant*
> *when I saw the prosperity of the wicked."*

I was craving attention and wanting desperately for someone to notice that I had something important to say. When I realized the types of articles that were getting recognition, what did this purveyor of truth do? She lied. I lied about my values, my morals, and my faith. No one ever asked me these questions directly, but I made sure Pete, my editor, realized I was willing to do whatever I needed to succeed.

Was that when the sleepless nights began, when I no

longer honored God?

> *"For they suffer no pain;*
> *their bodies are healthy and sleek.*
> *They are free of the burdens of life;*
> *they are not afflicted like others.*
> *Thus pride adorns them as a necklace;*
> *violence clothes them as a robe."*

What greater violence is there then to the unborn? *Lord, can you ever forgive what I've done in writing these articles?* I pray.

> *"Out of such blindness comes sin;*
> *evil thoughts flood their hearts.*
> *They scoff and spout their malice;*
> *from on high they utter threats."*

And if women don't have someone standing in support, full of grace, praying and encouraging them, like Jesus, to make the right choice, how can they be blamed? If you are told a lie over and over and over again, can the truth no longer be heard? Is that what has happened?

> *"They set their mouths against the heavens,*
> *their tongues roam the earth.*
>
> *So my people turn to them*
> *and drink deeply of their words."*

Why did I turn from You and seek earthly recognition? Because I wanted to, because I wanted it my way and not Your way or to wait for Your perfect timing, I continue.

I read each verse slowly to gain meaning and relevancy to my life right now allowing God's words minister to my soul.

> *"Yet I am always with you;*
> *You take hold of my right hand."*

"Lord, I was out of balance, running toward an elusive dream. Please hold on tight to me so I will not be seduced by lies again. Please forgive me," were the last words I pray tonight. Finally I fall into a peaceful sleep with His words on my lips.

❖ ❖ ❖

As the sun breaks through the window, I remain in bed determined to start this morning right by reconnecting with the Lord. I'm finally breathing again with no pangs of anger or anxiety. Now that I let go of my will, breathing has become natural again. Sitting in my childhood bed, I breathe in the peace of God and breathe out all my anxiety and worry. I again breathe in the mercy of God while I breathe out all judgment and condemnation.

Peace envelops me like my down comforter on this cold winter morning. I'm home again, and right with the Lord. It feels heavenly. My ever gracious and loving Father has welcomed me back, in spite of my sinfulness. His overwhelming presence is felt throughout my entire body and penetrates deep into my soul, as I realize no sin is too big for God to forgive. Nothing can separate us from His love, except saying no to Him. Maybe that is the real message I was sent here to share: God's abundant love and forgiveness.

Chapter 29
Christmas Cures Everything

"This is the day the Lord hath made; we will rejoice and be glad."
Psalm 118:24 (KJV)

Earl

How did Esther pull this celebration off? The house is decorated like Christmas elves showed up to help her. Esther does have a whole lot of friends who were immediately willing to jump in and help. Considering the amount of food in the kitchen, she must have thought Jason was bringing in his whole army battalion. What a difference a couple of weeks can make. Two weeks ago, Jo and I were half expecting to plan her funeral. The Lord obviously had different expectations, surpassing anything that I've been hoping and praying for. Jo accepting my marriage proposal would have been enough, but God had more in store for all of us. Not only did He cure our broken hearts, He brought two hurting families together. Who would have thought the whole Broden and Reynolds families would be right here in North Carolina celebrating the gift of our Savior together. Mom is probably singing "Glory Alleluia" louder than anyone in heaven today.

Holding Jo close, I enjoy the silence between us that allows me to drink in her beauty. I've never seen Jo look more amazing. The sparkle in her eyes, the expanse of her smile, it's as if she drank liquid sunshine. She's glowing, radiant, and indescribable. The Christmas tree could take a lesson or two from Jo in how to shine the love of Christ. This is an amazing day, and an even more amazing, is the woman that God has chosen for me.

Crazy how taking a stance and choosing the Lord's way, not mine or Jo's, was not the impossible task I had thought. My fear had been that I would lose Jo forever. Only through God's grace, His constant presence, and

undeniable truth was I able to hold strong and wait for
His perfect timing. Today is proof that doing it God's way,
not mine works! Thank You, Lord, for bringing us all back
together.

During the long drive to pick up Jo's laptop, she
asked a lot of questions, mostly about my father. It was
tough to realize, especially after the way I'd been preaching
to Jo about God's plan for her, that I wasn't paying much
attention to my own faith walk. If truth be told, and we're
doing a lot of that lately in this house, I hadn't truly forgiven
my father. Was fear holding me back: fear of his final
rejection, fear that letting my anger and resentment go
would excuse him? My biggest fear was opening my heart,
which between Mom's death, Dad's volatile behavior, and
Jo's rejection, had become pretty fragile. Not understanding
what total forgiveness looked and felt like, I had deceived
myself into believing I had forgiven him. This deception held
me in bondage to him, not allowing our relationship to heal.
I remembered Mom's words about how God shines brightest
on the things we try to keep hidden from Him. Forgiveness
was flashing in large neon lights. Mom was right, how could
I not forgive Dad when I know that the Lord, and Mom,
had already done so?

By taking a major leap of faith, flying down to Texas,
and finally seeing him face to face, it was impossible not to
forgive him. Hearing about his fears, his hopes, and his own
broken heart helped me see him, maybe for the first time, for
the man he really is. No matter how strong his bravado or
how thick his façade; Harry Broden is as vulnerable and
insecure as the rest of us. And God loves him, so who am I
to deny Dad my love and forgiveness?

Miracles are everywhere these last couple of weeks.
One I was not prepared for, seeing my Dad down on the
floor wrestling and playing with his grandsons. I never
remember him doing that with me. As the saying goes,
grandchildren are God's second chances to do it right! There
is proof to that right here in Esther's living room, Harry has
won over each of Deb's kids. God gives us all innumerable

number of chances to get it right with Him. Tonight I have hope that Dad will finally know God's love through the love of his grandchildren. It looks like he's on his way.

Esther

Joy and blessings are everywhere this Christmas Day. Evident in the joy radiating from Josie Beth's face and Earl's loving gaze as they sit, young lovers, holding hands by the fireplace. They're seeing one another for the first time through God's eyes, and it's a beautiful sight to behold. Today they exist in a world of their own, relishing one other's presence even amidst the chaos of three rambunctious boys, Christmas carols blaring, and the excited chattering of our family.

Josie Beth was right about the holidays. For too long, I was making a celebration happen and not celebrating what happened on this miraculous day.

" Lord, I've been so busy trying to prove myself worthy of Your gift of love, that I refused to accept it. Why was I so reluctant to receive it freely? I believed for all those years that I was not worthy of such a perfect love. Lord, today my heart and hands are open to receive all that You want to give me."

Being forgiven and set free for the first time in my life has definitely put pep in this old lady's step. What did the pastor tell me about my busyness? He always gave us something simple to remember his messages. B.U.S.Y. means Being Under Satan's Yoke. That's it. By not opening my heart to forgiving Charles, my parents, Josie Beth, and even myself, I was living under Satan's yoke. Guilt, shame, and regret are powerful weapons Satan used to keep me in bondage. Forgiveness, His and mine, is the most powerful defense against Satan's attacks.

"Please Lord; let me never forget that truth again. Looking at the joy on my Josie Beth's face, I know your timing was perfect. I almost doubted You Lord, but You reminded me through Your Word that Your ways are not my ways."

Jo

What an amazing delight to be sitting in front of Grandma's fireplace, snuggling with Earl on this cold Christmas Day. Finally my Christmas dinner wish has come true: we are just family. The extravaganza that Grandma would orchestrate each holiday had become an exhausting ritual.

'Josie Beth, if it was only our family it would be just the two of us, like every other meal,' Grandma would always say. My entire life our church, neighborhood, and anyone who showed up for dinner was all the only family I had. This year I wanted to know what it was like to be with my real family, and they are all here.

Being able to see the Christmas tree and fireplace, minus the obstruction of folding tables and mismatched chairs, is a welcome change from previous Christmases. Without the maze of tables and chairs, there is actually room to move around and enjoy the comfort and warmth of this room. Today we have only one table set in the dining room, and it looks like the Christmas dinner in my dreams.

Earl draws me closer into his arms allowing me to be with him and my thoughts. The true test of his love was when I fell into the pit of despair, betrayal, and grief. The fall to the bottom was painful but there he was reaching down to pick me up. His love for me moved beyond physical and emotional, it reached a spiritual level. Through our shared struggle with forgiveness, we became soul mates. Our relationship moved to a level that I did not even know existed.

"Lord, if this is how it feels to do it Your way and not mine, why did I wait so long! Your blessings surround me, letting me know the best gift ever was Your Son. Jesus is Your miraculous cure for this aching world." Giggling I wonder what Pete, the publishers, and some of my readers would feel about this side to the story: the side of the Christmas story that no one wants to talk about, the true reason for the celebration. That day will come soon as I present my third article for Pete's review. One thing I now know for sure, I am not remaining quiet about my faith. This news is too good not to share.

My desire to forgive Grandma, and ultimately my parents, whoever they are, brought me to my knees in prayer. Forgiveness is a powerful weapon, that's why Jesus kept reminding me to forgive, as I've been forgiven. During my long silent ride down to collect my laptop I was ready to shut the door on life with Esther Reynolds forever. But the words that Bob Betts had spoken to me, about the woman being caught in adultery and Jesus advocating for her, played like an endless loop in my head. What I thought was Bob preaching to me was actually the catalyst I needed to move to forgiveness. Grandma was that woman, that woman caught in adultery, caught having an abortion, caught helping with abortions, caught lying, and caught stealing a sickly, failed abortion called me. The stones were all in my hands, filled with condemnation, hatred and loathing for everything she did and for what she really is, a sinner.

Jesus asked me if were I willing to cast the first stone, and I was ready. If I could, I would have chosen a much more powerful and painful weapon to launch at her. Then Christ, lovingly and mercifully, revealed to me my own sins. He showed me the ugliness of my words and actions and the pain I had caused Grandma, Earl, Him, and myself by choosing my way over His. When I could finally see who He truly was, my Savior, and who Grandma was, His beloved daughter, the stones became too heavy to hold and impossible for me to throw. With the release of each stone, my heart opened wider to His forgiveness and his endless grace.

Noticing the final rays of sunlight leaving this day, I

turn to gaze out the frosted windows. Icy snowflakes begin swirling lazily past the window. Could we actually have a white Christmas? What fun if all of us were snowed in, even if for a day, where we could dance and sing to the carols. Chills vibrate up my arms, and Earl squeezes my hand and draws me closer. I love this man so much. Why did I ever refuse his wonderful gift of love?

One of the best parts of today is that I've never seen Earl happier or more at peace. There was always something hanging over him that I couldn't put my finger on. It was some kind of invisible wall that he erected around himself that; divided and separated us. Was I unconsciously afraid to commit to him fully because of this wall? I'm not sure. Finally this barrier came tumbling down. Now I know what it was. It has a name: lack of forgiveness, or, more accurately, not forgiving his dad.

After Earl returned from his dad's, he was a new man; his burden had been lifted. Once he opened his heart to total forgiveness, I opened my heart to him and marriage. Saying yes to Earl's proposal, this time, was so easy. There was no doubt, no confusion, no misunderstanding, no argument, and no need for compromise. We were now on the same side, Christ's side.

"What are you two waiting for? I'm not going to be around forever," Grandma had said. Her not-so-subtle prompting is how our Christmas Eve wedding happened. She was right, what was I waiting for? Did I want a big wedding, was I unsure of my decision, or was I unsure if Earl was the right guy? When I was clear on what I now wanted from my life and how I wanted to live it going forward, I agreed not to wait. Grandma was amazing; knocking on death's door two weeks ago, and now with a renewed spirit, she planned the whole wedding, including a family reunion for the Brodens, in just two days.

We had a beautiful ceremony held right here in my childhood hometown. My marvelous new family was all in attendance celebrating. The look on Earl's face as I walked down the aisle was all the wedding present I needed. I could see the deep and endless look of love in his eyes. Babs was kind enough to let me borrow her wedding gown; it was a beautiful lace antique that her mother had worn. Grandma's friends, including her pastor, made sure everything else was taken care of, from the stunning bouquet to the lovely wedding ceremony.

Deb, Jason, and the boys are all here. And it took an act of God, our wedding, for me to finally meet big, bad Harry Broden. He is nothing more than a big teddy bear needing a little "TLC," not just tender loving care, Harry needs The Lord's Cure. Grandma reeled him in for mega doses of love.

Grandma summons us all to the dinner table. After so many crazy holiday celebrations, it was so perfect to have just family, my new and complete family, at this beautifully set table. The white linen of the table cloth, the red of the Poinsettias, and the light flickering from the candles are welcome reminders of how pure we are through forgiveness, and how brightly the light of the Lord shines within us through His precious shed blood.

Christmas china and crystal surprise me. I had no idea Grandma owned anything this delicate and costly. She said it was her mom's, one of the few bright memories she has of her. Grandma shared how her mother forced herself out of bed each Christmas Day to set the Christmas table no matter how deep her darkness. Now I know why celebrating Christmas in such a big way is so important to Grandma, it was the only time she could count on her mother to come alive.

Breaking tradition, Grandma insists that I will not help her in the kitchen since it is, after all, my wedding reception. Thankfully Deb, Jason, and even Harry are ready to heed Grandma's commands and put this scrumptious smelling dinner on the table. This Christmas is so full of miracles. How can I begin to thank God for all the blessings He has given each of us sitting around this table tonight?

Grandma asks if anyone wants to say grace.

"I do, I do," Deb's youngest child, Doug, excitedly yells as he wildly raises his hand and jumps up on his chair. Thankfully, the prayer baton has been passed to a very worthy person, one of my new nephews. The prayers of a child are always the best: simple, poignant, and full of faith all at the same time.

Clearing his throat, Doug speaks loudly and proudly. He asks us all to bow our heads. "Lord, thank You for this dinner. It looks really good, and I can't wait to eat it. Also for having my dad back home safe. Boy, I missed him. Thanks for the new aunt; I really like Jo, and for a new Grandma. We all miss Gigi Dorothy, but Grandma Esther is pretty cool. And I'm really happy to have Pop-Pop Harry here with us all the way from Texas and for the X-Box he gave us. Amen."

Everyone laughs as he jumps down from his chair and runs around the dining room table high-fiving his older brothers. I have to agree, I could not have said it any better. His innocent prayer reminds me of my childlike prayers asking for my mom and dad to be alive. Now I have a father-in-law; maybe Harry is a partial answer to my prayer.

There is so much to be thankful for this Christmas. The burden we were all bearing has been lifted, and this house is filled with the light of Jesus, and the lightness of forgiveness. Glancing out the window, I see snowflakes piling up on the windowsill. Amongst all the dinner noise and laughter I hear the faint sound of "Silent Night, Holy Night" playing in the distance on the kitchen radio. Yes, it is a Holy Night. Our Lord came from very humble beginnings; and through this precious gift, God has given us the cure to all the aches, pains, heartbreaks, and disappointments that this life holds. It is proof to what Grandma's dear Papa taught her: Christmas cures everything.

Jo – Chapter 30
HIS WAY, NO LONGER MINE

*"Trust in the LORD with all your heart, on your own
understanding do not rely; in all your ways be mindful of him,
and he will make straight your paths."*
Proverbs 3:5-6 (NAB)

Next year is going to be my best year ever! Why? I've chosen to live my life His way and no longer mine. Since I made that life-defining decision two weeks ago, He has made my path straight. After arriving at Grandma's I re-read the third article I had written for the abortion series. I knew it was all a lie; written to keep my job and my followers. I knew with absolute certainty that the truth, my truth, had to be told. After hearing my birth story, it would be impossible for me not to write about abortion from any other perspective but pro-life. I'm alive, aren't I, and loving it!

Fortunately, I was able to stall sending Pete the original article. I was armed with a litany of excuses from Grandma being ill, which was true, to me getting married, another truth. But the stall was really done so I could sort out how to write the third article in a way that protects Grandma and does not make it look like I've gone crazy. Whatever my decision, I knew there was going to be career and life implications. Earl had asked to be my sounding board for future articles, and this time I took him up on it. He agreed with every decision I made on how to handle my story. What a relief to now be forging our life together, a new life, with Christ at the center.

There was no other way to deliver this new article to Pete except face to face. Three days after Christmas, and five days before the mandated deadline of January 2, I walk into Pete's office, hand him the article, and wait. Sitting down I watch carefully as Pete reads my story. The look on his face registers shock, disbelief, and then the one I was expecting, anger.

Standing up, he puts his hands on the desk, leans over, looks me right in the eye, and screams. "Good try Jo, but I'm not buying it. What kind of sick stunt are you trying to pull on me? Do you want to get both of us fired?"

"Pete, this is the truth. Not even three weeks ago I found out the circumstances of my birth. Our agreement was for me to write the third article from my perspective, correct? Well, after hearing the truth from my rescuer, the woman I thought was my paternal Grandmother, this is the article that I had to write."

"There is no way we are going to publish this piece of …," he screams as he rips up my article into minuscule pieces. "You have until January 2nd to deliver something I can print in this paper or you're fired." He pounds his desk to emphasize the gravity of the situation. "Do you understand?" he yells. It wasn't a question.

After years of being bullied, pushed around, and diminished for my faith and who I am, somewhere deep inside of me came this unwavering courage. I stand up and look Pete right back in the eyes. "I totally understand. That's exactly how I thought you would react. So I have something else I would like you to read." I pull another piece of paper out of my bag and hand it over to him.

"What the hell is this? You're resigning? You can't resign because I'm firing you."

"Thanks for the opportunity and the lesson Pete. Josie Beth is back, and she is not taking orders from anyone else except her real boss, Jesus. Good luck Pete and God bless you." I say this with a confidence I have never felt. The truth is empowering!

Courage is what I needed today to turn my back on what I thought was my dream job, the job I had spent ten long, hard years working to obtain. But I was given an endless supply of courage to walk out of Pete's office with my head held high and joy in my heart. "Thank You God," I shout out as I look up in praise. Pete on the other hand continues to rant at me, even as I walk away. "Your career is over. You will never, ever write for a metropolitan newspaper. I have connections." Even the wide-eyed stares of my former co-workers did not stop me as I cleaned out my desk.

Yeah right, I think. I have connections to, and mine is with the Master of the Universe. I am no longer cowering in fear, but celebrating my freedom. People will no longer silence me, because I finally found strength and freedom to do it God's way. What a relief to finally stop following the false demands of this world. I will no longer listen to bullies telling me I'm not good enough, and threatening me unless I do it their way.

No, I'm not foolish. I now know God has a better plan for my career. He planted a dream in my heart, a dream to write, to shift perspectives and seek the truth. Now the only truth I'm seeking is His truth. I've found an on-line Christian Magazine, *Contemporary Christian Woman*. The editor agreed to publish my third article in their next edition. Even better, they've asked me to bring my blog and byline, Two Sides to Every Story, over to the magazine. I will be writing a weekly blog and monthly feature articles. What two sides will I write about? Now that's become crystal clear—His Way, versus the world's. In my newfound confidence, I am no longer wavering or indecisive. I haven't had a sleepless night in weeks!

Since that long car ride back to reconcile with Grandmother, I knew that my quest to seek the truth is not over. This might sound crazy, but I want to find my mother. After hearing Liz and Nicole's stories and the pain they felt after their abortions, maybe my mother is also regretting her abortion. If it's God's plan, I'll find her and help erase her pain. This is a year of possibilities. Grandma is helping me with the information from where she worked when I was born. It might take some time, and it also might never happen. Whatever the outcome I'm okay, because in heaven I will know her name. I've already forgiven Grandma, my mother and father, and even all the bullies in my life. It's the only way I'm going to live my life going forward, in God's grace.

My first call after the New Year will be to Liz and Bob Betts asking for their forgiveness and help. I really blasted the mission of W.A.I.T., and Liz's abortion story in my so-called pro-life article. Who was I to judge their truth, when I am a failed abortion myself! Because of their work, they have a solid network and hopefully they will be able to help me find my mother.

The second call I need to make will be to Nicole. I need to apologize about how I diminished her pain. Nicole also knows the transformational power of the Lord. I've missed her friendship. I think we will become a strong, united force talking about women's issues from a Christian point of view. We fell into the trap of the worlds' lies, and the Lord rescued us. Now I'm excited what He can do *through* us. The thought of helping other women become free of the bondage of worldly judgment and condemnation, now that's a purpose worth pursuing. By leading them to, or back to, the Way, the Truth and the Life they will know who their real advocate is, Jesus Christ.

I am hopeful, but even if all of these new dreams never happen, I have all that I need. My new life with Earl, the job with *Contemporary Christian Women*, my new family, and knowing the Lord is right by my side, it is all I have ever hoped for and more. I just thought it was impossible to dream such huge dreams. I've got it all—I'm truly successful, the success that Earl's mother had desired for him, heart and soul success. For planting this seed of truth in Earl's heart, I am forever grateful to Dorothy Broden. What I now know, with absolute certainty, is that a little baby, the innocent Christ child was Father God's plan from the beginning of time to save His wounded and hurting children, to heal hearts and souls, and even to save wretches just like me. Proving to me time and time again that Christmas does indeed cure everything.

Thank you for taking your precious time to read this book. If you are anything like us leaving the characters behind can be such a sad experience. We love the characters so much that we are currently writing a sequel. With our busy schedules we are not sure what the release date will be so we will keep you informed on our Facebook Fan page: Christmas Cures Everything and website. .

Please continue the journey with us by signing up as "fans" on our website. You can use the QR code to link you. There we are providing free book study questions on acceptance, forgiveness, and struggles. You will also find us blogging about our lives as wives, mothers, grandmothers, sisters and authors.

Again, thank you for reading our book and our hope is that it has changed your heart as much as it has changed ours.

Love,
Diane and Marie

About the authors

Marie Ralbusky is a mother of two awesome daughters Heather and Amy with their husbands Kevin and Dustin. She has been blessed with five wonderful granddaughters: Katie, Jackie, Abbie, Torie and Claire. Marie taught for 30 years and now is happy to be at home with her husband of 41 years Emil watching her granddaughters, quilting and writing.

Marie and her husband have been in the pro-life movement for over 30 years. It wasn't until they were team members on Rachel Vineyard post-abortion healing retreats did they see how these men and women were also abortion victims. Through these retreats Marie has witnessed the pain of post-abortion and the healing power of God's forgiveness.

Marie would like her readers to know that God does not have a pan scale for sins. If willing to ask God's forgiveness He is waiting for you with open arms.

Diane Belz is a "recovering executive" and has shared similar challenges that some of the main characters endured in this story; an insatiable desire to succeed, the guilt and shame she felt after becoming pregnant before marriage and the pain of losing her adult daughter, Jessica.

Diane learned how living life her way resulted in a soul-killing struggle. Only by choosing His way, not hers, did she finally obtain the soul satisfying life she always desired.

Diane continues to share her struggles and her desire to help others struggling to find soul satisfying success through her podcast and blog, Living Your MORE.

Diane has been married to her wonderful husband Joe for 39 years, the father of all her children, Jessica, Tyson and Geoffrey. Diane has been blessed with the additions to her family of loving daughter-in-laws Suzette and Thera and two granddaughters Isabella and Sofia.